PENG

THE COSMOPOLITAN BOOK OF SHORT STORIES

Kate Figes was born in 1957 and graduated with a BA in Arabic and Russian from the Polytechnic of Central London. She worked for six years for the publishing house Pandora Press before moving to *Cosmopolitan* magazine where she is Fiction Editor. Her first book, *Because of Her Sex – The Myth of Equality for Women in Britain*, was published in 1994. She reviews fiction regularly for BBC Radio 4's *Kaleidoscope*.

THE COSMOPOLITAN BOOK OF SHORT STORIES

Edited by Kate Figes

PENGUIN BOOKS

PENGUIN BOOKS

Published by the Penguin Group
Penguin Books Ltd, 27 Wrights Lane, London W8 5TZ, England
Penguin Books USA Inc., 375 Hudson Street, New York, New York 10014, USA
Penguin Books Australia Ltd, Ringwood, Victoria, Australia
Penguin Books Canada Ltd, 10 Alcorn Avenue, Toronto, Ontario, Canada M4V 3B2
Penguin Books (NZ) Ltd, 182–190 Wairau Road, Auckland 10, New Zealand

Penguin Books Ltd, Registered Offices: Harmondsworth, Middlesex, England

1 3 5 7 9 10 8 6 4 2

Filmset in 10/13pt Monophoto Bembo by Datix International Ltd, Bungay, Suffolk

Printed in England by Clays Ltd, St Ives plc

CONTENTS

Acknowledgements vii

Introduction ix

LORRIE MOORE
Community Life 1

ALISON LURIE
The Pool People 18

FAY WELDON
Pains 32

FRANK RONAN
Handsome Men are Slightly Sunburnt 41

ANGELA CARTER
Lizzie's Tiger 58

AMY BLOOM
Love is Not a Pie 72

ELIZABETH MCCRACKEN
It's Bad Luck to Die 87

HELEN SIMPSON
Last Orders 100

RACHEL CUSK
Wellborers and Sinkers 109

BARBARA GOWDY
Presbyterian Crossing 117

PAM HOUSTON
Cowboys are My Weakness 133

MARGARET ATWOOD
The Bog Man 147

JOSEPH O'CONNOR
Mothers were All the Same 164

CAROL SHIELDS
Mrs Turner Cutting the Grass 177

DAVID MAMET
A Family Vacation 186

TATYANA TOLSTAYA
The Poet and the Muse 191

MARY GAITSKILL
Tiny, Smiling Daddy 204

Notes on the Authors 217

ACKNOWLEDGEMENTS

Thanks are due to the copyright holders of the following short stories for permission to reproduce them in this volume:

MARGARET ATWOOD: to Bloomsbury Publishing Ltd for 'The Bog Man' from *Wilderness Tips*, copyright © Margaret Atwood 1991.

AMY BLOOM: to Curtis Brown Group Ltd for 'Love is Not a Pie' from *Come to Me* (Macmillan Publishers Ltd, 1994), copyright © Amy Bloom, 1994.

ANGELA CARTER: to the Estate of Angela Carter, c/o Rogers, Coleridge & White Ltd, 20 Powis Mews, London W11 1JN, for 'Lizzie's Tiger', first co-commissioned by *Cosmopolitan* and BBC Radio for publication in September 1991, and now collected in *American Ghosts and Old World Wonders* (Chatto & Windus, 1993), copyright © Angela Carter, 1991.

RACHEL CUSK: to the author and Lutyens & Rubenstein Agency, c/o 231 Westbourne Park Road, London W11 1EB, for 'Wellborers and Sinkers', copyright © Rachel Cusk, 1993.

MARY GAITSKILL: to the author for 'Tiny, Smiling Daddy', copyright © Mary Gaitskill, 1993.

BARBARA GOWDY: to HarperCollins Publishers for 'Presbyterian Crossing' from *We So Seldom Look on Love*, copyright © Barbara Gowdy, 1993.

PAM HOUSTON: to the author and the Darhansoff & Verrill Literary Agency, c/o Tessa Sayle Agency, 11 Jubilee Place, London SW3 3TE, for 'Cowboys are My Weakness' from her collection of stories *Cowboys are My Weakness* (Virago Press, 1993), copyright © Pam Houston, 1992.

ALISON LURIE: to Reed Consumer Books for 'The Pool People' from *Women and Ghosts* (William Heinemann Ltd, 1994), copyright © Alison Lurie, 1994.

DAVID MAMET: to Faber & Faber Ltd for 'A Family Vacation' from *Writing in Restaurants*, copyright © David Mamet, 1988.

ELIZABETH MCCRACKEN: to the author and Curtis Brown Group Ltd, c/o Tessa Sayle Agency, 11 Jubilee Place, London SW3 3TE, for 'It's Bad Luck to Die' from *Here's Your Hat What's Your Hurry?* (Secker & Warburg, 1993), copyright © Elizabeth McCracken, 1993.

LORRIE MOORE: to the author and the Melanie Jackson Agency, c/o Rogers, Coleridge & White Ltd, 20 Powis Mews, London W11 1JN, for 'Community Life', first published in *The New Yorker* and subsequently in *Cosmopolitan* in November 1994, copyright © Lorrie Moore, 1994.

JOSEPH O'CONNOR: to Reed Consumer Books for 'Mothers were All the Same' from *True Believers* (Sinclair-Stevenson, 1991), copyright © Joseph O'Connor, 1991.

FRANK RONAN: to the author, c/o Rogers, Coleridge & White Ltd, 20 Powis Mews, London W11 1JN, for 'Handsome Men are Slightly Sunburnt', copyright © Frank Ronan, 1995.

CAROL SHIELDS: to Fourth Estate Ltd for 'Mrs Turner Cutting the Grass' from *Various Miracles*, copyright © Carol Shields, 1994.

HELEN SIMPSON: to Reed Consumer Books for 'Last Orders' from *Dear George* (William Heinemann Ltd, 1995), copyright © Helen Simpson, 1993.

TATYANA TOLSTAYA: to Virago Press for 'The Poet and the Muse' from *Sleepwalker in a Fog*, copyright © Tatyana Tolstaya, 1991; English translation copyright © Jamey Gambrell, 1991.

FAY WELDON: to the author for 'Pains', copyright © Fay Weldon, 1972.

INTRODUCTION

As Fiction Editor for *Cosmopolitan* magazine I have read thousands of short stories, some by the very famous, some by the not so famous and some by the totally unknown. While many were good, few left a resounding, lasting impression that haunted me afterwards or made me catch my breath with wonder. But the stories collected here are a selection of the wonders, some of those that we are proud to have published, some of them for the first time, in *Cosmopolitan* in the past four years.

It never ceases to amaze me how different the image of *Cosmopolitan* is from its content. Almost daily I find myself explaining to those who are not regular readers that we don't publish Mills & Boon romances, that we don't just publish stories about relationships, and no, we don't extract only sex scenes from novels. The most ignorant and dangerous misconception people have is that because *Cosmo* is a 'woman's magazine' (read, incidentally, by large numbers of men), those women reading it are only interested in what publishers insist on calling in their rather quaint way 'women's fiction': sagas and historical romance, while the boys get on with the nitty gritty hard stuff of fiction (which of course gets the serious review coverage). This is highly patronising. Young women today want to read all sorts of things. I see women on trains and buses reading everything from macho writers such as Thomas Harris and Stephen King to serious non-fiction tomes on biology or the nature of civil war. But I have never seen any woman, young or old, reading a Barbara Cartland novel. Women today buy and read more fiction than men, but they buy and read a whole range of material which does not necessarily fall into the highly limited and derogatory term 'women's fiction', and the range of writers that we have published over the years recognises that fact.

Every month, *Cosmopolitan* publishes an extract from a brand-new novel or short story by well-known authors or by outstanding newcomers. Over the past few years we have published extracts from Michael Ondatjee's *The English Patient*, Angela Carter's *Wise Children*, Margaret Atwood's *The Robber Bride*, Adam Thorpe's *Ulverton*, Ben Elton's *Gridlock*, Nicholson Baker's *Vox*, William Trevor's *Felicia's Journey*, Lucy Ellmann's *Varying Degrees of Hopelessness*, Marina Warner's *Indigo*, Armistead Maupin's *Maybe the Moon* and Ruth Rendell's *The Crocodile Bird* – to name but quite a few. We have also introduced countless new names from Britain and around the world to a massive audience with fiction from wonderful writers such as Tatyana Tolstaya, Amy Bloom, Rachel Cusk, Barbara Gowdy and Jeffrey Eugenides; names that will surely become as well known in years to come as those of Angela Carter and Margaret Atwood. An audience of over 2 million women and men read *Cosmopolitan* every month, and we are determined not to underestimate the intelligence of those readers by publishing the trash churned out month after month by publishing houses and targeted specifically at women. Instead we give women the very best fiction available, never assuming it to be somehow over their heads.

Cosmopolitan magazine also holds regular short story and poetry competitions with work submitted by well-known names as well as previously unpublished writers. We also stage a unique event in the literary calendar. The *Cosmopolitan* Book Day is held in October and attracts roughly 500 readers and passionate book buyers each year. A host of literary stars attend the day, delivering lectures and readings as well as joining in discussions on specific topics. Paul Theroux described his experience of the *Cosmo* Book Day as 'a thousand times more interesting than a literary lunch', and many other writers and readers would agree with him. The Book Day seems to bridge the gap between intimidating literary festivals, which sprawl over a week and cover half the countryside, and the one-off 'writer in a bookshop' event, which often leaves the reader feeling faintly unsatisfied. At the Book Day writers and readers are in the same hall throughout the day and consequently an intimacy builds up as previous sessions often come up in discussion. Writers meet each other as well as readers, and the readers are presented with the highlights of the literary year. Many come year after year and lasting friendships have developed at the Book Day.

There seems little point in including extracts from some of the many novels that we have published over the years in *The Best of Cosmopolitan Fiction*. Most are now available in paperback and the point in publishing the extract was to give the reader a taste of something new as it was published. Short stories though are different. They are complete in themselves and many of those collected here are not available in other volumes of short stories, either as anthologies or complete volumes by the author. They simply disappear from view as the magazine goes off sale at the end of the month. These are, I suppose, my favourites, for while the excellence of work is a given, taste inevitably enters the selection process. It is interesting that it was only as I looked back through past issues of the magazine and drew up a list of authors that I noticed how many of these stories had been written by women, and how few by men. I am not anti men's writing and I certainly read and enjoy a great deal of fiction by men; indeed we publish a great many extracts from their novels. I think women are genuinely more interested in reading and writing the short story as a literary form. Virtually all of the major female novelists have written short stories as well, while many of the men don't. Peter Ackroyd, Ian McEwan, Paul Bailey and Kazuo Ishiguro are known avoiders of the short story form, while Margaret Atwood, Shena Mackay, Angela Carter, Alison Lurie, Fay Weldon and Ruth Rendell are known for their numerous collections.

The subject matter of the stories is rich and diverse. Many explore the nature of relationships with great tenderness and sophistication – from Amy Bloom's marvellous tale of a successful triangular relationship, to Lorrie Moore's sad tale of unrequited love. Helen Simpson and Fay Weldon write with wit and honesty about giving birth, while Rachel Cusk and Barbara Gowdy write with pathos and understanding about children. 'Lizzie's Tiger' by Angela Carter was commissioned by *Cosmopolitan* and BBC Radio 3 and was sadly to be one of the last short stories that Angela wrote before she died. Joseph O'Connor is a marvellous new writer, one of the growing number of men interested in writing about relationships from a man's point of view. His story of a young Irish couple in London is both vivid and moving, while

David Mamet's voice of a father on holiday with his family, who can't wait to get back to work, has an honest and entertaining ring to it, but speaks with hope for a dying breed of men. These are warm, funny and stimulating short stories from a wide range of exceptionally talented writers. Read and enjoy them.

KATE FIGES
November 1994

Lorrie Moore

COMMUNITY LIFE

When Olena was a little girl, she had called them lieberries – a fibbing fruit, a story store – and now she had a job in one. She had originally wanted to teach English Literature, but when she failed to warm to the graduate study of it, its French-fried theories – a vocabulary of arson! – she'd transferred to library school, where everyone was taught to take care of books, tenderly, as if they were dishes or dolls.

She had learned to read at an early age. Her parents, newly settled in Vermont from Tirgu-Mures in Transylvania, were anxious that their daughter learn to speak English, to blend in with the community in a way they felt they probably never would, and so every Saturday they took her to the children's section of the Rutland library and let her spend time with the librarian, who chose books for her and sometimes even read a page or two out loud, though there was a sign that said 'Please be quiet boys and girls.' No comma.

Which made it seem to Olena that only the boys had to be quiet. She and the librarian could do whatever they wanted.

She had loved the librarian.

And when Olena's Romanian began to recede altogether, and in its stead boomed a slow, rich, English-speaking voice, not unlike the librarian's, too womanly for a little girl, the other children on her street became even more afraid of her. 'Dracula!' they shouted. 'Transylvaniess!' they shrieked, and ran.

'You'll have a new name now,' her father told her on the first day of first grade. He had already changed their last name from Todorescu to Resnick. His shop was called Resnick's Furs. 'From here on in, you will no longer be Olena. You will have a nice American name, Nell.'

'You make to say the name,' her mother said. 'When the teacher tell you Olena, you say, "No, Nell." Say "Nell."'

'Nell,' said Olena. But when she got to school, the teacher, sensing something dreamy and outcast in her, clasped her hand and exclaimed, 'Olena! What a beautiful name!' Olena's heart filled with gratitude and surprise, and she fell in, adoring and mute, close to the teacher's hip.

From there on in, only her parents, in their throaty Romanian accents, ever called her Nell – her secret, jaunty American self existing only for them.

'Nell, how are the other children at the school?'

'Nell, please to tell us what you do.'

Years later, when they were killed in a car crash on the Farm-to-Market Road, and the Nell who had never lived died with them, Olena numbly rearranging the letters of her own name on the envelopes of the sympathy cards she received, discovered what the letters spelled. Olena: 'Alone.' The word was a body walled in the cellar of her, a whiff and a forecast of doom like an early, rotten spring – and she longed for the Nell-that-never-lived's return. She wished to start all over again, to be someone living coltishly in the world, not someone hidden away behind books, with a carefully learned voice and a sad past.

She missed her mother the most.

The library Olena worked in was one of the most prestigious university libraries in the Midwest. It housed a large collection of rare and foreign books, and she had driven across several states to get there, squinting through the splattered tempera of insects on the windshield, watching for the dark tail of a possible tornado, and getting sick, painfully, in Indiana, along I-80, in the rest rooms of the service plazas named for dead Hoosiers. The ladies' rooms there had had electric eyes for the toilets, the sinks, the hand dryers, and she'd set them all off by staggering in and out of the stalls or leaning into the sinks. 'You the only one in here?' asked a cleaning woman. 'You the only one making this racket?' Olena had smiled, a dog's smile; in the yellowish light everything seemed tragic and ridiculous and unable to stop. The flatness of the terrain gave her vertigo, she decided: that was it. The land was windswept; there were no smells. In Vermont she had felt cradled by mountains. Now, here, she would have to be brave.

But she had no memory of how to be brave. Here it seemed, she had no memories at all. Nothing triggered them. And once in a while, when she gave voice to the fleeting edge of one, it seemed like something she was making up.

Olena first met Nick at the library in May. She was temporarily positioned at the reference desk, hauled out from her ordinary task as the supervisor of foreign cataloguing, to replace someone who was ill. Nick was researching statistics on municipal campaign spending in the state. 'Haven't stepped into a library since I was 18,' he said. He looked at least 40.

She showed him where he might look. 'Try looking there,' she said, writing down the names of indexes, but he kept looking at *her*. 'Or here.'

'I am managing a county-board-seat campaign,' he said. 'The election is not until the fall but I'm trying to get a jump on things.'

His hair was a coppery brown, threaded through with silver. There was something animated in his eyes, like pond life. 'I just wanted to get some comparison figures. Will you have a cup of coffee with me?'

'I don't think so,' she said.

But he came back the next day and asked her again.

The coffee shop near campus was hot and noisy, crowded with students, and Nick loudly ordered espresso for both himself and Olena. She usually didn't like espresso – its gritty, cigarish taste. But a kind of distortion was in the air, something that bent you a little; it caused your usual self to grow slippery, to wander off and shop, to get blurry, bleed, bevel with possibility. She drank fast, with determination and a sense of adventure. 'I guess I'll have a second,' she said, and wiped her mouth with a napkin.

'I'll get it,' said Nick, and when he came back he told her more about the campaign he was running. 'It's important to get the endorsements of the neighbourhood associations,' he said. He ran a bratwurst and frozen yogurt stand called Please Squeeze & Bratwursts. He had got to know a lot of people that way. 'I feel alive and relevant, living life like this,' he said. 'I don't feel like I've sold out.'

'Sold out to what?' she asked.

He smiled. 'I can tell that you're not from around here,' he said. He raked his hand through the various metals of his hair. '*Selling out*. Like, doing something you never really wanted to do, and getting paid too much for it.'

'Oh,' she said.

'When I was a kid, my father said to me, "Sometimes in life, son, you're going to find you have to do things you don't want to do," and I looked him right in the eye and said, "No fucking way."' Olena laughed. "I mean, you probably always wanted to be a librarian, right?'

She looked at all the crooked diagonals of his face and couldn't tell whether he was serious. 'Me?' she said. 'I first went to graduate school to be an English professor.' She sighed, switched elbows, sinking her chin into her other hand. 'I did try,' she said. 'I read Derrida. I read Lacan. I read *Reading Lacan*. I read *Reading "Reading Lacan"* – and that's when I applied to library school.'

'I don't know who Lacan is,' he said.

'He's, well . . . You see, that's why I like libraries: no whats or whys. Just, "Where is it?"'

'And *where* are you from?' he asked, his face briefly animated by his own clever change of subject. 'Originally?' There was, it seemed, a way of spotting those not native to the town. It was a college town, attractive and dull, and it hurried its transients along – the students, gypsies, visiting scholars and comics – with a motion not unlike peristalsis.

'Vermont,' she said.

'Vermont!' Nick exclaimed, as if it were exotic, which made her glad she hadn't said something like Transylvania. He leaned towards her, confidentially. 'I have to tell you: I own one chair from Ethan Allen.'

'You do?' she smiled. 'I won't tell anyone.'

'Before that, however, I was in prison, and didn't own a stick.'

'Really?' she asked. She sat back. Was he telling the truth? As a girl, she had been very gullible, but she had always learned more that way.

'I went to school here,' he said. 'In the Sixties. I bombed a warehouse where the military was storing research supplies. I got 12 years.' He paused, searching her eyes to see how she was doing, how *he* was doing. Then he fetched back his gaze, like a piece of jewellery he'd merely wanted to show her, quick. 'There wasn't supposed to be anyone there. We'd checked it all out in advance, but this poor asshole named Lawrence Sperry – Larry Sperry! Christ, can you imagine having a name like that?'

'Sure,' said Olena.

Nick looked at her suspiciously. 'He was in there, working late. He lost a leg and a eye in the explosion. I got the federal pen in Winford. Attempted murder.'

The thick coffee coated his lips. He had been looking steadily at her, but now he looked away.

'Would you like a bun?' asked Olena. 'I'm going to get a bun.' She stood, but he turned and gazed up at her with such disbelief that she sat back down again, sloppily, side-saddle. She twisted forward, leaned into the table. 'I'm sorry. Is that all true, what you just said? Did that really happen to you?'

'*What?*' His mouth fell open. 'You think I'd make that up?'

'It's just that, well, I work around a lot of literature,' she said.

'Literature,' he repeated.

She touched his hand. She didn't know what else to do. 'Can I cook dinner for you some night? Tonight?'

There was a blaze in his eye, a concentrated seeing. He seemed for a moment able to look right into her, to know her in a way that was uncluttered by actually knowing her. He seemed to have no information or misinformation, only a kind of photography, factless but true.

'Yes,' he said, 'you can.'

Which was how he came to spend the evening beneath the cheap stained-glass lamp of her dining room, its bar-room red, its Schlitz-Tiffany light, and then to spend the night, and not leave.

Olena had never lived with a man before. 'Except my father,' she said, and Nick studied her eyes, the streak of blankness in them, when she said it. Though she had dated two different boys in college, they were the kind who liked to leave early, to eat breakfast without her, at smoky greasy spoons, to sit at the counter with large men in blue windbreakers, read the paper, get their cups refilled.

She had never been with anyone who had stayed. Anyone who had moved in his box of tapes, his Ethan Allen chair.

Anyone who had had lease problems at his old place.

'I'm trying to bring this thing together,' he said, holding her in the middle of the afternoon. 'My life, the campaign, my thing with you – I'm trying to get all my birds to land in the same yard.' Out the window there was an afternoon moon like a golf ball, pocked and stuck. She looked at the calcified egg of it, its coin face, its blue neighbourhood of nothing. Then she looked at him. There was the pond life again in his eyes, and in the rest of his face a hesitant, warm stillness.

'Do you like making love to me?' she asked, at night during a thunderstorm.

'Of course. Why do you ask?'

'Are you satisfied with me?'

He turned towards her, kissed her. 'Yes,' he said. 'I don't need a show.'

She was quiet for a long time. 'People are giving shows?'

The rain and wind rushed down the gutters, snapping the branches of the weak trees in the side yard.

He had her inexperience and self-esteem in mind. At the movies, at the beginning, he whispered, 'Twentieth Century Fox. Baby, that's you.' During a slapstick part, in a library where card catalogues were up-ended and scattered wildly through the air, she broke into a pale, cold sweat, and he moved towards her, hid her head in his chest, saying, 'Don't look, don't look.' At the end, they would sit through the long credits – gaffer, best boy, key grip.

'That's what *we* need to get,' he said. 'A grip.'

'Yes,' she said. 'And a negative cutter.'

Other times, he encouraged her to walk around the house naked. 'If you got it, do it.' He smiled, paused, feigned confusion. 'If you do it, have it. If you flaunt it, do it.'

'If you have it, got it,' she added.

'If you say it, mean it.' And he pulled her towards him like a dancing partner with soft shoes and the smiling mouth of love.

But too often she lay awake wondering. There was something missing. Something wasn't happening to her – or was it to him? – while, all through the summer, thunderstorms set the sky on fire as she lay awake listening for the train sound of a tornado that never came, although the lightning ripped open the night and the trees were lit like things too suddenly remembered, then left indecipherable again in the dark.

'You're not feeling anything, are you?' he finally said. 'What's wrong?'

'I'm not sure,' she said cryptically. 'The rainstorms are so loud in this part of the world.' The wind from a storm blew through the screens and caused the door to the bedroom to slam shut. 'I don't like a door to slam,' she whispered. 'It makes me think someone is angry.'

At the library there were Romanian books coming in – Olena was to skim them, read them just enough to proffer a brief description for the catalogue listing. It dismayed her that her Romanian was so weak, that it had seemed almost to vanish, a mere handkerchief in a stairwell, and that daily now another book arrived to reprimand her.

She missed her mother the most.

On her lunch break, she went to Nick's stand for a frozen yogurt. He looked tired, bedraggled, his hair like sprockets. 'You want the Sperry Cherry or the Lemon Bomber?' he asked. These were his joke names, the ones he threatened really to use someday.

'How about apple?' she said.

He cut up an apple and arranged it in a paper dish. He squeezed yogurt from a chrome machine. 'There's a fund-raiser tonight for the Teetlebaum campaign.'

'Oh,' she said. She had been to these fund-raisers before. At first she had liked them, glimpsing corners of the town she would never have seen otherwise. Nick leading her out into them, Nick knowing everyone, so her life seemed filled with possibility, with hopefulness. But finally she felt the events were too full of dreary, glad-handing people talking incessantly of their camping trips out West. They never really spoke to you. They spoke towards you. They spoke at you. They spoke on you, near you. They believed themselves crucial to the welfare of the community. They didn't read books. 'At least they're *contributors to the community*,' said Nick. 'At least they're not sucking the blood of it.'

'Lapping,' she said.

'What?'

'Gnashing and lapping. Not sucking.'

He looked at her in a doubtful, worried way. 'I looked it up once,' she said.

'Whatever.' He scowled. 'At least they care. At least they're trying to give something back.'

'I'd rather live in Russia,' she said.

'I'll be back around ten or so,' he said.

'You don't want me to come?'

In truth, she wasn't very impressed with Ken Teetlebaum. Perhaps Nick had figured this out. Though Ken had the support of the local leftover left, there was something fatuous and vain about him. He tended to do little isometric leg exercises while you were talking to him. Often, he took out a Woolworths photo of himself and showed it to people. 'Look at this,' he'd say. 'This was back when I had long hair. Can you believe it?' And people would look and see a handsome, teenaged boy who bore only a slight resemblance to the puffy Ken Teetlebaum of today. 'Don't I look like Eric Clapton?'

'Eric Clapton would never have sat in a Woolworths photo booth like some high-school girl,' Olena said, in the caustic blurt that sometimes afflicts the shy. Ken looked at her in a laughing, hurt sort of way, and after that he stopped showing the photo around.

'You can come if you want to.'

Nick reached up, smoothed his hair, and looked handsome again. 'Meet me there.'

The fund-raiser was in the upstairs room of a local restaurant called Dutch's. She paid ten dollars, went in, and ate a lot of raw cauliflower and hummus before she saw Nick back in a far corner talking to a woman in jeans and a brown blazer. She was the sort of woman that Nick might twist around to look at in restaurants: her fiery auburn hair cut bluntly in a pageboy. She had a pretty face, but the hair was too severe, too separate and tended-to. Olena herself had long, disorganised hair, and she wore it pulled back messily in a clip. When she reached up to wave to Nick, and he looked away without acknowledging her, back towards the auburn pageboy, she kept her hand up and moved it back, to fuss with the clip. She would never fit in here, she thought. Not among these jolly, activist-clerk types. She preferred the quiet poet-clerks of the library. They were delicate and territorial, intellectual, and physically unwell. They sat around at work, thinking up Tom Swifties: *I have to go to the hardware store, he said wrenchingly.*

Would you like a soda? he asked spritely.

They spent weekends at the Mayo Clinic. 'An amusement park for hypochondriacs,' said a cataloguer named Sarah. 'A cross between Lourdes and *The New Price is Right*,' said someone else named George. These were the people she liked: the kind you couldn't really live with.

She turned to head towards the ladies' room and bumped into Ken. He gave her a hug hello, and then whispered in her ear, 'You live with Nick. Help us think of an issue. I need another issue.'

'I'll get you one at the issue store,' she said, and pulled away as someone approached him with a heartily extended hand and a false, booming 'Here's the man of the hour.' In the bathroom, she stared at her own reflection. In an attempt at extroversion, she had worn a tunic with large slices of watermelon depicted on the front. What had she been thinking of?

She went into the stall and slid the bolt shut. She read all the graffiti on the back of the door. 'Anita loves David S.' 'Christ + Diane W.' It was good to see that, even in a town like this, people could love each other.

'Who were you talking to?' Olena asked Nick later, at home.

'Who? What do you mean?'

'The one with the Plasticine hair.'

'Oh, Erin? She does look like she does something to her hair. It looks like she hennas it.'

'It looks like she tacks it against the wall and stands underneath it.'

'She's head of the Bayre Corners Neighbourhood Association. Come September, we're really going to need her endorsement.'

Olena sighed, looked away.

'It's the democratic process,' said Nick.

'I'd rather have a king and queen,' she said.

The following Friday, the night of the Fish-Fry Fund-Raiser at the Labour Temple, was the night Nick slept with Erin of the Bayre Corners Neighbourhood Association. He arrived back home at seven in the morning and confessed to Olena, who, when Nick hadn't come home, had downed half a packet of Dramamine to get to sleep.

'I'm sorry,' he said, his head in his hands. 'It's a Sixties thing.'

'A Sixties thing?' Olena was fuzzy, zonked from the Dramamine.

'You get all involved in a political event, and you find yourselves sleeping together. She's from that era too. It's also that, I don't know, she just seems to really care about her community. She's got this reaching, expressive side to her. I got caught up in that.' He was sitting down, leaning forward on his knees, talking to his shoes. The electric fan was blowing on him; his hair was moving gently, like weeds in water.

'A Sixties thing?' Olena repeated.

'A Sixties thing, what is that – like "Easy to Be Hard"?' It was the song she remembered best. But now something switched off in her. The bones in her chest hurt. Even the room seemed changed – brighter and awful. Everything had fled her, run away to become something else. She started to perspire under her arms, and her face grew hot. 'You're a murderer,' she said. 'That's finally what you are, what you'll always be.' She began to weep so loudly that Nick got up and closed the windows. Then he came back and held her – who else was there to hold her? – and she held him, too.

Nick bought Olena a large garnet ring, a cough drop set in brass. He did the dishes ten days in a row. She had a tendency to go to bed right after supper and sleep, heavily, needing the escape. She had become afraid of going out – restaurants, shops, the tension in her shoulders, the fear gripping her face when she was there, as if people knew she was a foreigner and a fool – and for 15 additional days he did the cooking and shopping. His car was always parked on the outside of the driveway, and hers was always in first, close, blocked off, as if to indicate who most belonged to the community, to the world, and who most belonged tucked away from it, in a house. Perhaps in bed. Perhaps asleep.

'You need more life around you,' said Nick, cradling her, though she'd gone stiff and still. His face was plaintive and suntanned, the notes and varnish of a violin. 'You need a greater sense of life around you.' Outside, there was the old-rot smell of rain coming.

'How have you managed to get a suntan when there's been so much rain?' she asked.

'It's summer,' he said. 'I work outside, remember?'

'There are no sleeve marks,' she said. 'Where are you going?'

She had become afraid of the community. It was her enemy. Other people, other women.

She had, without realising it at the time, learned to follow his gaze, learned to know his lust, and when she did go out, to work at least, his desires remained memorised within her. She looked at the attractive women he would look at. She turned to inspect the face that went with every pageboy haircut she saw from behind and passed in her car. She looked at them furtively or squarely – it didn't matter. She appraised their eyes and mouths and wondered about their bodies. She had become him: she longed for these women. But she was also herself, and so she despised them. She lusted after them, but she also wanted to beat them up.

A rapist.

She had become a rapist, driving to work in a car. But, for a while, it was the only way she could be.

She began to wear his clothes – a shirt, a pair of socks – to keep him next to her, to try to understand why he had done what he'd done. And in this new empathy, in this pants role, as if in an opera, she thought she understood what it was to make love to a woman, to open the hidden underside of her, a secret food, to thrust yourself up in her, to feel her arching and thrashing like a puppet, to watch her later when she got up and walked around without you, oblivious of the injury you'd done her (you'd surely done her). How could you not love her, gratefully, marvelling? She was so mysterious, so recovered, an unshared thought enlivening her eyes; you wanted to follow her for ever.

A man in love. That was a man in love. So different from a woman.

A woman cleaned up the kitchen. A woman gave and hid, gave and hid, like someone with a May basket.

Olena made an appointment with a doctor. Her insurance covered her only if she went to the university hospital, so she made an appointment there.

'I've made a doctor's appointment,' she said to Nick, but he had the water running in the bath tub and didn't hear her. 'To find out if there's anything wrong with me.'

When he got out, he approached her with nothing on but a towel. He pulled her close to his chest and lowered her to the floor, right there in the hall by the bathroom door. Something was swooping back and forth in an arc above her. Mayday, Mayday. She froze.

'What was that?' She pushed him away.

'What?' He rolled over on his back and looked.

Something was flying around in the stairwell – a bird.

'A bat,' he said.

'Oh, my God!' cried Olena.

'The heat can bring them out in these old rental houses,' he said, standing and rewrapping his towel. 'Do you have a tennis racket?'

She showed him where it was. 'I've only played tennis once,' she said. 'Do you want to play tennis sometime?'

But he proceeded to stalk the bat in the dark stairwell.

'Now, don't get hysterical,' he said.

'I'm already hysterical.'

'Don't get – There!' he shouted, and she heard the thwack of the racket against the wall, and the soft drop of the bat to the landing.

She suddenly felt sick. 'Did you have to kill it?' she said.

'What did you want me to do?'

'I don't know. Capture it. Rough it up a little.' She felt guilty, as if her own loathing had brought about its death. 'What kind of bat is it?'

She tiptoed up to look, to try to glimpse its monkey face, its cat teeth, its pterodactyl wings, like beet leaves. 'What kind? Is it a fruit bat?'

'Looks pretty straight to me,' said Nick. With his fist, he tapped Olena's arm lightly, teasingly.

'Will you stop it? Maybe it's a brown bat. It's not a vampire bat, is it?'

'I think you have to go to South America for those,' he said. 'Take your platform shoes!'

She sank down on the steps, pulled her robe tighter. She felt for the light switch and flicked it on. The bat, she could now see, was small and light-coloured, its wings folded in like a packed tent – a mouse with backpacking equipment. It had a sweet face, like a deer's, though blood drizzled from its head. It reminded her of a cat she'd seen once as a child, shot in the eye with a BB.

'I can't look anymore,' she said, and went back upstairs.

He appeared a half hour later, standing in the doorway. She was in bed, a book propped in her lap – a biography of a French feminist, which she was reading for the hairdo information.

'I had lunch with Erin today,' he said.

Olena stared at the page. Snoods. Turbans and snoods. You could go for days in a snood. 'Why?'

'A lot of different reasons. For Ken, mostly. Erin's still head of the Neighbourhood Association, and he needs her endorsement. I just wanted to let you know. Listen, you've gotta cut me some slack.'

Olena grew hot in the face again. 'I've cut you some slack,' she said. 'I've cut you a whole forest of slack. The whole global slack forest has been cut for you.' She closed the book. 'I don't know why you cavort with these people. They're nothing but a bunch of clerks.'

He'd been trying to look pleasant but now he winced a little. 'Oh, I see,' he said. 'Miss High-Minded. You, whose father made his living off furs. Furs!' He took two steps towards her, then turned and paced back again. 'I can't believe I'm living with someone who grew up on the proceeds of tortured animals!'

She was quiet. This lunge at moral fastidiousness was something she'd noticed a lot in the people around here. They were not good people. They were not kind. They played around and lied to their spouses. But they recycled their newspapers!

'Don't drag my father into this.'

'Look, I've spent five years of my life working for peace and free expression. I've been in prison already. I've lived in a cage! I don't need to live in another one.'

'You and your free expression! You who can't listen to me for two minutes!'

'Listen to you what?'

'Listen to me when I' – here she bit her lip a little – 'when I tell you that these people you care about, this hateful Erin What's-her-name, they're just small, awful, nothing people.'

'So they don't read enough books,' he said slowly. 'Who the fuck cares?'

The next day, Nick was off to a meeting with Ken at the Senior Citizens' Association. The host from *Jeopardy* was going to be there, and Ken wanted to shake a few hands, sign up volunteers. The host from *Jeopardy* was going to give a talk.

'I don't get it,' Olena said.

'I know.' Nick sighed, the pond life treading water in his eyes. 'But, well – it's the American way.' He grabbed his keys, and the look that quickly passed over his face told her this: she wasn't pretty enough.

'I hate America,' she said.

Nonetheless, he called her at the library during a break. She'd been sitting in the back with Sarah, thinking up Tom Swifties, her brain ready to bleed through her ears, when the phone rang. 'You should see this,' he said. 'Some old geezer raises his hand, I call on him, and he stands up and the first thing he says is, "I had my hand raised for ten whole minutes, and you kept passing over me. I don't like to be passed over. You can't just pass over a guy like me, not at my age."'

Olena laughed, as Nick wanted her to.

This hot dog's awful, she said frankly.

'We've got all these signs up that say "Teetlebaum for Tort Reform."'

'Sounds like a Wallace Stevens poem,' she said.

'Yeah, I don't know what I expected. But the swirl of this whole event has not felt right.'

She's a real dog, he said cattily.

She was quiet, deciding to let him do the work of this call.

'Do you realise that Ken's entire softball team just wrote a letter to the *Star*, calling him a loudmouth and a cheat?'

'Well,' she said, 'what can you expect from a bunch of grown men who pitch underhand?'

There was some silence. 'I care about us,' he said finally. 'I just want you to know that.'

'Okay,' she said.

'I know I'm a pain in the ass to you,' he said. 'But you're an inspiration to me, you are.'

I like a good sled dog, she said huskily.

'Thank you for just – for saying that,' she said.

'I just wish you'd get involved in the community, help out with the campaign. Give of yourself. Connect a little with something.'

At the hospital, Olena got up on the table and pulled the paper gown tight around her, her feet in the stirrups. The doctor took a plastic speculum out of a drawer. 'Anything particular seem to be the problem today?' asked the doctor.

'I just wanted you to look and tell me if there's anything wrong,' said Olena.

The doctor studied her carefully. 'There's a class of medical students outside. Do you mind if they come in?'

'Excuse me?'

'You know this is a teaching hospital,' she said. 'We hope that our patients won't mind contributing to the education of our medical students by allowing them in during an examination. It's a way of contributing to the larger medical community, if you will. But it's totally up to you. You can say no.'

Olena clutched at her paper gown. *There's never been an accident, she said recklessly*. 'How many of them are there?'

The doctor smiled quickly. 'Seven,' she said. 'Like dwarfs.'

'They'll come in and do what?'

The doctor was growing impatient, looked at her watch. 'They'll participate in the examination. It's a learning visit.'

Olena sank back down on the table. She didn't feel that she could offer herself up in this way. *You're only average, he said meanly.*

'All right,' she said. 'Okay.'

Take a bow, he said sternly.

The doctor opened the door and called down the corridor. 'Class?'

They were young, more than half of them men, and they gathered around the examination table in a horseshoe shape, looking slightly ashamed, sorry for her, no doubt, the way art students sometimes felt sorry for the shivering model they were about to draw. The doctor pulled up a stool between Olena's feet and inserted the plastic speculum – the stiff, widening arms of it uncomfortable, embarrassing. 'Today we will be doing a routine pelvic examination,' the doctor announced loudly, and then she got up again, went to a drawer, and passed out rubber gloves to everyone.

Olena went a little blind. A white light, starting at the centre, spread to the black edges of her sight. One by one, the hands of the students entered her or pressed on her abdomen, felt hungrily, innocently, for something to learn from her, in her.

She missed her mother the most.

'Next,' the doctor was saying. And then again. 'All right. Next?'

Olena missed her mother the most.

But it was her father's face that suddenly loomed before her now; his face at night in the doorway of her bedroom, coming to check on her before he went to bed; his bewildered face, horrified to find her lying there beneath the covers, touching herself and gasping; his whispered 'Nell? Are you okay?' and then his vanishing, closing the door loudly, to leave her there, finally for ever – to die and leave her there feeling only her own sorrow and disgrace, which she would live in as if it were a coat.

There were rubber fingers in her, moving, wriggling around, but not like the others. She sat up abruptly, and the young student withdrew his hand, moved away. 'He didn't do it right,' she said to the doctor. She pointed at the student. 'He didn't do it correctly!'

'All right, then,' said the doctor, looking at Olena with concern and alarm. 'All right. You may all leave,' she said to the students.

The doctor herself found nothing. 'You are perfectly normal,' she said. But she suggested that Olena take vitamin B, and listen quietly to music in the evenings.

Olena staggered out through the hospital parking lot, not finding her car at first, and then, when she found it, strapping herself in tightly, as if she were something wild.

She went back to the library and sat at her desk. Everyone had gone home already. In the margins of her notepad she wrote, 'alone as a book, alone as a desk, alone as a library, alone as a pencil, alone as a catalogue, alone as a number, alone as a notepad.' Then she, too, left, went home, made herself tea. She felt separate from her body, felt herself dragging it up the stairs as if it were a big handbag, its leathery hollowness something you could cut up and give away, stick things in. She lay between the sheets of her bed, sweating, perhaps from the tea. The world felt over to her, used up, off to one side. There were no more names to live by.

One should live closer. She had lost her place, as in a book.

One should live closer to where one's parents were buried.

Waiting for Nick's return, she felt herself grow dizzy, float up towards the ceiling, and look down on the handbag. Tomorrow, she would get an organ donor's card, an eye donor's card, as many cards as she could get. She would show them all to Nick. 'Nick! Look at my cards!'

And, when he didn't come home, she remained awake through the long night, through the muffled thud of a bird's hurling itself against the window, through the thunder approaching and leaving like a voice, through the Frankenstein light of the storm. Over her house, in lieu of stars, she felt the bright heads of her mother and father, searching for her, their eyes beamed down from the sky.

'Oh, there you are,' they said. 'Oh, there you are.'

But then they went away again, and she lay waiting, fist in her spine, for the grace and fatigue that would come – surely it must come – of having given so much to the world.

Alison Lurie

THE POOL PEOPLE

Clary Graber's husband had warned her against staying with his mother for three weeks, but Clary decided to go to Key West that April anyhow. She was determined to get four-year-old Kate out of grey, drizzling Boston. Her daughter had had a runny, wet cold, and a worrying little cough on and off ever since Christmas. It was dreadful to see her snuffling around the apartment day after day, pale and limp and whiny, not her normal self at all. But outdoors, in the sun . . .

'Sure, it might help,' Ron said. 'But you're going to be irritated and bored out of your mind there, darling.'

'I don't see why; we all had a good time last year,' said Clary, who sometimes congratulated herself on her ability to get on with her mother-in-law, unlike many of her married friends.

'Yeah,' Ron grinned. 'For four days.'

'And I think it was really nice of June to invite us.' Clary didn't mention that she'd suggested the visit herself. 'Besides, you're going to be in Brussels most of next month.'

'OK, if that's what you want.'

Even after a week in Key West, during which she often had to admit that Ron had had a point, Clary knew she'd been right to come. Kate's sniffles had dried up almost overnight, and in a few days the cough was gone, too, and she was full of energy and joy. It was marvellous to watch her in June's pool, paddling about at the shallow end in her ruffled swimsuit and orange life jacket, sailing leaves or a yellow plastic boat full of plastic Ninja Turtles.

It was the first time that either Clary or Kate had really swum there. Ron always insisted on going to the beach; he didn't care for his mother's pool. It was an unusual shape: long and trapezoid, and Ron said that when he did laps he kept banging into the sides. He disliked the noise of the pool machinery, and the way the water bulged and seethed and churned below the surface at the deep end, as if it were coming to the boil. It gave him a queasy feeling, exactly like June's cooking, he said.

Clary saw absolutely nothing wrong with June's pool. Because it was so deep, and heavily shaded most of the day, it hadn't become stale and warm at the end of the season. The water remained limpidly cool, with a shifting pattern in its depth of white reflections on aquamarine, like delicate wire netting. Its constant flow was silky, sensual, caressing; and the hum of the filter peaceful, almost soporific. Clary thought that what Ron had really wanted, as usual, was to get away from his mother.

Ever since they'd met, Clary had felt sorry for June Graber. Some people might have said that was ridiculous, because June was healthy and remarkably attractive for 58, and she was also extremely well off, having been married to three very rich men. But you had to feel sorry for somebody whose son made jokes about her behind her back and who didn't appear to have any real friends.

It was true, June knew a lot of people in Key West, but she didn't seem to know them very well. According to articles Clary had read, the town was supposed to be full of interesting types, but June didn't seem to have met any of them. Her acquaintances were all well-to-do retired people, mildly and monotonously interested in travel, real estate, home improvement, tropical gardening, and their own ailments. These people also had less than no interest in children; they tended to become anxious as soon as they saw Kate. It was written all over their faces that they were afraid she would damage their rice-paper screens or their hand-blown crystal, or that Kate herself would be injured by their spoilt and irritable pets. Of course it would have been more sensible to leave Kate at home with a sitter, but in Key West during the season, sitters are a vanished species; all the local teenagers were working in shops or restaurants.

After a couple of disastrous encounters, Clary decided that it would be easier, not to mention less boring, to take Kate away whenever June's friends came over, and stay home when June was invited out.

Kate didn't mind being alone; she carried on long conversations with her plastic Turtles, and with two imaginary friends called Davy and Big Bill who lived in the pool.

Clary recognised the names, which were those of the carpenters who had been remodelling June's Key West house last year. Kate had made friends with them, following them about and feeding them animal crackers, her favourite food. Davy, who was small and dark and handsome, and sometimes wore a purple T-shirt with the slogan GAY IS GOOD, told Kate long stories about his dog. Big Bill, a large, slow-moving, muscular young man with three children of his own, made her a set of blocks out of ends of lumber, carefully shaped and sanded.

Kate's current Davy and Big Bill were not exactly like the ones she had known; they were blue, and you could see right through them. Some days they were in the pool, she explained to her mother, and other days they weren't.

Clary, however, had no friends in Key West, imaginary or otherwise. The only adults she had spoken to now in days, besides her mother-in-law, were Rusty and Joy, two handsome, deeply tanned, slightly spacy Key Westerners who came twice a week to clean and service the pool.

But she was reconciled to being bored. A more serious disappointment was her mother-in-law's lack of interest in Kate. June had always been, or pretended to be, dotingly fond of her granddaughter, and Clary had assumed she'd want to spend time with her. She had imagined how, during this time, she herself would be exploring the shops and art galleries, or out on the reef, snorkelling through a cool pale-green universe of brilliantly hued coral and sparkling fish. Instead, she literally couldn't go anywhere alone.

'It's so long since I had a small child,' June had explained when Clary first suggested that she might take Kate somewhere. 'I'd feel much more comfortable if you came, too.'

Another thing that Clary hadn't fully realised was that her mother-in-law was a compulsive talker; she had thought of her, simply, as lively and voluble. But in the past there'd always been other listeners around; now Clary was the only one. The moment June entered the room she began a monologue, even if Clary was reading to Kate or watching the news on TV. She followed her daughter-in-law from room to room, out to the pool and back, talking and talking, and if Clary was going anywhere, June always volunteered to come along.

The only time June was quiet was during and just after her daily swim. She did laps every morning for 20 minutes in a silvery or aqua dressmaker suit, her carefully streaked and set gold hair bunched under a white rubber cap, her leathery bronze shoulders glistening. When she came out and lay dripping on one of the chaises longues, she seemed for a little while to be a different person, with a different, peaceful, sated expression.

'Oh, that felt wonderful,' she might murmur, or 'I wish I could stay in the water for ever.' Then for up to 15 minutes she would lie silent, her eyes closed.

Occasionally June spoke of films or TV programmes, but her usual topics were goods and services. Each morning she drove back and forth across the island in her rented Buick Le Sabre with the air-conditioning turned to high, prowling the end-of-season sales. She returned at lunch time with news of reconnaissance, attack, skirmish, and defeat or triumph in her battle for the most desirable food, drink, clothing and household furnishings and services. ('Would you believe it, there's not such a thing as a down cushion/salad spinner/scissor sharpener on this entire island . . . I tried Sears first, and this absolutely imbecile salesgirl said she'd never heard of them. And then I went to Strunk's. I'm positive I saw some there last year, only the man denied it . . . He was incredibly rude, and I told him so. I said . . .')

June's most extended narrative concerned the remodelling of her house. Its basic theme was the delay, deception, and waste of expensive materials that had taken place during construction. These were, June declared in a favourite phrase, 'mind-boggling'. ('I used to wonder, when I was a kid, you know, how you boggled a mind,' Ron had remarked once. 'I figured you did it with some kind of mechanical gismo, kind of like a toggle switch.' Clary hadn't laughed: she'd had her own troubles with workmen.)

Now she heard the saga again, with additions and elaborations. There'd been nothing but trouble from the first, according to June.

The job had been delayed literally for months because of objections from Historic Preservation of Key West, and their ridiculous rules about everything from the colours of paint you could use to the seven feet you were supposed to leave on each side of your lot, though half the houses in town were jammed up smack against the property line. But if you were a local, as far as June could see, whatever you wanted to build was just fine. She got so furious at one point that she threatened to sue Historic Preservation, which she might as well have done, because after her lawyer talked her out of it, the old biddies on the board raised even more objections and her architect had to redraw the plans at a frightful cost (figures supplied).

Several times during the summer, June had had to come down to keep an eye on things.

'The heat was frightful, totally exhausting, but I truly believe that if I hadn't been here they would never have lifted a finger,' she announced. It was just after lunch and she was sitting by the patio table, chain-smoking, while Clary tried to read the *Times* and Kate, humming softly to herself, coloured a paper napkin. Overhead high, shredded clouds drifted across a pale, light-suffused sky: leaves rustled down one by one from the banyan and sapodilla trees; and the bare, blunt fingers of the frangipani invisibly unfolded sprays of creamy stars.

'You cannot picture how slowly they were working,' June continued, breaking the calm.

'Mm,' Clary said. In fact she could picture it. Key West was a leisurely, laidback place: the speed limit, even on the highway to the airport, was 35 miles an hour. June Graber, however, was used to life on the fast track. She didn't decelerate in Key West; maybe, after nearly 60 years in Manhattan, she didn't know how.

'Of course, the contractor was never around when I wanted him,' she told Clary, stubbing out her Kent and lighting another, 'and those two carpenters of his were impossible. Half the time they were just pretending to be working. I'd look out of the window and I'd see Big Bill carrying a piece of pipe around the side of the house, and five minutes later I'd see him carrying the same pipe back.

'And then, if I asked that big good-looking oaf what he thought he was doing, he wouldn't answer. It turned out he had a hearing problem, but even when I came up close and positively shouted he just kept nodding stupidly and repeating "Yes, ma'am. Right you are, ma'am." And on top of that, he was a born-again Christian. For a while he was actually trying to convert me.' June laughed shrilly. 'He kept leaving these smarmy evangelistical tracts around the house, and once he told me that if I would let Christ into my heart I would find peace, can you imagine the nerve?'

'Mm,' said Clary. I wish to God you *would* find peace, she thought, and then, ashamed of herself, added, 'Awfully annoying.'

'Awfully. And I very soon found out I had to watch them every minute, or else something was sure to go wrong. Well, for example, one day I was having a sprout sandwich here on the deck, and I glanced up and saw that Davy – you remember him, that tough-looking little homosexual – was getting far more paint on my aralias than he was on my fence.' June indicated the leggy, rustling shrubs that edged her back yard. 'The contractor had asked me please not to talk to the crew, to come to him if I had any problem. But really, he was never there half the time, and if I saw somebody doing something stupid right under my nose, I was going to mention it. I had no intention of paying for sloppy work and the waste of expensive materials. That's exactly what I said.'

'Yes, I remember your telling me,' prompted Clary, hoping to urge June towards the end of this familiar episode.

'So when I saw that Davy simply splashing paint everywhere, naturally I spoke up. I said I'd never seen such carelessness. I'd been watching him for 15 minutes, I said, and he wasn't worth 16 dollars an hour. Well, I don't know if I told you . . .'

'You told me,' Clary murmured.

'. . . he became incredibly offensive. At first he didn't even answer me, he simply slammed down his wet paintbrush right on the tiles, you can still see the mark if you move that pincushion cactus, and stood up and started to walk away.

'So naturally I followed him. "Where do you think you're going?" I asked, but really quite calmly and nicely. "I'm paying for your time," I said, "and I'd really like you to listen when I speak to you." Well, then Davy turned round. He pulled his arm away and screamed at me.

"Oh, go to hell, lady!" He positively screamed.' June looked at Clary for a reaction.

'Very rude,' she said, feeling as if she were repeating lines in a play.

'Yes. That's exactly what he said, shouted really, and then he climbed on his motorbike and rode off. Can you imagine?'

'Mm,' Clary said. If only June would stop talking for just a moment, she thought. And we'll be here for nearly two more weeks.

'Well, of course I was furious. I told my contractor he had to fire Davy, but he persuaded me to give him another chance. What a mistake that was, but I guess I have a soft heart.' June placed her manicured hand on washed aquamarine silk above the relevant spot.

'Of course, after Davy came back he was terribly sulky for a while, but I tried to overlook it. And then later I found out he'd had the nerve to tell people *he'd* decided to give *me* another chance, because I was obviously under the influence of negative forces from some previous-life personality.

'Absolutely. He said that. He was one of those New Age types, he always wore a crystal round his neck on a chain.' June made the same face she had made at a restaurant the night before over some doubtful soft-shell crabs. 'My private opinion is, they were probably all three of them on drugs.'

'Mm.' Clary raised and turned the pages of the *Times*, but June didn't take the hint.

'Right before I left for New York in July,' she continued, 'I came back to the house unexpectedly at lunch time, and what did I see?'

'Yes, I know, you saw . . .'

'Just let me tell you,' June interrupted. 'I saw Big Bill sitting on the edge of my pool, dangling his beefy legs in the water and eating a sloppy-joe sandwich. Davy was there, too, lying beside him smoking, and his long, greasy hair was wet, which proved that he had been swimming.

'Well, I made a big effort: I controlled myself and didn't say anything until I saw Mac, and then I told him I'd prefer it if the crew didn't eat on the job or use my pool. Just that, very politely. I didn't contradict him when he pretended they hadn't been swimming, or say anything about not wanting bits of bread and tomatoes and cigarette ashes and long, greasy hair in the water I swam in every day. I think that was perfectly reasonable,' June finished, on a note of enquiry.

'Mm, certainly,' Clary agreed, looking at the pool as it rocked in the sun-dappled shade like a cool, pure trapezoid of ice-blue Perrier.

'But that's the kind of help you get down here,' June sighed. 'The cleaner we had last winter . . .'

Briefly June was diverted, but soon she resumed the saga of the house. After she went back to New York, she said, everything began to go wrong. She could tell from the photos – thank God she had absolutely demanded photos with the weekly statement. The bedroom windows had four panes instead of nine, and the closet shelf divider was completely off-centre, and they'd used this hideous grey grout between the salmon-pink tiles in the bathroom and hung the mirror horizontally instead of vertically. Naturally she insisted that everything be done over.

'And then, can you believe it, Mac expected me to pay for their errors. It simply didn't make sense. I sometimes think that he was deliberately allowing things to go wrong, maybe subconsciously. A friend of mine, she's a therapist, and she said it sounded to her like Mac was a passive-aggressive personality who was working out his hostility to more successful members of society by screwing up my house along with his own career.'

About this time, June said, it became nearly impossible to get hold of Mac on the phone. Even if she called him at 11 p.m. after the rates went down, he'd have his machine on. Or else his wife would answer, and Clary couldn't imagine how rude *she* was. '"Mac has to get up in six hours to work on your house, and I'm not going to wake him now for you or God herself." That's exactly how she put it, she was some kind of feminist nut.'

Clary, with difficulty, suppressed any comment; but one was supplied by Kate, who was now playing on the deck under a red hibiscus. 'She goes, n' she goes, n' she goes on,' Kate sang, pushing a plastic truck laden with plastic Turtles along a track between two boards.

Warming to her subject, lighting another cigarette, June described the final battle. She related how she had paid to have her Key West phone turned on so she could reach Mac on the job, and how often he wasn't there. 'I'd call and Big Bill or Davy would tell me that he was at the lumberyard. And then I'd call back an hour later and they'd say he was at City Hall. Well, eventually I blew up. "God damn it," I said, "I'm tired of hearing your lame excuses. Do you know what these calls are costing me?"'

Perhaps predictably, when June phoned the following day her Key West number did not answer, though she tried it for over an hour, becoming more and more upset and furious. Finally she called her next-door neighbour, an elderly woman with arthritis. She was sorry to bother her, June said, but she had to know what the hell was going on at her house.

Reluctantly, the neighbour agreed to investigate. While the phone charges rapidly piled up, she went slowly next door and came slowly back to tell June that nobody was home. After further persuasion, she went out into her yard, climbed on to a bench and looked over the wall. She returned to report that the fellows who were working over at June's place probably hadn't heard the phone or the bell on account of they were in the pool. Wishing not to cause trouble, she neglected to mention that they were in the pool without any clothes on, though this came out later. 'Yes. Buck naked, in my pool. Can you imagine?' (June spoke, it struck Clary, with a mixed thrill of horror and sexual excitement. She was reminded of something embarrassing a drunken elderly man had said to her at a Key West party a year ago: 'Age calls to youth. I've got a giant crush on you, Clary, just like June's got the hots for those good-looking workmen of hers.')

As soon as she hung up, June Graber continued, she started dialling her Key West number again, and she kept at it for over two hours, until Mac finally answered.

If anything could have made the situation worse then, she said, it was his attitude. He didn't apologise or try to pretend he didn't know what had been going on; instead he laughed.

'For Christ's sake, Mrs Graber,' he said. 'It's nearly 95 degrees out today. That's goddam hot, and the guys were on their lunch break. Anyhow, if you're not here, what difference does it make?'

'Well, I answered that question. I said it wasn't merely that his crew had deliberately contravened my orders. He'd also allowed someone who could very well be infected with AIDS to use the pool. "You're not going to deny that Davy is a homosexual, I suppose," I told him.'

Mac did not try to deny this, June said. Instead, could you believe it, he started to act as if she were at fault and not him. He claimed that there was nothing wrong with Davy, and that anyhow you couldn't get AIDS from swimming in the same pool as an infected person.

'"Yes, that's what the so-called experts tell us," I said to him,' June declared. '"They tell us the water is safe to drink and the wax on apples doesn't cause cancer and a whole lot of things like that, and later you find out they were lying. I'm taking no chances," I said.

'Well, then Mac changed his tune. "All right," he said to me, but very unpleasantly, you know. "If it bothers you so much, I'll tell the guys to stay out of the pool."'

June took a breath, preparing for the climax. 'You know what I said to him? I said, "I don't want you to tell them anything. I want all three of you off my property this afternoon."' She smiled, reliving her victory. 'I told him, "I don't ever want to see you or those lazy bums you've got working for you again." That's exactly what I said.' She blew a self-congratulatory cloud of smoke.

Of course, June added, Mac had tried to argue with her. 'But I simply wouldn't listen, though it meant I had to fly back down to Key West and find another builder (what a frightful job that was, I'll tell you all about it later). And then Mac had the gall to send in a final bill for over 3,000 dollars, when I'd already paid far more than the work was worth. The way I figure it, he was lucky I didn't sue him for contaminating my pool.'

June smiled, ground out her cigarette, and looked round. 'And what did you do this morning, Katie?' she called to her granddaughter.

'Played with the pool people,' Kate said.

'They came today? Now that is rather annoying.' June frowned. 'Monday and Thursday are their days, you know, Clary, and I really can't have . . .'

'It's not your regular pool people she means,' Clary said. 'Not Rusty and Joy.'

'Uh-uh,' Kate agreed, walking a plastic Turtle across the deck towards her grandmother. 'Davy and Big Bill.'

Uncharacteristically, June was silent. She had gone pale under her leathery tan, and her expression was one of strain, even panic.

'Kate hasn't really seen Davy and Big Bill, I'm sure,' Clary reassured her. 'She's just remembered them from last year, and used their names for her imaginary friends. You know, back home she has an imaginary rabbit, it takes baths with her. Are Davy and Big Bill rabbits, too, darling?'

'Nope. Like ordinary people, 'cept they're blue.'

'You see, June, they're blue,' Clary laughed. 'And they don't come in from the street like ordinary people, do they?'

Kate shook her head. 'Live in pool,' she explained, pointing downwards into the water. 'They said, when was my Grammy coming to swim at night again? We want to play with her. That's you,' she told June. 'You're my Grammy.'

June sat frozen; she opened her mouth but seemed for once unable to speak. Either she disapproved of imaginary friends, Clary thought, or she was furious at Kate's term of address. She had already said several times that she didn't want to be called Grammy, Grandma, or Granny ('It always makes me feel like some pathetic little old lady. Why can't Kate say "June", like everyone else in the family?').

The following day it turned very hot, and when Rusty came to clean the pool, Clary brought him iced tea.

'Thanks,' he said, leaning against the shady side of the house. 'Nice and peaceful here. You'd never know . . .' He paused.

'Never know what?'

'Well.' He took another long swallow. 'All that bad business last fall.'

'You mean the way those workmen behaved to Mrs Graber?' No doubt everyone in town's heard that story by now, Clary thought.

Rusty gave her a hard look. 'Hell, no. I mean the shitty way she behaved to them, excuse me. And what happened afterwards.'

'Really?' said Clary. 'What happened afterwards?'

'Well,' he looked across the deck to where Kate was digging in a flowerbed. 'After she fired those guys, and wouldn't pay what she owed, you know about that?'

'Yes,' Clary said. 'At least, that is . . .' She frowned.

'Well, they were up the creek. It wasn't so hard on Mac. He had a couple of repair jobs lined up, and some savings. But Big Bill had a wife and three children under six, and he really needed the money. So when this character he knew asked him to drive a load of never-mind-what to an address in Atlanta, for a thousand dollars, he said okay. You never heard any of this?'

'No.'

'Hell, maybe I shouldn't . . .'

'Go on.'

'Well. Okay. Big Bill, he made it the first time, but on the second trip he ran into a police roadblock just north of Summerland Key. He freaked out and turned the truck round and started back, and a couple of cops started after him. Pretty soon he got to speeding, and when he came to the construction on the bridge he lost control and crashed through a barrier and was DOA at Keys Memorial Hospital.'

'Oh, that's awful.' Clary set down her iced tea; her fingers felt frozen. 'I'm really sorry . . .'

'And then Davy. You heard about that?' Clary shook her head. 'He didn't have any family responsibilities, but he was paying out over 80 dollars a week for AZT. He tried to get on the county programme, but they had a six-week waiting period. So he got antsy and took off for San Francisco, where he'd heard the situation was better, only he ran into more red tape there. Sold his bike and was sleeping in a park. Round about Thanksgiving he decided he couldn't take waiting around to get sick and die, so he jumped off some big building they have out there.'

'Oh, awful,' Clary repeated. 'But I really don't think June – Mrs Graber – knows any of this, or she wouldn't be so . . .' She paused, unable to think of a neutral term.

'She knows,' Rusty said. 'She knows, all right, because I told her when she got down here just before Christmas.'

On Clary's arrival in Key West, June had declared that she was going to give a cocktail party for her. Clary had thanked her mother-in-law politely, but now that the gift had been presented she wasn't enjoying it much. Under an orange-stained rapidly fading sunset, two dozen well-preserved, ageing people in strangely youthful garb –

fire-engine red slacks, Hawaiian shirts, yellow Bermuda shorts, and purple ruffled sundresses – stood around the illuminated pool with drinks in their hands. As dusk fell, the water glowed brighter and brighter, an almost supernatural turquoise; but they turned their backs on it, absorbed in news of local real-estate transactions and their own homes, plants, pets, and ailments.

June, in pink silk patio pyjamas, wove continually among her guests, urging them to try the conch fritters. Clary stood by the shallow end watching her daughter sail leaves and hibiscus flowers in the water and listening to a discussion of restaurants in Bermuda, where she had never been and had no wish to go.

Suddenly, at the other end of the pool, there was a commotion. June Graber, or so it appeared later, had taken a step backwards and fallen in. There were screams and splashing, increasing to a crescendo as several of June's guests, most of them over 60 and more or less woozy with alcohol, jumped in to save her, some on top of each other.

Almost at once the slippery trapezoid of water was full of thrashing multicoloured bodies, the air of confused, hysterical cries. Other guests waded in past Kate, or threw green and magenta-flowered chair cushions that, though intended as life preservers, acted as weapons.

It was fully dark before all the would-be rescuers were helped from the pool, or sloshed themselves out of it, bruised and dazed. June Graber was removed, too, in the midst of the chaos. Apparently she had hit her head on something and sunk almost at once. Though several volunteers, and later an ambulance crew, tried to revive her, they all failed.

Clary didn't witness these vain efforts; at the first glimpse of that heavy, sodden pink thing, she had hurried Kate into the house.

Back in Boston, once the shock had worn off, Clary and Ron's main concern was for Kate. A child's first experience of death was important, and had to be handled tactfully.

'You see, darling,' Clary concluded. 'That's why you always have to wear your life jacket when you're around water, because you can't always be thinking about being careful all the time. Grammy wasn't thinking about it, so she walked backwards and fell into the pool.'

'No,' Kate said.

'How do you mean, no?' Clary hugged Kate anxiously.

'Grammy didn't walk backwards. Big Bill grabbed on her leg and pulled, and then Davy pushed her down in the water.'

'Oh, no, honey,' her father protested.

But in spite of anything her parents could say, Kate stuck to her version. When they continued to press her, she burst into tears, and it took the best efforts of both Clary and Ron to calm her.

'Kate doesn't really understand about death yet, she's just too young,' Clary said later. 'When I put her to bed tonight she told me that your mother is living in the pool in Key West.'

'She said something like that to me, too,' Ron agreed. 'I think maybe it's just a way of denying that she'll never see June again, because the loss is still too painful.'

'Ye-es.' It was painful for Ron, Clary thought – far more than she would have guessed. But really June didn't mean anything to Kate. It was just as well that they had never been close.

Clary pictured June's house in Key West, now on the market, since Ron had refused to go there ever again. She could see the back yard clearly in her mind: the shutters would be closed now, the deck furniture under plastic covers. But the outside spotlights, intended to deter burglars, would have come on automatically at dusk, bathing the palms and hibiscus in their unnatural glow. The pool would be full; the real-estate agent thought that it looked better to prospective buyers.

The water is as cool and clear and silver green as ever, Clary thought: rippling out from the inlets with the same slow, silky bubbling and churning, the same low continuing hum. And there are the same leafy reflections on the surface. And the same shifting lattice patterns on the bottom – as if someone were slowly shaking a net in which, down at the deep end, shadowy blue figures were moving.

Fay Weldon

PAINS

A Story of Most Contemporary Women

Paula lies amazed on the bed, like some poor butterfly with a pin driven through its middle. Can these be the contractions which indicate the beginning of labour? Or perhaps of false labour, or perhaps indeed, being more like pains than contractions, indigestion from the curry fetched in that evening by her kind, thoughtful and radically-minded husband from the local takeaway curry-in-a-hurry house. Who knows?

Paula, at the moment, feels she knows all too little. She does expect, however, soon to know more. The central heating has lately been repaired and there is a hole in the floor where the service engineers have carelessly removed a pipe. So Paula can now hear what is going on in the room below.

More has been going on down there, Paula suspects, than ought to have been.

At the moment her husband Deakey is opening the door to members of the local Women's Liberation Group. Paula has had an upsetting day, as Deakey has told her at least eight times this evening, and, being eight-and-a-half months' pregnant, has sensibly agreed to miss the meeting and has taken to her bed.

Outside, the moon rises.

'We live in an odd part of London,' Paula and Deakey will explain at dinner parties. 'Not exactly smart but it's a solid Edwardian house, with good soil for rose growing. We like roses. Well, who doesn't, but we especially like not those great modern, plastic-looking roses, but the little old-fashioned ones that smell. Yes, that kind of rose attracts greenfly, white-fly, aphids, slugs, and every invisible worm that ever flew in the night in the howling storm, but we think they do smell just wonderful.

Paula and Deakey like everything together, think everything together, change their views together, spray pests together, feel together, are together. We believe this, they say: we do that, we have found out the other. In and out of each other's apron pockets for a full seven years.

'Why shouldn't a man wear an apron just like a woman!' cried Deakey only last night, home at seven as usual from the Civil Service, wielding the garlic crusher like a man, slavering the nut-roast with garlic slime. 'Careful the baby doesn't come out smelling of garlic,' said a friend. There are usually friends about. Paula and Deakey are a very pleasant couple. Anyone would like them. Paula's contraceptive loop fell out one night, which is why she is pregnant. Paula and Deakey are not perfect, which makes them the more endearing.

The moon rises a little further and now shines in upon Paula. It is a full moon. Every full moon, regular as clockwork, Paula's curse has come upon her; until eight months ago, that is; until the unplanned slipping of the loop and the consequent stoppage of blood. What is this? This rusty red stuff? Why now? Merely the body's habit, thinks Paula, wriggling painfully on her contractual pin; what a wonderful thing the body is! It carries its own remembrances.

Perhaps Deakey should be with his Paula at this moment of their joint life? When the moon shines and her body aches? No, thinks Paula. No need for that: Deakey is with me in spirit anyway and, besides, someone has to answer the door. If Paula lies quiet and still, the pains will stop. The quieter she lies, the better she will hear. The rest she can imagine. Marta is arriving. Marta is always the last to come, snorting and jeering. Now they'll all be sitting down in the familiar, conspiratorial ring. 'Male liberal,' Marta will be sneering at Deakey's back as he goes to make coffee, as, if she were black she would say, disparagingly, 'White, white Liberal!' and the others will be nodding their heads and appearing to agree, but thinking how nice to have a husband like Deakey, if only they had, instead of having to pacify their own, having to placate, lie, make coffee in advance, leave extra-special dinners to warm up in the oven, if they want to be allowed out to attend. Well, a meeting such as this one is regarded as domestic treachery. Yes, it is treachery. Female complaints made public. All men do when they're together, everyone knows, is drink, tell funny stories and contemplate exercising their rights: there is no treachery inherent in this. But women shouldn't tell.

And what are the women doing now but telling? Do they not go fully conscious, hand in hand, where once they only went in dreams; one by one they return to that far back world of matriarchy and of Mother Right, and come back to tell the tale of it. Not so much a hen party, this, more a cosmic conspiracy. If it gets too powerful, delves too deep, the sun itself might go out. Don't forget your key when you go out, wife – you might not get back in again. He's serious.

Why hasn't Paula sealed the hole in the bedroom floor? Because Paula needs to know what's going on. Paula suspects that her husband Deakey sometimes has it off in the room below with Audrey, the woman next door. Audrey is married to an adulterous husband. For all anyone knows, the condition is catching. Who is to say what goes on when our eyes are closed and we sleep, as Paula would be sleeping now, if it were not that the Great Lassoer in the sky keeps circling her round her middle and tugging tight, and has woken her. Listen now. Down below.

'The fact is,' bejewelled Rachel is saying, her knees held tight together, 'and as Engels was the first to point out, the nuclear family is founded on the open or concealed domestic slavery of the wife. Within the family, man is the bourgeois and the wife the proletariat. I think we could usefully examine the implications.'

Oh, Deakey. Deakey and Audrey. If it were true, it would be more than mere adultery, it would be treachery. Paula has said as much to Deakey. Deakey, however, maintains that if there is any treachery it lies in Paula's own paranoia, albeit more pronounced than usual by her advanced state of pregnancy. So Deakey and Paula looked up paranoia as it relates to pregnancy in their various books on childbirth and human response and discovered only one mildly-related reference, namely that acute womb envy in the male can predispose to destructive promiscuity. 'Nonsense!' cried Deakey, dismissing the author as Freudian-orientated, and Paula was obliged to agree. Nonsense! All the same, she consulted the midwife, who said she'd never heard of destructive promiscuity but did remark that all men were the same and told a sorry tale of how she once delivered a 16-year-old junkie girl of twins. The mother lay on a double bed between two men who, when asked, declined to move over, but lay just where they were while the midwife worked over and round them. 'Such a nicely spoken girl, too,' said the midwife. The midwife had taken the twins to hospital, she said, wrapped in her raincoat, but the girl never called to collect them.

What can Paula hear now? Is that Audrey's voice amongst the others? It is. It is. Why is Audrey here? She doesn't belong to the group. What is being plotted? A soft little female voice. Audrey's.

'Deakey said come and I know Paula's keen, so I did but I mean I *like* being a woman,' says Audrey. 'I mean, what's wrong with it? I mean, it's all a bit ridiculous, isn't it, all this bra-burning, and why do they make themselves so *plain*? Present company excepted, of course. A woman has a duty to make herself look attractive. I'm happy as I am. I love being feminine and looked after by my husband.'

'Adulteress,' cries Paula in her heart. 'Hypocrite!'

Whoosh and wheesh and there's water everywhere and the Abyssinian or wherever bedcover from Liberty's, with an embroidered Tree of Life upon it, embedded with little pieces of mirror, is not just probably ruined but is rendered cold and uncomfortable to lie upon. What, is Paula now incontinent? Has rage made her thus? Was it like this when she was a little child?

'Little girls don't wet the bed,' said Paula's Mama, 'only nasty little boys.' And she washed and cleaned and ironed on, saying, 'I sacrificed everything for you, my Paula – my career, my fame, my fortune. Your father didn't want a working wife and mother, so now I'll grit my teeth for ever as I smile at you, my little bed-wetting Paula.' Whoosh and wheesh.

'But is the paternalistic society a function of only capitalism, or of civilisation itself – ?' Dandy is asking, in her blue-chip voice. Everyone hates it when Dandy speaks.

To a butterfly, thinks Paula, a pin must feel like an RSJ. A rolled steel joist, the kind you support whole houses by, from within.

'Do you mean function or symptom?' snaps Sybil. 'Make up your mind. If you're a revolutionary, not a radical, you're in the wrong group –'

'Oh dear,' simpers Audrey. 'Oh dear, it's much too deep for me.'

And now Deakey can be heard opening the door and saying: more coffee anyone? Paula's still lying down, says Deakey: she went to a relaxation class this evening and it's exhausted her, ha ha.

It did. It did. Paula hurried home early from the Clinic, wondering what she would find. But when she passed Audrey's house, there was Audrey just ordinarily at her kitchen window. She even smiled as Paula went by, waving her wooden spoon. Making jam, her usual strawberry jam no doubt, and that was when Paula suddenly felt exhausted. Paula found Deakey calmly smoking a herbal cigarette in the living room, but such a sense of sudden departure in the air, such a scent of passion spent, that the baby kicked its heels in the pelvic what-have-you as an ostrich might bury its head in the sand, and shock ran through poor paranoid Paula, and she'd never in all her life felt so tired.

Why was Audrey smiling so at her window? Audrey's adulterous husband was away on business with his PA. Why should Audrey smile? Only one thing can make a betrayed wife smile, and that's betrayal on her own account.

Why should Deakey be smoking last year's Christmas present herbal cigarette at six in the evening, if not to cover something up, fog the scent of betrayal?

A plot, cried Paula. Paranoia, cried Deakey. You insult me! 'But we always think alike,' pleaded Paula. 'You know we do!' and Deakey buried his face in his hands.

'Do men have feelings the same way as women do?' asks Rachel now, down below. 'That's what I always want to know.'

'No,' says Sybil. 'They don't. Oh no! Or if they do, they invalidate them in relation to the degree of their involvement with male institutions. The nicest men will murder, sacrifice, betray, die in the name of patriotism, religion, efficiency, progress and even the Civil Service.' Or that's what Paula supposes Sybil says. It is usually something like that.

A very small, rare buttefly flutters hopelessly in Paula's belly: a very large RSJ, one fit to keep up Centrepoint, pins it to the bed.

What I need, thinks Paula presently, is to consult one of the many books on the shelf which will tell me what the symptoms of labour are. Though I'm sure this is far, far worse than labour, which is a perfectly natural process, could possibly be. Paula sits up, falls off the bed, lies where she falls. If she moves, she feels she will do herself an injury. It is not comfortable being eight months' plus pregnant at the best of times, as Deakey has lately said to Paula when she gets into bed. He keeps himself carefully and considerately to the far side of the bed, away from her – why?

'Nursery schools,' says Philippa. 'That's the answer to all our problems. How I hate and despise Dr Bowlby and his myth of mother-care! If hell were not a male institution, I should wish him there. I suggest we lobby the Council, Monday.'

'For lobby, read lob,' mutters Dandy. 'A few broken windows should work wonders.'

'We are not an extremist group. Go join the Maoists!' shouts Sybil.

Deakey, where are you, Deakey? No, no, these can't be contractions. They're pains. This beautiful red rose opening inside, bursting from bud to bloom, thrusting everything aside to make room for it. Why can't you be here to admire it?

An ear to the ground. Well, it's there already. Paula still lies where she fell: the voices from below are louder now.

'Segregated toilets in infant schools,' Philippa is saying.

'That's where the whole thing starts.'

'Deakey,' Paula had said that afternoon, finding her husband smoking last year's herbal cigarette, 'Audrey's been here, with you. You and she are having a sexual relationship.'

'What nonsense,' said Deakey. 'Audrey's at home making jam. She wouldn't leave jam on the cooker to burn. Our marriage is founded on truth. You and I are equal partners in it.'

'You're laughing at me,' said Paula. 'And you know I have no sense of humour.'

'I have enough for both of us,' said Deakey. 'That is why we have this perfect marriage.'

'It's happened because I'm having the Women's Lib meeting here tonight,' said Paula. 'It's revenge. If I cancel it, will you stop seeing Audrey?'

'For one thing,' elaborated Deakey a little later, as he washed up the plates after the take-away curry. 'I am all for Women's Liberation. We both agree that women are a persecuted majority. For another, I am not having a sexual relationship with Audrey. She's half-witted and wouldn't understand the term. Would you like me to bring your slippers? You must be tired, back from your relaxation class.'

'I don't like the way you keep saying "I",' said Paula. 'It always used to be "we".'

'There are two of you now,' Deakey had said. 'It makes all the difference,' and Paula had lumbered up the stairs and started to cry – why is it always Paula who cries, never Deakey? – fallen asleep, woke to what cannot be labour, for in labour one does not have pains, only contractions, all the books agree – and to hear Deakey opening the door to the Liberation Group, including tonight, for no apparent reason, Audrey.

Another red rose bursts into flower. A whole bush of vulgar floribundas bloom inside, forcing even the RSJ to bend and buckle.

'You are more than me, double what you were. I must look after myself,' Deakey said to Paula. Yes, he did, and baby buried his ostrich head further in the sand which is now growing these amazing flowers.

Downstairs the ladies' slips are showing. The slips are made of barbed wire, worn like hair shirts, excoriating – all women have them, apparently, keep them in their bottom drawers, in readiness.

Marta throws her wedding ring across the room. Tomorrow it will slip beneath one damp-raised lino tile and be lost for ever. Paula can envisage it.

'Why should I have to come home from work and cook and clean,' cries Marta, 'while he sits watching the ads on the telly and says, "Why aren't you like the one on the screen who's wiping paint?"'

He, he, he.

'The Pill made me so depressed I had to have shock treatment,' whispers Philippa, 'and the loop made me flood, all month, and the cap gives me nervous eczema, and he won't wear anything – what shall I do? If I say no, he'll be off.'

'Well, we're Jewish,' murmurs Rachel. 'I only had daughters, so he made this other woman pregnant, and you know my youngest son Benjamin, well, he's hers, not mine. I've never told anyone till now.'

'Oh God, oh God,' says Sybil, 'I'm not all that pretty, am I? I met this man; I thought it was true love. He took me to his flat; all night we made love. I told him I loved him. He left the room, he said for cigarettes, and when he got back into bed, it was another man. His flatmate. He'd had a good lay, he must have said, and passed the news on. Well, so I am. Who cares?'

'What I want to know,' says Dandy darkly, 'is why do they show female orgasm on the media and never male?'

'Women's Lib, Housebound Wives, Group Therapy, what's the difference?' says Audrey, bright and trite as ever. 'It always sounds the same.'

They go. Paula hears them depart. Doors open and close. There is silence. Then:

'Stay a little, Audrey,' says Deakey. Paula hears. Audrey stays.

'Consider the tapeworm,' Paula hears Deakey saying to Audrey. 'Accord it all virtue. A complete set of male and female organs in each of its 50–200 proglottides: it spends its entire life copulating, in all its sections, with itself?" It's the kind of thing Paula would love Deakey to say to her but, of course, Deakey only says it to Audrey, who doesn't understand a word of it. 'Let me be your tapeworm, Audrey,' says Deakey now.

'Thank you, Deakey, but what would Paula think? What would she say?' asks Audrey.

'Paula is in no position to say anything,' says Deakey. 'Paula's too pregnant to think and asleep upstairs in any case.'

Do they kiss, do they copulate? Does Deakey tie Audrey's centre even tighter to her cosy fate, wrapping his 210 proglottides around her? Paula scarcely cares.

Pain. Quite definite pain. What is that noise? Is it Paula? A volcano? Addition or subtraction? The beginning of everything, wrenching more matter out of less? Division, multiplication? Strain and push: don't tear the sheets either, you naughty girl.

Push, rend, slither, pop, baby's here. Baby cries.

'Dear God, what's that?' says Deakey.

It's a boy.

Frank Ronan

HANDSOME MEN ARE SLIGHTLY SUNBURNT

Katie's place was at the top of the lowering grey town that rose the steep hill from the river. Her house stank sweet with decay. The only parts of it that were clear or clean were tracks along the floor between the rooms, where Katie had dragged herself on her bottom for the past 30 years. On fine days she would sit on the doorstep for the company of passing traffic and children. There was a fat spaniel called Barney, who visited her at the same hour each afternoon and sat with her while she fed him fig rolls or coconut creams. She got the meals-on-wheels but aside from that, as far as anyone could tell, she lived on biscuits and tea. What she did about the other end of things was a great mystery. There had never been a lavatory in the house, and no one had the indelicacy to ask a question like that of a small woman of such dignity and independence.

She went in one of those hot months that do not happen every year in County Wexford. A month when she had long hours on her threshold beaming her smile and blinking in the sunshine; when the passing people seemed to have more time to stop with her, as if time had been slowed by the strength of the heat. A time of long mornings when people walked with the limpidness of foreigners, temporarily forgetting that their anatomies had evolved for scuttling through the rainstorms, and evenings which stayed light until near closing time when the pubs were full of pinkened sandy drinkers on weekends when the population of the town had flooded down to the seaside and back again. She liked the smell of hot tar off the road, and was not yet so short-sighted that she couldn't tell who went into Langan's bar across the way, and how they came out of it.

Young men, like Emmet Marshall, would nod to her and ask her how she was, their skins glowing in the evening, on their return from Carnivon, the strand where all the real townspeople went to take their sunshine. And she would answer that she was grand, boy, grand, and hadn't it been a lovely day, thank God. And Emmet, or it might be his cousin Brian, would pass along to their grandmother's big house two doors down and push against a door that they had never known to be locked before bedtime. And say hello to the aunt and go to the tin and take a lump of whatever cake was in it and make their way up to the foot of the big wooden bed. Elbows rested on the bedstead and mouthful of cake, ready to tell the soft gossip of the summer, and hear what they had missed in the town that day: who had died and who had nearly died and who had been taken up to John Of God's for the cure.

Emmet Marshall's grandmother would rouse herself from her doze or her crossword upon his entrance and, giving his face a matter-of-fact glance of appraisal, would begin the conversation by saying, 'Handsome men are slightly sunburnt.' No matter that by now he was deeply tanned, the compliment was still given, and he would take it with the becoming sheepishness of youth. It was a phrase that came from somewhere in her childhood, and she had used it all the summers he could remember, from when he was small enough to believe anything she said. She used to show him her few remaining strands of red hair and thrill him by telling him that she had been a tinker girl before she married his grandfather. There were elaborate stories of travels with an ass and cart, and of saucepan mending, and beautiful lies of her being wooed by the man from the town on account of her long flaming hair. The child Emmet would listen, in a cataract of detail which allowed no room for questions.

As she had been in fiction she was these days in fact. At 18 and back from Carnivon he listened now as she told him what visitors she had had that day, and what the visitors had to say for themselves. Every few minutes her hearing aid would whistle and she would put a hand behind her ear to adjust it, swearing like a navvy. It astonished him sometimes that she had news to tell; that anyone got a word in at all from the foot of her bed. It could only be that she was a creature of extrapolation and could read a great deal into the monosyllables that she occasionally allowed to others. He would stay in her company until it was time to change into a white shirt and make his way down to the Royal Hotel, where he would serve behind the main bar until 11.00 and, on disco nights, behind the bar upstairs until three. It was good work for the summer even though the pay wasn't great because it left you free to be outdoors in the daytime.

The evening of the big fire in Brogue Lane he arrived in her room expecting her to have all the details, but she seemed preoccupied with other matters.

'Did you hear about the fire?' he said.

'Mrs Hammond was up telling me about it. Wasn't it terrible? She brought me the flowers out of her garden. Aren't they lovely?'

She indicated a bowl of roses on her bedside table that he had taken no notice of so far. She always had flowers there and one bloom was much like another to him, camouflaged among the clutter that she needed to have within her reach.

'There's one of them is a bit like a rose I had years ago. I lost it since but I remember sending a slip of it down to Katie in the war. I'd lay any money it's in her garden still. We'll find out soon enough, I suppose.'

There was an uncharacteristically long pause in her talk while she studied the rose, a small pale pink thing of the kind that could hardly be desired but might be treasured once it was owned. Emmet wondered what it was that was happening soon to give them access to Katie's garden, but didn't ask, since he had deduced from his grandmother's tone that he should know already.

'I've been thinking what we're to do with Katie's house,' she said.

For a moment, in his alarm, he couldn't remember whether he had seen Katie on her doorstep that evening. Perhaps he hadn't noticed, preoccupied with the curls of smoke from the direction of Brogue Lane.

'She isn't dead, is she?' he said. It was a natural reaction, in a town where the last rites seemed to outnumber all the other sacraments put together.

His grandmother gave him a withering look. 'You're a great listener,' she said, sarcastically. 'It's been common knowledge the last month they're moving her up to the new estate. The poor craythur won't know where she is.'

'Oh,' Emmet said, unheeded by his grandmother, who went on to speculate how Katie might cope with running water and electricity and all the essentials she had lived without in apparent contentment.

At the next lull in her flow he said, 'So what has her house to do with us?'

'It's mine,' she said, in astonishment at how little her grandson knew of the business of others. 'It's the last of the houses your grandfather bought, God rest him.' And then she caught hold of the subject of her dead husband's goodness, and how he used to sing to her in bed every morning (all of Emmet's aunts had pronounced this to be a fantasy), and how there hadn't been a pauper in the town whom he wouldn't go out of his way to help, if he could (and that was allowed by the aunts to be true).

Emmet had faint memories of his grandfather, a harassed man who had given him half a crown on Sundays to buy ice-cream. There was a vague recollection of the discovery, after his death, that he had owned several small houses in the town. Apparently, he had had the habit, whenever he heard of an impending eviction, of buying the house in question and allowing the tenant to continue to live in it rent free. He had not been a wealthy man, but comfortable by the standards of the town, and in any case none of the houses had been of the kind that commanded a great price in those days. And, being modest in his charity, not even his family had known of these purchases until the reading of his will.

Rather than ask more questions of his grandmother, and give her the great satisfaction she would derive from his ignorance, Emmet listened on, piecing the story together from the unnecessary detail in her speech and half-remembered dribs of family gossip.

She had a proposition for him. The house was not worth selling or renting in its present condition, and she had enough money from the sale of the back field to do it up nicely. What had been considered a slum dwelling 50 years ago was now ideal for the kind of girls who came to work in the banks. Two or three quiet single girls could share it and pay a good rent between them. First, the house had to be cleared, and that was something Emmet could do. She would pay him well. She knew he was saving money to go travelling on the Continent before the summer was out.

'You needn't be paying me, Gran. It's no bother. I'll do it anyway.'

'I wouldn't be asking you if I wasn't going to pay you,' she said. 'It's hard work. You'll take the money.'

Two days later Katie was gone and, by all accounts, delighted with her new lifestyle. She boiled the electric kettle 20 times a day for the pleasure of it. There were still schoolchildren to pass her doorway in the afternoon, though not so much traffic, and she still sat beaming on the threshold. Barney somehow rediscovered her; everyone said the dog was a marvel, and the half-mile daily trot up the hill to the new estate for his fig roll helped to mitigate the effect of the biscuit on his waistline.

After his grandmother had spent an enjoyable morning on the telephone negotiating the hire of a skip, Emmet set to work. The task was destructive enough to be satisfying and sufficiently archaeological to be interesting. There were rotten stair banisters to be kicked down, and layers of paint and wallpaper so thick that the rooms they were taken from seemed twice the volume once they were stripped. Stacks of papers and magazines and calendars that went back to the beginning of the century were sorted through but, in the end, thrown away in their entirety. Katie's hoarding had been so indiscriminate that any separation of the worthwhile was no task for a man working in full spate, and within two hours of entering the house Emmet had become more bulldozer than human. He worked in a frenzy, his blood up, sweating in the baking heat and choking in clouds of dust and plaster dust. When he could no longer breathe he would retreat into the yard and saw down ash trees that were sprouting from the foundations, and hack down brambles and Russian vine, all the time keeping an eye out for the rose his grandmother claimed had once grown there and was there still. He had no doubt of the rose's existence because he knew that his grandmother had the ability to know things she had never witnessed. She might fantasise about the past, but her knowledge of the present was keen and hard and independent of anything so banal as fact.

The only incident that blighted the euphoria of the work happened halfway through the first morning. He was standing by an open window upstairs. Two women had stopped in the street and were peering into the house.

'Shocking,' said one.

'And the money them Marshalls have.'

'That's the way. Them that have it hang on to it.'

'Still, you'd think they'd be ashamed to be keeping the poor old thing in them conditions.'

He reported the conversation to his grandmother at lunchtime, expecting her rage to match his own. But she only shrugged her shoulders. 'I'd expect no less. We gave the woman a roof over her head when her own family wouldn't come up the street to make her a cup of tea. The only way to get thanks in this town is to do nothing.'

And then she was away on one of her pet subjects. How there had been women in the town who would get up at seven and sweep the footpath outside their front doors to gain the reputation of being great housekeepers, before going back to bed for the morning while the dirt piled up in their kitchens. And the women who really did keep clean houses never had time to be sweeping the pavements and were considered slovenly as a result. Then her talk turned to wives who belittled their husbands in public, and finished with a profound piece of advice he had heard often before.

'If you ever find yourself married to a woman who does that, just let her belittle you once, just the once, and you're to hit her a clout, as hard as you can, and walk out the door and never go back to her. Because once a woman has that in her, there's no cure for it, and you'll never be happy with her. Promise me that much, boy.'

'Yes, Gran.' There was no need to say more. You couldn't argue with her at the best of times, and her least palatable opinions were her most sacred. He waited for her instruction on choosing a wife, but this time it didn't come. When it did, the crux of it was that to marry outside his class would be a recipe for disaster. The advice might have some basis in logic except that his grandmother's ideas of class were so constrained that any alliance permitted by her would be forbidden by the law as incestuous.

Instead she said, 'You're looking tired. Is the work going well?'

'Grand,' he said, straightening his back so as not to look tired.

Towards the end of the morning on the second day, with the skip already three quarters full, Brian put his head round the door to see how the work was progressing. Emmet's cousin was a year and a bit younger than him, but close enough in sensibility for the two to be able to talk, and far enough behind in experience for them to have something to talk about. Emmet stopped working and put the sledgehammer down, sitting himself on a pile of rubble.

'Rather you than me,' Brian said, surveying the wreckage.

'It's clear enough now. You should have seen it yesterday. The woman never threw anything out. Have you seen the skip in the yard?'

They went outside, and expletives were muttered over the skip and its contents.

'You've saved nothing?' Brian said.

'What was good was half rotten, and what wasn't would take a lifetime to separate. I thought it may as well all go while I was at it.'

'Still, it's terrible to see a woman's life in a skip.'

'Anything she wanted she must have taken with her.'

'I suppose.'

Despite what he had said, Emmet felt there was a sadness in looking at what was in the skip, and thinking of the vigorous carelessness with which he had thrown the stuff in. There was nothing of value, but a lot that had been precious. For some reason he thought of the rose, hoping he would find it, as if that might in some way mitigate his brutal handling of Katie's past.

Brian said, 'You look thirsty. Will you knock off for a pint across the road?'

Emmet went into the house and looked for his shirt, wiping his face with it before putting it on. 'That'll do,' he said. 'The more rakish the more takish.'

So it was that he entered Langan's bar with the glow of labour and sunburn about him. After he had brought their pints to the table he nodded towards the bar and asked Brian who the girl behind it was.

'Surely you know Fiona? She used to have longer hair. Old Langan's niece. He gave her a job here for the summer.'

'She seems very friendly.' Emmet smiled over at the smiling barmaid, wondering why, if Brian knew who she was, he had never noticed her before. She had the looks of a Langan: the square chin and the good teeth. His consideration of her might have stopped there but she came out from behind the bar, ostensibly to collect the empty glasses from the tables.

'Working hard?' she said, eyeing the dust on Emmet's boots. 'It's a bit hot for that kind of carry on.'

Emmet heard himself say, 'It's the heat that gets your juices up,' surprised by the salaciousness in his own voice. She laughed at him flirtatiously and gave the table she had cleared a perfunctory wipe.

When she was safely behind the bar again, Brian spoke out of the corner of his mouth. 'You're a fast worker.' He was looking at Emmet with sly admiration.

Emmet felt there was nothing to do but take the compliment. He was not, in his own experience, a fast worker, but the reverse. A few words of banter with a seemingly lascivious girl on a hot day was not going to change that. But working hard and feeling healthy and making money had given him a self-confidence to which he was not accustomed. He thought he might be letting Brian down if he made a denial of sexual charisma. He said nothing.

Brian took his silence for self-assurance and said, 'I bet you a tenner you couldn't get her into bed within the week.'

Emmet laughed, at the ludicrousness of the bet, and at Brian's misreading of the situation. He knew that Brian would interpret the laughter differently; that in his excitable virginity he would hear only the hunting cry of the sexually successful male. This did not seem the time to disillusion him with his own half-formed concepts of romantic love.

'You're on,' he said, mentally putting aside the tenner as already lost.

*

You might say that it was a whirlwind romance. He asked her if she was going down to the disco at the Royal that night, and she said that she might be, and both of them contrived to make it seem as casual as possible. He said that he worked behind the bar there, and she said that she knew that already. By ten that evening he was regretting Brian's wager. If she didn't appear he would lose face, and if she did come her appearance would be marred by the bet. He liked her enough to want anything that might happen to be on his own terms and in his own time. When she turned up for the disco the pleasure he felt was mixed with shame. He wanted to sleep with her, but not for the sake of a ten pound note. She sat at the bar counter, fending off the local Romeos and chatting to Emmet whenever he had a moment to stand still, and he, under the pressure of it, found himself putting sly vodkas into the glass of Coke he kept for himself under the counter.

It was about half-past three when they walked up the hill together, and the linking of their arms was unpremeditated. So too was the way in which their arms remained linked at the point where she should have turned for her own house but came with him instead to his grandmother's.

'It's coffee, I suppose,' he said.

'I suppose,' she said.

He felt awkward putting the kettle on, and worse when he said, 'I'd better go up. She gets worried if she's awake and I don't look in.'

He put his head round his grandmother's door. She was asleep in the lamplight, propped up on her pillows with her glasses halfway down her nose and a heavy book open on her chest. Although he had made no noise he had been standing there for only a couple of seconds when her soft snoring gave way to a start and her eyes opened.

'Howiyah?' he said. 'I just got in.'

'Are you on your own?' she said.

He might have been astonished by the question, but he knew, from years of experience, that there was little could be hidden from her, despite her deafness and confinement. You had to be careful when you chose the shade of whiteness of your lies.

'No,' he said. 'One of the lads came in with me. We're having coffee. Do you want anything?'

If she had asked who his visitor was he would have been put on the spot, but she let it pass and switched off her hearing aid as a token gesture of cynicism.

'No,' she said, settling down in her bed and putting her glasses and book to the side. 'Thanks for asking. Don't be up all night. The skip man is coming in the morning.'

Fiona Langan had skin that was faintly freckled without being pale, and a sort of asymmetry that came from one of her nipples being inverted, though it could pop out if she became excited enough. Emmet decided that it was the nipple that made him as lustful as he was, writhing illicitly on the sitting-room carpet, 14 feet below the bed of his sleeping grandmother. After half an hour of them doing every other thing they could think of, he felt that if they didn't fuck soon he would burst, and when she told him that she had never had an orgasm with a man, he did burst, clenching his teeth so that what might have been a roar was no more than a grunt.

'Sorry,' he said. 'I got a bit carried away.'

She observed the pool of sperm by her hip bone and said, 'It's just as well. I'm not on the pill.'

He suggested that he fetch his condoms out of their hiding place, and knew instantly from her expression that he had said the wrong thing.

'I'm not doing it with those yokes,' she said. 'Don't be disgusting.'

He took her head in his hands, hoping, somehow, to bring her back to a state of mind where the concept of disgust would not figure. 'I felt I let you down, that's all,' he said. 'I wanted to make it up to you. There's no reason why you shouldn't get as much out of it as I did.'

He kissed her, and for a moment she was tender again, though sad with it. Just as his hand was moving down to the flat of her stomach she said, 'I'd better go home. I'll be killed for getting in this late.' And then, having freed herself of his arms, her expression brightened, and she said, 'So what are you doing tomorrow?'

'Work.'

'Me too. Will you be coming in at lunchtime?'

'Into Langan's? I could. I have the night off though. What are you doing?'

'I suppose I could skive off if it was in a good cause.'

'I'll think of something.'

By that time they were both smiling, retrieving garments from across the floor and restoring themselves to a state of dress which would make conversation easier between people who, however intimate they had been, barely knew each other.

When she had gone and he had undressed again, he spent some time in front of the mirror before getting into bed, trying to decide whether he was handsome or not. Old women thought he was, and said so, but there was no great satisfaction in being attractive to people who were wise enough to look beyond the superficial. He wasn't interested in whether he was perceived as being a good person: he was as good as he needed to be, and that much he knew already. His mother used to tell him that he was handsome, but he was a child then, and she was somewhat prejudiced. There was no one he knew well enough to ask straight out. In any case, anyone who cared about him would tell him that he was, to spare his feelings, and anyone who didn't care would tell him that he wasn't, to put him in his place.

The image in the mirror changed back and forth between ugly and handsome until, finally, he could discern no more than that he was tired and sunburnt and, remembering that the skip man would arrive in a few hours, that he should go to bed. His last thought before sleep, as he was reviewing the events of the evening, was that, whatever he was, he was not irresistible.

The good weather and the hard work of the morning brought him to his senses and for a few days he and Fiona went about like any other couple that were going out together. They slow-danced at the Five Counties disco and walked in the early evenings, talking easily and liking each other without question. The opportunity didn't seem to arise for another frenzied tussle on the sitting-room carpet, though they spoke, from time to time, of curing her ignorance of coital orgasm, as though it was assumed between them that it was something which would happen naturally in due course.

Brian handed him a tenner one day, assuming, without asking, that that had been the way things had gone. Emmet took the money without comment, making it understood by the gravity of his demeanour that what had once been a joke was now serious and private. The bet, though regrettable, had to be honoured, one way or another. Silence on the matter would bring the least dishonour possible to the subject of the bet.

Brian spoiled things by asking him if he would go on seeing her now the money was won. All Emmet could answer was, 'I'll see how things go, I suppose.'

Sunday was the last good day before the weather broke. Like a couple they rode bicycles out to the Rower for the afternoon, such ease between them that he sang as they cycled and she made no remark on his tunelessness, seeming not to notice it in her happiness. As they returned, a light drizzle fell on them, and she said that rainwater was a good hair conditioner, and it somehow never occurred to them that the best of the summer might be over. As they dismounted at the gates of her house he proposed that she should accompany him to Dublin the following weekend.

If he had had an ear for the minute detail of town gossip he might have known what to expect when she brought him into her house that day. It was well known that her mother had been several times for the cure, with no sign of improvement. Mrs Langan's condition was of the quiet, homely kind that stopped at her threshold, and she had won a certain amount of respect and sympathy for her containment of it, in a town where it seemed that no family was untouched by the problem and there was no one who should be unaware of the depths to which you could be brought by it.

She seemed inordinately pleased to see Emmet, and said at once, 'You're the image of your father,' as though it was the greatest compliment that could be bestowed.

'I know,' was all Emmet could reply. His acknowledgement sounded ungracious in the light of her enthusiasm, but there was no way of telling her that he was being as polite as was possible.

She offered him a drink, making an unsteady gesture towards the sideboard with her own glass, and told him to help himself. Fiona said something about having to get changed, which was the reason they had stopped by in the first place, and left the room. As she went he looked for a trace of embarrassment on her features. He could see none. He knew, from his own experience, that embarrassment would be long gone, replaced with irritation, and that irritation was easier to mask.

The sideboard was well equipped, as though life in this house was one long cocktail party. There was even a full bucket of ice and a sliced lemon. While he had his back turned Mrs Langan said, 'How is your father these days?'

'Grand. I think. I don't see much of him. I'm stopping at Granny's.'

He found her eyes rivetted to his face when he turned towards her. 'He was a great looker. Always had a good colour on him. Out, chasing sheep with his da. That was long before he met your mother, God rest her. I never knew her very well.'

'She never liked the town much,' he said, knowing it would turn the tables and return some of the discomfort that she, unawares, had been making him feel.

'You'll have to tell him I was asking after him.'

He thought that might be the closure of the subject, but when he looked at her he could see a weepy look to her eyes. He couldn't help wondering how she managed to keep the house and herself in such good condition, such cleanliness and order. There was something pathetic about the carefulness of her appearance, as though, every morning, she had to prove to herself that she had some dignity left, and as though there was dignity in smartness.

'I was very fond of him,' she said. 'Did he ever tell you I did a line with him?'

'No.'

'It was a long time ago.'

He tried not to show his alarm. He had no wish to hear any more about his father's youth, or to hear comparisons and have it implied that he and his father were the same at the same age. It was bad enough looking like the man and being identifiable all over the town as Jimmy Marshall's son, without the abandoned loves of Jimmy Marshall's youth weeping over him as though he were Jimmy Marshall reborn. He prayed that Fiona would return before the woman began to weep properly, and Fiona did. Having swapped one pair of jeans for another and stuck a brush through her hair she was ready to go out for the night. He put his half-empty glass down and began to back towards the door.

'Thanks for the drink. It was lovely meeting you.'

'You're not going off on me already?'

'Sorry. We're late. I said to Gran I'd be back by half past.' He didn't say half-past what, since he wasn't wearing a watch and had no idea what time it was.

'You'll have to come back for a proper visit. Fiona, I was telling him about when I used to go out with his dad. Next time I'll get the photos out and you'll stay longer.'

As they walked up Bewley Street with his bicycle between them, they spoke of the coincidence of their parents having been sweethearts once, ignoring the more patent thing they had in common. He knew how she would be feeling about it; that she would be entertaining the futile hope that he had noticed nothing out of the ordinary; that it would seem that her mother was doing nothing more than having a well-earned little drink to herself on a Sunday afternoon. And he didn't want to tell her that he knew how she felt, because that would entail his admission that he knew how he himself felt, and that admission was a long way in the future still.

'God,' he said, 'what if they'd got married?'

'Apparently,' she said, 'they nearly did.'

'You knew about it?'

'She started talking about it the minute she heard I was going out with you.'

'You never told me.'

'It didn't seem important.'

'Well, it isn't. It's just funny, that's all. Funny peculiar. Not that I'm anything like him or you're anything like her.'

'Maybe,' she said. 'God knows what they were like at our age.'

'People don't change,' he said, more because he wished it than because he had had the time to observe it.

And she agreed with him, because if it was true that people couldn't change then her mother was blameless, and pitying the helpless is easier than railing against the obstinate.

He finished clearing Katie's house that week. A rose bush did emerge from the undergrowth at the back of the house, gnarled and decrepit enough to have been planted there in the war. The bush was blind, so there was no way of telling if it was the right rose or not. Under his grandmother's instruction he took cuttings from it and planted them in a pot which she kept on her bedroom windowsill. She discussed the rose so earnestly that he wished, for her sake, it was the right one, or that if it was another rose that she would be dead before it flowered and never know the disappointment of it. She was not a woman upon whom you would wish disappointment.

It was a week of steady rain, and there was no new sunburn by which his grandmother could remark upon his handsomeness in the evenings, but Fiona looked at him from time to time as though she took enjoyment from what she was seeing, and that, in some ways, was better.

Each time he saw her he felt a little warmer towards her. There was nothing too girlie or pretentious about her. If they came to a barbed-wire fence while out walking she would cross it without comment, not flapping or shrieking the way most girls would. If he said what was on his mind she would not seize on it as though she had been waiting to be offended all along. There was nothing in it that could be called love, on his part, but having known love once he had no desire to repeat the agonies of that state.

They looked forward to the weekend in Dublin. There was a party to go to on the Saturday, and a flat they could have to themselves while his older brother was away pursuing some indelicate entanglement of his own. The freedom of a double bed where they could have sex like adults and not have to neck like adolescents.

At the end of the week he reminded his grandmother that he would be away, and she asked him where he would be staying, and he told her.

'Is Fiona going up with you?' she said.

'Yes.'

'And where will she be staying?'

'I don't know. Some friends of hers, I suppose.'

He had spoken the lie that was required of him. Whether she believed it or not was immaterial. She asked him if he was all right for money, and he said that he was, and she gave him some anyway so that, she said, he wouldn't have to be dipping into his savings. Knowing that he had no choice in the matter he took it without a struggle of conscience.

He sensed the change before they arrived in Dublin. Or so it seemed in retrospect. Not that she changed in any way: but that, it would seem, was the problem. She remained the same while he and the world about them changed. Though he saw it at once he did not acknowledge it for 24 hours. He had other things on his mind: an itch for consummation, and the sudden freedom of a city.

The rain was heavier in Dublin and steady, and his brother's flat was dark with it. Over the double bed there was a semi-erotic photograph which might pass for art if a difficult question were asked. The sheets were clean, which was only noticeable in contrast to the state of everything else. He managed to find enough scrags and ends in the kitchen cupboards to put together a sort of pasta supper. They ate to the sound of a wet Alsatian howling from the rooftops and a distant, ignored burglar alarm. They went to bed, and they went so far, and she said, 'No.'

'What's the matter?'

'I might get pregnant.'

Before he had time to think he'd said, 'I thought you would have sorted all that out by now. You've had plenty of time.'

By then there was no way of salvaging the situation, but still he took a deep breath and said, 'Look, I brought the condoms, just in case.'

'I told you. I won't do it with those.'

'Why not?'

'I just won't. They're not reliable. I had a fright once.'

'For Christ's sake,' he said. 'It was you wanted the fucking orgasm.'

When she wept he held her, although he was almost shaking with his own rage, or perhaps his own lust. It was hard to tell. She fell asleep and he stayed awake, holding her and hating her and trying to find reasons for it.

All the next day, every time he looked at her, she seemed out of place. He spoke to her as little as possible, and when he did he spoke sharply. It was when she put on a pair of dungarees to go to the party that his sudden dislike of her found a focus. She asked him if she looked all right, and he said that she did, without looking. He wondered how he had never noticed before how unsophisticated she was; how he could have ended up doing a line with such a culchie. At home the dungarees had looked fine; almost fashionable, but there they seemed like a white frock at a funeral.

He ignored her at the party while he talked to a girl who told him that he had a great tan, and who was prepared to argue the merits of Bunyon with him. They were laughing about the puddles and the horsepads when Fiona came up to them. He had noted, with a terrible satisfaction, that she had found no one to talk to, and he knew, maliciously, that she would have no idea what he and the new girl were talking about. She asked him for the keys of the flat and said that she'd had enough. He gave her the keys and carried on his conversation as though he barely knew her.

She was gone when he returned in the morning prepared, in the euphoria of conquest, to be quite civilised about the whole thing. There was a note on the door saying the keys were with a neighbour. If it ever crossed his mind, in the time that followed, that he should make any amends, he never got the chance. Although you wouldn't think it possible, in a town that small and that lowering, that he should never see her again.

Angela Carter

LIZZIE'S TIGER

When the circus came to town and Lizzie saw the tiger, they were living on Ferry Street, in a very poor way. It was the time of the greatest parsimony in their father's house; everyone knows the first $100,000 is the most difficult and the dollar bills were breeding slowly, slowly, even if he practised a little touch of usury on the side to prick his cash in the direction of greater productivity. In another 10 years' time, the war between the states would provide rich pickings for the coffin-makers, but, back then, back in the Fifties, well – if he had been a praying man, he would have gone down on his knees for a little outbreak of summer cholera or a touch, just a touch of typhoid. To his chagrin, there had been nobody to bill when he had buried his wife.

For, at that time, the girls were just freshly orphaned. Emma was 13, Lizzie four – stern and square, a squat rectangle of a child. Emma parted Lizzie's hair in the middle, stretched it back over each side of her bulging forehead and braided it tight. Emma dressed her, undressed her, scrubbed her night and morning with a damp flannel, and humped the great lump of little girl around in her arms whenever Lizzie would let her, although Lizzie was not a demonstrative child and did not show affection easily, except to the head of the house, and then only when she wanted something. She knew where the power was and, intuitively feminine in spite of her gruff appearance, she knew how to court it.

That cottage on Ferry – very well, it was a slum; but the undertaker lived on unconcerned among the stiff furnishings of his defunct marriage. His bits and pieces would be admired today if they turned up freshly beeswaxed in an antique store, but in those days they were plain old-fashioned, and time would only make them more so in that dreary interior, the tiny house he never mended, eroding clapboard and diseased paint, mildew on the dark wallpaper with a brown pattern like brains, the ominous crimson border round the top of the walls, the sisters sleeping in one room in one thrifty bed.

On Ferry, in the worst part of town, among the dark-skinned Portuguese fresh off the boat with their earrings, flashing teeth and incomprehensible speech, come over the ocean to work the mills whose newly erected chimneys closed in every perspective, every year more chimneys, more smoke, more newcomers, and the peremptory shriek of the whistle that summoned to labour as bells had once summoned to prayer.

The hovel on Ferry stood, or, rather, leaned at a bibulous angle on a narrow street cut across at an oblique angle by another narrow street, all the old wooden homes like an upset cookie jar or broken gingerbread houses lurching this way and that way, and the shutters hanging off their hinges and windows stuffed with old newspapers and the snagged picket fence and raised voices in unknown tongues and howling of dogs who, since puppyhood, had known of the world only the circumference of their chain. Outside the parlour windows was nothing but rows of counterfeit houses that sometimes used to scream.

Such was the anxious architecture of the two girls' early childhood.

A hand came in the night and stuck a poster, showing the head of a tiger, on to a picket fence. As soon as Lizzie saw the poster, she wanted to go to the circus, but Emma had no money, not a cent. The 13-year-old was keeping house at that time, the last skivvy just quit with bad words on both sides. Every morning, Father would compute the day's expenses, hand Emma just so much, no more. He was angry when he saw the poster on the fence; he thought the circus should have paid him rental for the use. He came home in the evening, sweet with embalming fluid, saw the poster, purpled with fury, ripped it off, tore it up.

Then it was suppertime. Emma was no great shakes at cookery and Father, dismissing the possibility of another costly skivvy until such time as plague struck, already pondered the cost-efficiency of remarriage; when Emma served up her hunks of cod, translucently uncooked within, her warmed-over coffee and a dank loaf of baker's bread, it almost put him in a courting mood, but that is not to say his meal improved his temper. So that, when his youngest climbed kitten-like upon his knee and, lisping, twining her tiny fingers in his gunmetal watch-chain, begged small change for the circus, he answered her with words of unusual harshness, for he truly loved his last daughter, whose obduracy recalled his own.

Emma unhandily darned a sock.

'Get that child to bed before I lose my temper!'

Emma dropped the sock and scooped up a Lizzie, whose mouth set in dour lines of affront as she was borne off. The square-jawed scrap, deposited on the rustling straw mattress – oat straw, softest and cheapest – sat where she had been dropped and stared at the dust in a sunbeam. She seethed with resentment. It was moist midsummer, only six o'clock and still bright day outside.

She had a will of iron, this one. She swung her feet on to the stool upon which the girls climbed down out of bed, thence to the floor. The kitchen door stood open for air behind the screen door. From the parlour came the low murmur of Emma's voice as she read *The Providence Journal* aloud to Father.

Next door's lean and famished hound launched itself at the fence in a frenzy of yapping that concealed the creak of Lizzie's boots on the back porch. Unobserved, she was off – off and away! – trotting down Ferry Street, her cheeks pink with self-reliance and intent. She would not be denied. The circus! The word tinkled in her head with a red sound, as if it might signify a profane church.

'That's a tiger,' Emma had told her as, hand in hand, they inspected the poster on their fence.

'A tiger is a big cat,' Emma added instructively.

How big a cat?

A *very* big cat.

A dumpy, red-striped regular cat of the small domestic variety greeted Lizzie with a raucous mew from atop a gatepost as she stumped determined along Ferry Street; our cat, Ginger, whom Emma, in a small ecstasy of sentimental whimsy presaging that of her latter protracted spinsterhood, would sometimes call Miss Ginger, or even, Miss Ginger Cuddles. Lizzie, however, sternly ignored Miss Ginger

Cuddles. Miss Ginger Cuddles sneaked. The cat put out a paw as Lizzie brushed past, as if seeking to detain her, as if to suggest she took second thoughts as to her escapade, but, for all the apparent decision with which Lizzie put one firm foot before the other, she had not the least idea where the circus might be and would not have got there at all without the help of a gaggle of ragged Irish children from Corkey Row, who happened by in the company of a lean, black and tan, barking dog of unforeseen breed that had *this* much in common with Miss Ginger Cuddles, it could go whither it pleased.

This free-ranging dog with its easy-going grin took a fancy to Lizzie and, yapping with glee, danced around the little figure in the white pinafore as it marched along. Lizzie reached out to pat its head. She was a fearless girl.

The child-gang saw her pet their dog and took a fancy to her for the same reason as crows settle on one particular tree. Their wild smiles circled round her. 'Going to the circus, are ye? See the clown and the ladies dancing?' Lizzie knew nothing about clowns and dancers, but she nodded, and one boy took hold of one hand, another of the other, so they raced her off between them. They soon saw her little legs could not keep up their pace, so the 10-year-old put her up on his shoulders where she rode like a lord. Soon they came to a field on the edge of town.

'See the big top?' There was a red-and-white striped tent of scarcely imaginable proportions, into which you could have popped the entire house on Ferry, and the yard too, with enough room to spare inside for another house, and another – a vast red-and-white striped tent, with ripping naphtha flares outside and, besides this, all manner of other tents, booths and stalls, dotted about the field, but most of all she was impressed by the great number of people, for it seemed to her that the whole town must be out tonight, yet, when you looked closely at the throng, nowhere at all was anyone who looked like she did, or her father did, or Emma; nowhere that old New England lantern jaw, those ice-blue eyes.

She was a stranger among these strangers, for all here were those the mills had brought to town, the ones with different faces. The plump, pink-cheeked Lancashire mill-hands, with brave red neckerchiefs; the sombre features of the Canucks imbibing fun with characteristic gloom; and the white smiles of the Portuguese, who knew how to enjoy themselves, laughter tripping off their tipsy-sounding tongues.

'Here y'are!' announced her random companions as they dumped her down and, feeling they had amply done their duty by their self-imposed charge, they capered off among the throng, planning, perhaps, to slither under the canvas and so enjoy the shows for free, or even to pick a pocket or two to complete the treat, who knows?

Above the field, the sky now acquired the melting tones of the end of the day, the plush, smoky sunsets unique to these unprecedented industrial cities, sunsets never seen in this world before the age of steam that set the mills in motion that made us all modern.

At sunset, the incomparably grave and massive light of New England acquires a monumental, a Roman sensuality; under this sternly voluptuous sky, Lizzie abandoned herself to the unpremeditated smells and never-before-heard noises – hot fat in a vat of frying doughnuts; horse dung; boiling sugar; frying onions; popping corn; freshly churned earth; vomit; sweat; cries of vendors; crack of rifles from the range; singsong of the white-faced clown, who clattered a banjo, while a woman in pink fleshings danced upon a little stage. Too much for Lizzie to take in at once, too much for Lizzie to take in at all – too rich a feast for her senses, so that she was taken a little beyond herself and felt her head spinning, a vertigo, a sense of profound strangeness overcoming her.

As unnoticeably small as she was, she was taken up by the crowd and tossed about among insensitive shoes and petticoats, too close to the ground to see much else for long; she imbibed the frenetic bustle of the midway through her nose, her ears, her skin that twitched, prickled, heated up with excitement so that she began to colour up in the way she had, her cheeks marked with red, like the marbling on the insides of the family Bible. She found herself swept by the tide of the crowd to a long table where hard cider was sold from a barrel.

The white tablecloth was wet and sticky with spillage and gave forth a dizzy, sweet, metallic odour. An old woman filled tin mugs at the barrel spigot, mug after mug, and threw coins on to other coins into a tin box – splash, chink, clang. Lizzie clung on to the edge of the table to prevent herself being carried away again. Splash, chink, clang. Trade was brisk, so the old woman never turned the spigot off and cider cascaded on to the ground on the other side of the table.

The devil got into Lizzie, then. She ducked down and sneaked in under the edge of the tablecloth, to hide in the resonant darkness and crouch on the crushed grass in fresh mud, as she held out her unobserved hands under the discontinuous stream from the spigot until she collected two hollowed palmsful, which she licked up, and smacked her lips. Filled, licked, smacked again. She was so preoccupied with her delicious thievery that she jumped half out of her skin when she felt a living, quivering thing thrust into her neck in that very sensitive spot where her braids divided. Something moist and intimate shoved inquisitively at the nape of her neck.

She craned round and came face to face with a melancholy piglet, decently dressed in a slightly soiled ruff. She courteously filled her palms with cider and offered it to her new acquaintance, who sucked it up eagerly. She squirmed to feel the wet quiver of the pig's curious lips against her hands. It drank, tossed its pink snout, and trotted off out the back way from the table.

Lizzie did not hesitate. She followed the piglet past the dried-cod smell of the cider-seller's skirts. The piglet's tail disappeared beneath a cart piled with fresh barrels that was pulled up behind the stall, Lizzie pursued the engaging piglet to find herself suddenly out in the open again, but this time in an abrupt margin of pitch black and silence. She had slipped out of the circus grounds through a hole in its periphery and the dark had formed into a huge clot, the night, whilst Lizzie was underneath the table; behind her were the lights, but here only shadowy undergrowth, stirring, and then the call of a night bird.

The pig paused to rootle the earth, but when Lizzie reached out to stroke it, it shook its ears out of its eyes and took off at a great pace into the countryside. However, her attention was immediately diverted from this disappointment by the sight of a man who stood with his back to the lights, leaning slightly forward. The cider-barrel spigot sound repeated itself. Fumbling with the front of his trousers, he turned round and tripped over Lizzie, because he was a little unsteady on his feet and she was scarcely to be seen among the shadows. He bent down and took hold of her shoulders.

'A small child,' he said, and belched a puff of acridity into her face. Lurching a little, he squatted right down in front of her, so they were on the same level. It was so dark that she could see of his face only the hint of a moustache above the pale half moon of his smile.

'Small girl,' he corrected himself, after a closer look. He did not speak like ordinary folks. He was not from around these parts. He belched again, and again tugged at his trousers. He took firm hold of her right hand and brought it tenderly up between his squatting thighs.

'Small girl, do you know what *this* is for?'

She felt buttons; serge; something hairy; something moist and moving. She didn't mind it. He kept his hand on hers and made her rub him for a minute or two. He hissed between his teeth: 'Kissy, Kissy from missy?'

She *did* mind that and shook an obdurate head; she did not like her father's hard, dry imperative kisses, and endured them only for the sake of power. Sometimes Emma touched her cheek lightly with unparted lips. Lizzie would allow no more. The man sighed when she shook her head, took her hand away from his crotch, softly folded it up on its fingers and gave her hand ceremoniously back to her.

'Gratuity,' he said, felt in his pocket and flipped her a nickel. Then he straightened up and walked away. Lizzie put the coin in her pinafore pocket and, after a moment's thought, stumped off after the funny man along the still, secret edges of the field, curious as to what he might do next.

But now surprises were going on all round her in the bushes, mewings, squeaks, rustlings, although the funny man paid no attention to them, not even when a stately fat woman rose up under his feet, huge as a moon and stark naked but for her stays, but for black cotton stockings held up by garters with silk rosettes on them, but for a majestic hat of black leghorn with feathers. The woman addressed the drunken man angrily, in a language with a good many k's in it, but he ploughed on indifferently and Lizzie scuttled unseen after, casting an inquisitive backward glance. She had never seen a woman's naked breasts since she could remember, and this pair of melons jiggled entrancingly as the fat woman shook her fist in the wake of the funny man before she parted her thighs with a wet smack and sank down on her knees again in the grass in which something unseen moaned.

Then a person scarcely as tall as Lizzie herself, dressed up like a little drummer boy, somersaulted – head over heels – directly across their paths, muttering to himself as he did so. Lizzie had just the time to see that, although he was small, he was not shaped quite right, for his head seemed to have been pressed into his shoulders with some violence, but then he was gone.

Don't think any of this frightened her. She was not the kind of child that frightens easily.

Then they were at the back of a tent, not the big, striped tent, but another, smaller tent, where the funny man fumbled with the flap much as he had fumbled with his trousers. A bright mauve, ammoniac reek pulsed out from this tent; it was lit up inside like a Chinese lantern and glowed. At last he managed to unfasten it and went inside. He did not so much as attempt to close up after him; he seemed to be in as great a hurry as the tumbling dwarf, so she slipped through too, but as soon as she was inside, she lost him, because there were so many other people there.

Feet of customers had worn all the grass from the ground and it had been replaced by sawdust, which soon stuck all over the mudpie Lizzie had become. The tent was lined with cages on wheels, but she could not see high enough to see what was inside them, yet, mixed with the everyday chatter around her, she heard strange cries that did not come from human throats, so she knew she was on the right track.

She saw what could be seen: a young couple, arm in arm, he whispering in her ear, she giggling; a group of three grinning, gaping youths, poking sticks within the bars; a family that went down in steps of size, a man, a woman, a boy, a girl, a boy, a girl, a boy, a girl, down to a baby of indeterminate sex in the woman's arms. There were many more present, but these were the people she took account of.

The gagging stench was worse than a summer privy and a savage hullabaloo went on all the time, a roaring as if the sea had teeth.

She eeled her way past skirts and trousers and scratched, bare legs of summer boys until she was standing beside the biggest brother of the staircase family at the front of the crowd, but still she could not see the tiger, even if she stood on tiptoe, she saw only wheels and the red-and-gold base of the cage, whereon was depicted a woman without any clothes, much like the one in the grass outside only without the hat and stockings, and some foliage, with a gilded moon and stars. The brother of the staircase family was much older than she, perhaps 12, and clearly of the lower class, but clean and respectable-looking, although the entire family possessed that pale, peculiar look characteristic of the mill operatives. The brother looked down and saw a small child in a filthy pinafore peering and straining upwards.

'*Veux-tu voir le chat grand, ma petite?*'

Lizzie did not understand what he said, but she knew what he was saying and nodded assent. Mother looked over the head of the good baby in the lace bonnet as her son heaved Lizzie up in his arms for a good look.

'*Les poux . . .*' she warned, but her son paid her no heed.

'*Voilà, ma petite!*'

The tiger walked up and down, up and down; it walked up and down like Satan walking about the world and it burned. It burned so brightly, she was scorched. Its tail, thick as her father's forearm, twitched back and forth at the tip. The quick, loping stride of the caged tiger; its eyes like yellow coins of a foreign currency; its round, innocent, toy-like ears; the stiff whiskers sticking out with an artificial look; the red mouth from which the bright noise came. It walked up and down on straw strewn with bloody bones.

The tiger kept its head down, questing hither and thither though in quest of what might not be told. All its motion was slung from the marvellous haunches it held so high you could have rolled a marble down its back, if it would have let you, and the marble would have run down an oblique angle until it rolled over the domed forehead on to the floor. In its hind legs the tense muscles keened and sang. It was a miracle of dynamic suspension. It reached one end of the cage in a few paces and whirled around upon itself in one liquid motion; nothing could be quicker or more beautiful than its walk. It was all raw, vivid, exasperated nerves. Upon its pelt it bore the imprint of the bars behind which it lived.

The young lad who kept hold of her clung tight as she lunged forwards towards the beast, but he could not stop her clutching the bars of the cage with her little fingers and he tried but he could not dislodge them. The tiger stopped in its tracks halfway through its mysterious patrol and looked at her. Her pale-blue Calvinist eyes of New England encountered with a shock the flat, mineral eyes of the tiger.

It seemed to Lizzie that they exchanged this cool regard for an endless time, the tiger and herself.

Then something strange happened. The svelte beast fell to its knees. It was as if it had been subdued by the presence of this child, as if this little child of all the children in the world, might lead it towards a peaceable kingdom where it need not eat meat. But only 'as if'. All we could see was, it knelt. A crackle of shock ran through the tent: the tiger was acting out of character.

Its mind remained, however, a law unto itself. We did not know what it was thinking. How could we?

It stopped roaring. Instead it started to emit a rattling purr. Time somersaulted. Space diminished to the field of attractive force between the child and the tiger. All that existed in the whole world now were Lizzie and the tiger.

Then, oh! Then . . . it came towards her, as if she was winding it to her on an invisible string by the exercise of pure will. I cannot tell you how much she loved the tiger, nor how wonderful she thought it was. It was the power of her love that forced it to come to her, on its knees, like a penitent. It dragged its pale belly across the dirty straw towards the bars where the little soft creature hung by its naked fingers. Behind it followed the serpentine length of its ceaselessly twitching tail.

There was a wrinkle in its nose and it buzzed and rumbled and they never took their eyes off one another, though neither had the least idea what the other meant.

The boy holding Lizzie got scared and pummelled her little fists, but she would not let go a grip as tight and senseless as that of the newborn.

Crack! The spell broke.

The world bounded into the ring.

A lash cracked round the tiger's carnivorous head, and a glorious hero sprang into the cage brandishing in the hand that did not hold the whip a three-legged stool. He wore fawn britches, black boots, a bright red jacket frogged with gold, a tall hat. A dervish, he: he beckoned, crouched, pointed with the whip, menaced with the stool, leaped and twirled in a brilliant ballet of mimic ferocity, the dance of the Taming of the Tiger, to whom the tamer gave no chance to fight at all.

The great cat unpeeled its eyes off Lizzie's in a trice, rose up on its hind legs and feinted at the whip like our puss Ginger feints at a piece of paper dangled from a string. It batted at the tamer with its enormous paws, but the whip continued to confuse, irritate and torment it and, what with the shouting, the sudden, excited baying of the crowd, the dreadful confusion of the signs surrounding it, habitual custom, a lifetime's training, the tiger whimpered, laid back its ears and scampered away from the whirling man to an obscure corner of the stage, there to cower, while its flanks heaved, the picture of humiliation.

Lizzie let go of the bars and clung, mud stains and all, to her young protector for comfort. She was shaken to the roots by the attack of the trainer upon the tiger and her four-year-old roots were very near the surface.

The tamer gave his whip a final, contemptuous ripple around his adversary's whiskers that made it sink its huge head on the floor. Then he placed one booted foot on the tiger's skull and cleared his throat for speech. He was a hero. He was a tiger himself, but even more so, because he was a man.

'Ladies and gentlemen, boys and girls, this incomparable tiger known as the Scourge of Bengal, and brought alive-oh to Boston from its native jungle but three short months before this present time, now, at my imperious command, offers you a perfect imitation of docility and obedience. But do not let the brute deceive you. Brute it was, and brute it remains. Not for nothing did it receive the sobriquet of Scourge for, in its native habitat, it thought nothing of consuming a dozen brown-skinned heathen for its breakfast and follow up with a couple of dozen more for dinner!'

A pleasing shudder tingled through the crowd.

'This tiger,' and the beast whickered ingratiatingly when he named it, 'is the veritable incarnation of blood lust and fury; in a single instant, it can turn from furry quiescence into 300 pounds, yes, 300 pounds, of death-dealing fury.

'The tiger is the cat's revenge.'

Oh, Miss Ginger, Miss Ginger Cuddles, who sat mewing censoriously on the gatepost as Lizzie passed by; who would have thought you seethed with such resentment!

The man's voice dropped to a confidential whisper and Lizzie, although she was in such a state, such nerves, recognised this was the same man as the one she had met behind the cider stall, although now he exhibited such erect mastery, not a single person in the tent would have thought he had been drinking.

'What is the nature of the bond between us, between the Beast and Man? Let me tell you. It is fear. Fear! Nothing but fear. Do you know how insomnia is the plague of the tamer of cats? How all night long, every night, we pace our quarters, impossible to close our eyes for brooding on what day, what hour, what moment the fatal beast will choose to strike?

'Don't think I cannot bleed, or that they have not wounded me. Under my clothes, my body is a palimpsest of scars, scar upon scar. I heal only to be once more broken open. No skin of mine is not scar tissue. And I am always afraid, always; all the time in the ring, in the cage, now, this moment – this very moment, boys and girls, ladies and gentleman, you see before you a man in the grip of mortal fear.

'Here and now I am in terror of my life.

'At this moment I am in this cage within a perfect death trap.'

Theatrical pause.

'But,' and here he knocked the tiger's nose with his whipstock, so that it howled with pain and affront, 'but . . .' and Lizzie saw the secret frog he kept within his trousers shift a little, '. . . *but* I'm not half so scared of the big brute as it is of me!'

He showed his red maw in a laugh.

'For I bring to bear upon its killer instinct a rational man's knowledge of the power of fear. The whip, the stool, are instruments of bluff with which I create his fear in my arena. In my cage, among my cats, I have established a hierarchy of *fear* and among my cats you might well say I am *top dog*, because I know that all the time they want to kill me, that is their project, that is their intention . . . but as for them, they just don't know what I might do next. No, sir!'

As if enchanted by the notion, he laughed out loud again, but by now, the tiger, perhaps incensed by the unexpected blow on the nose, rumbled out a clear and incontrovertible message of disaffection and, with a quick jerk of its sculpted head, flung the man's foot away so that, caught off balance, he half toppled over. And the tiger was no longer a thing of stillness, of hard edges and clear outlines, but a whizz of black and red, maw and canines, in the air. On him.

The crowd immediately bayed.

But the tamer, with enormous presence of mind, seeing as how he was drunk, and, in the circumstances, with almost uncanny physical agility, bounced backwards on his boot-heels and thrust the stool he carried in his left hand into the fierce tiger's jaws, leaving the tiger worrying, gnawing, destroying the harmless thing, as a ragged black boy quickly unlatched the cage door and out leapt the tamer, unscathed, amidst hurrahs.

Lizzie's stunned little face was now mottled all over with a curious reddish purple, with the heat of the tent, with passion, with the sudden access of enlightenment.

To see the rest of the stupendous cat act, the audience would have had to buy another ticket for the Big Top, besides the ticket for the menagerie, for which it had already paid, so, reluctant on the whole to do that, in spite of the promise of clowns and dancing ladies, it soon got bored with watching the tiger splintering the wooden stool, and drifted off.

'*Eh bien, ma petite*,' said her boy-nurse to her in a sweet, singsong, crooning voice. '*Tu a vue la bête! La bête du cauchemar!*'

The baby in the lace bonnet had slept peacefully through all this, but now began to stir and mumble. Its mother nudged her husband with her elbow.

'*On va, Papa?*'

The crooning, smiling boy brought his bright pink lips down on Lizzie's forehead for a farewell kiss. She could not bear that; she struggled furiously and shouted to be put down. With that, her cover broke and she burst out of her disguise of dirt and silence; half the remaining gawpers in the tent had kin who had been bleakly buried by her father, the rest owed him money. She was the most famous daughter in all Fall River.

'Well, if it ain't Andrew Borden's little girl! What are they Canucks doing with little Lizzie Borden?'

Amy Bloom

LOVE IS NOT A PIE

In the middle of the eulogy at my mother's boring and heartbreaking funeral, I began to think about calling off the wedding. August 21 did not seem like a good date, John Wescott did not seem like a good person to marry, and I couldn't see myself in the long white silk gown Mrs Wescott had offered me. We had gotten engaged at Christmas, while my mother was starting to die; she died in May, earlier than we had expected. When the minister said, 'She was a rare spirit, full of the kind of bravery and joy which inspires others,' I stared at the pale blue ceiling and thought, 'My mother would not have wanted me to spend my life with this man.'

After the funeral, we took the little box of ashes back to the house and entertained everybody who came by to pay their respects. Lots of my father's law school colleagues, a few of his former students, my uncle Steve and his new wife, my cousins (whom my sister Lizzie and I always referred to as Thing One and Thing Two), friends from the old neighbourhood, before my mother's sculpture started selling, her art world friends, her sisters, some of my friends from high school, some people I used to babysit for, my best friend from college, some friends of Lizzie's, a lot of people I didn't recognise. I'd been living away from home for a long time, first at college, now at law school.

My sister, my father, and I worked the room. And everyone who came in my father embraced. It didn't matter whether they started to pat him on the back or shake his hand, he pulled them to him and hugged them so hard I saw people's feet lift right off the floor.

My father was in the middle of squeezing Mrs Ellis, our cleaning lady, when he saw Mr DeCuervo come in, still carrying his suitcase. He about dropped Mrs Ellis and went charging over to Mr DeCuervo, wrapped his arms around him, and the two of them moaned and rocked together in a passionate, musicless waltz. My sister and I sat down on the couch, pressed against each other, watching our father cry all over his friend, our mother's lover.

When I was eleven and Lizzie was eight, her last naked summer, Mr DeCuervo and his daughter, Gisela, who was just about to turn eight, spent part of the summer with us at the cabin in Maine.

That July, the DeCuervos came, but without Mrs DeCuervo, who had to go visit a sick someone in Argentina, where they were from. That was okay with us. Mrs DeCuervo was a professional mother, a type that made my sister and me very uncomfortable. She told us to wash the berries before we ate them, to rest after lunch, to put on more suntan lotion, to make our beds. She was a nice lady, she was just always in our way. My mother had a few very basic summer rules: don't eat food with mould or insects on it; don't swim alone; don't even think about waking your mother before 8 a.m. unless you are fatally injured or ill. That was about it, but Mrs DeCuervo was always amending and adding to the list, one apologetic eye on our mother, who was pleasant and friendly as usual and did things the way she always did. She made it pretty clear that if we were cowed by the likes of Mrs DeCuervo, we were on our own. They got divorced when Gisela was in her second year at Mount Holyoke.

We liked pretty, docile Gisela, and bullied her a little bit, and liked her even more because she didn't squeal on us, on me in particular. We liked her father, too. We saw the two of them, sometimes the three of them, at occasional picnics and lesser holidays. He always complimented us, never made stupid jokes at our expense, and brought us unusual, perfect little presents. Silver barrettes for me the summer I was letting my hair grow out from my pixie cut; a leather bookmark for Lizzie, who learned to read when she was three. My mother would stand behind us as we unwrapped the gifts, smiling and shaking her head at his extravagance.

When they drove up, we were all sitting on the porch. Mr DeCuervo got out first, his curly brown hair making him look like a giant dandelion, with his yellow T-shirt and brown jeans. Gisela looked just like him, her long, curly brown hair caught up in a bun, wisps flying around her tanned little face. As they walked toward us, she took his hand and I felt a rush of warmth for her, for showing how much she loved her daddy, like I loved mine, and for showing that she was a little afraid of us, of me, probably.

Mr DeCuervo and Gisela fitted into our routine as though they'd been coming to the cabin for years, instead of just last summer. We had the kind of summer cabin routine that stays with you forever as a model of leisure, of life being enjoyed. We'd get up early, listening to the birds screaming and trilling, and make ourselves some breakfast; cereal or toast if the parents were up, cake or cold spaghetti or marshmallows if they were still asleep. My mother got up first, usually. She'd make a cup of coffee and brush and braid our hair and set us loose. If we were going exploring, she'd put three sandwiches and three pieces of fruit in a bag, with an army blanket. Otherwise, she'd just wave to us as we headed down to the lake.

We'd come back at lunchtime and eat whatever was around and then go out to the lake or the forest, or down the road to see if the townie kids were in a mood to play with us. I don't know what the grown-ups did all day; sometimes they'd come out to swim for a while, and sometimes we'd find my mother in the shed she used for a studio. But when we came back at five or six, they all seemed happy and relaxed, drinking gin and tonics on the porch, watching us run toward the house. It was the most beautiful time.

At night, after dinner, the fathers would wash up and my mother would sit on the porch, smoking a cigarette, listening to Aretha Franklin or Billie Holiday or Sam Cooke, and after a little while she'd stub out her cigarette and the four of us would dance. We'd twist and lindy and jitterbug and stomp, all of us copying my mother. And pretty soon the daddies would drift in with their dish towels and their beers, and they'd lean in the doorway and watch. My mother would turn first to my father, always to him, first.

'What about it, Danny? Care to dance?' And she'd put her hand on his shoulder and he'd smile, tossing his dish towel to Mr DeCuervo, resting his beer on the floor. My father would lumber along gamely, shuffling his feet and smiling. Sometimes he'd wave his arms around and pretend to be a fish or a bear while my mother swung her body easily and dreamily, sliding through the music. They'd always lindy together to Fats Domino. That was my father's favourite, and then he'd sit down, puffing a little.

My mother would stand there, snapping her fingers, shifting back and forth.

'Gaucho, you dance with her, before I have a coronary,' said my father.

So Mr DeCuervo would shrug gracefully and toss the two dish towels back to my father. And then he'd bop toward my mother, his face still turned toward my father.

They only danced the fast dances, and they danced as though they'd been waiting all their lives for each song. My mother's movements got deeper and smoother, and Mr DeCuervo suddenly came alive, as though a spotlight had hit him. My father danced the way he was, warm, noisy, teasing, a little overpowering; but Mr DeCuervo, who was usually quiet and thoughtful and serious, became a different man when he danced with my mother. His dancing was light and happy and soulful, edging up on my mother, turning her, matching her every step. They would smile at all of us, in turn, and then face each other, too transported to smile.

'Dance with Daddy some more,' my sister said, speaking for all three of us. They had left us too far behind.

My mother blew Lizzie a kiss. 'Okay, sweetheart.'

She turned to both men, laughing, and said, 'That message was certainly loud and clear. Let's take a little break, Gauch, and get these monkeys to bed. It's getting late, girls.'

And the three of them shepherded the three of us through the bedtime rituals, moving us in and out of the kitchen for milk, the bathroom for teeth, toilet, and calamine lotion, and finally to our big bedroom. We slept in our underwear and T-shirts, which impressed Gisela.

'No pyjamas?' she had said the first night.

'Not necessary,' I said smugly.

We would lie there after they kissed us, listening to our parents talk and crack peanuts and snap cards; they played gin and poker while they listened to Dinah Washington and Odetta.

One night, I woke up around midnight and crossed the living room to get some water in the kitchen and see if there was any strawberry shortcake left. I saw my mother and Mr DeCuervo hugging, and I remember being surprised and puzzled. I had seen movies; if you hugged someone like you'd never let them go, surely you were supposed to be kissing, too. It wasn't a Mummy-Daddy hug, partly because their hugs were defined by the fact that my father was eight inches taller and a hundred pounds heavier than my mother. These two looked all wrong to me; embraces were a big pink-and-orange man enveloping a small, lean black-and-white woman who gazed up at him. My mother and Mr DeCuervo looked like sister and brother, standing cheek-to-cheek, with their broad shoulders and long, tanned, bare legs. My mother's hands were under Mr DeCuervo's white T-shirt.

She must have felt my eyes on her, because she opened hers slowly.

'Oh, honey, you startled us. Mr DeCuervo and I were just saying good night. Do you want me to tuck you in after you go to the bathroom?' Not quite a bribe, certainly a reminder that I was more important to her than he was. They had moved apart so quickly and smoothly I couldn't even remember how they had looked together. I nodded to my mother; what I had seen was already being transformed into a standard good-night embrace, the kind my mother gave to all of her close friends.

When I came back from the bathroom, Mr DeCuervo had disappeared and my mother was waiting, looking out at the moon. She walked me to the bedroom and kissed me, first on my forehead, then on my lips.

'Sleep well, pumpkin pie. See you in the morning.'

'Will you make blueberry pancakes tomorrow?' It seemed like a good time to ask.

'We'll see. Go to sleep.'

'Please, Mummy.'

'Okay, we'll have a blueberry morning. Go to sleep now. Good night, nurse.' And she watched me for a moment from the doorway, and then she was gone.

My father got up at five to go fishing with some men at the other side of the lake. Every Saturday in July he'd go off with a big red bandanna tied over his bald spot, his Mets T-shirt, and his tackle box, and he'd fish until around three. Mr DeCuervo said that he'd clean them, cook them, and eat them but he wouldn't spend a day with a bunch of guys in baseball caps and white socks to catch them.

I woke up smelling coffee and butter. Gisela and Lizzie were already out of bed, and I was aggrieved; I was the one who had asked for the pancakes, and they were probably all eaten by now.

Mr DeCuervo and Lizzie were sitting at the table, finishing their pancakes. My mother and Gisela were sitting on the blue couch in the living room while my mother brushed Gisela's hair. She was brushing it more gently than she brushed mine, not slapping her on the shoulder to make her sit still. Gisela didn't wiggle, and she didn't scream when my mother hit a knot.

I was getting ready to be mad when my mother winked at me over Gisela's head and said, 'There's a stack of pancakes for you on top of the stove, bunny. Gauch, would you please lift them for Ellen? The plate's probably hot.'

Mr DeCuervo handed me my pancakes, which were huge brown wheels studded with smashed purpley berries; he put my fork and knife on top of a folded paper towel and patted my cheek. His hand smelled like coffee and cinnamon. He knew what I liked and pushed the butter and the honey and the syrup toward me.

'Juice?' he said.

I nodded, trying to watch him when he wasn't looking; he didn't seem like the man I thought I saw in the moonlight, giving my mother a funny hug.

'Great pancakes, Lila,' he said.

My mother smiled and put a barrette in Gisela's hair. It was starting to get warm, so I swallowed my pancakes and kicked Lizzie to get her attention.

'Let's go,' I said.

'Wash your face, then go,' my mother said.

I stuck my face under the kitchen tap, and my mother and Mr DeCuervo laughed. Triumphantly, I led the two little girls out of the house, snatching our towels off the line as we ran down to the water, suddenly filled with longing for the lake.

'Last one in's a fart,' I screamed, cannonballing off the end of the dock. I hit the cold blue water, shattering its surface. Lizzie and Gisela jumped in beside me, and we played water games until my father drove up in the pick-up with a bucket of fish. He waved to us and told us we'd be eating fish for the next two days, and we groaned and held our noses as he went into the cabin, laughing.

There was a string of sunny days like that one: swimming, fishing with Daddy off the dock, eating peanut butter and jelly sandwiches in the rowboat, drinking Orange Crush on the porch swing.

And then it rained for a week. We woke up the first rainy morning, listening to it tap and dance on the roof. My mother stuck her head into our bedroom.

'It's monsoon weather, honeys. How about cocoa and cinnamon toast?'

We pulled on our overalls and sweaters and went into the kitchen, where my mother had already laid our mugs and plates. She was engaged in her rainy day ritual: making sangria. First she poured the orange juice out of the big white plastic pitcher into three empty peanut butter jars. Then she started chopping up all the oranges, lemons, and limes we had in the house. She let me pour the brandy over the fruit, Gisela threw in the sugar, and Lizzie came up for air long enough to pour the big bottle of red wine over everything. I cannot imagine drinking anything else on rainy days.

Rainy days were basically a series of snacks, more and less elaborate, punctuated by board games, card games, and whining. We drank soda and juice all day, ate cheese, bananas, cookies, bologna, graham crackers, Jiffy popcorn, hard-boiled eggs. The grown-ups ate cheese and crackers and drank sangria.

The daddies were reading in the two big armchairs, my mother had gone off to her room to sketch, and we were getting bored. When my mother came downstairs for a cigarette, I was writing my name in the honey that had spilled on the kitchen table, and Gisela and Lizzie were pulling the stuffing out of the hole in the bottom of the blue couch.

'Jesus Christ, Ellen, get your hands out of the goddamn honey. Liz, Gisela, that's absolutely unacceptable, you know that. Leave the poor couch alone. If you're so damn stir-crazy, go outside and dance in the rain.'

The two men looked up, slowly focusing, as if from a great distance.

'Lila, really . . .' said my father.

'Lila, it's pouring. We'll keep an eye on them now,' said Mr DeCuervo.

'Right. Like you were.' My mother was grinning.

'Can we, Mummy, can we go in the rain? Can we take off our clothes and go in the rain?'

'Sure, go naked, there's no point in getting your clothes wet and no point in suits. There's not likely to be a big crowd in the yard.'

We raced to the porch before my mother could get rational, stripped and ran whooping into the rain, leaping off the porch onto the muddy lawn, shouting and feeling superior to every child in Maine who had to stay indoors.

We played Goddesses-in-the-Rain, which consisted of caressing our bodies and screaming the names of everyone we knew, and we played ring-a-ring-a-rosy and tag and red light/green light and catch, all deliciously slippery and surreal in the sheets of grey rain. Our parents watched us from the porch.

When we finally came in, thrilled with ourselves and the extent to which we were completely, profoundly wet, in every pore, they bundled us up and told us to dry our hair and get ready for dinner.

My mother brushed our hair, and then she made spaghetti sauce while my father made a salad and Mr DeCuervo made a strawberry tart, piling the berries into a huge red, shiny pyramid in the centre of the pastry. We were in heaven. The grown-ups were laughing a lot, sipping their rosy drinks, tossing vegetables back and forth.

After dinner, my mother took us into the living room to dance, and then the power went off.

'Shit,' said my father in the kitchen.

'Double shit,' said Mr DeCuervo, and we heard them stumbling around in the dark, laughing and cursing, until they came in with two flashlights.

The daddies accompanied us to the bathroom and whispered that we could skip everything except peeing, since there was no electricity. The two of them kissed us good night, my father's moustache tickling, Mr DeCuervo's sliding over my cheek. My mother came into the room a moment later, and her face was as smooth and warm as a velvet cushion. We didn't stay awake for long. The rain dance and the eating and the storm had worn us out.

It was still dark when I woke up, but the rain had stopped and the power had returned and the light was burning in our hallway. It made me feel very grown-up and responsible, getting out of bed and going around the house, turning out the lights that no one else knew were on: I was conserving electricity.

I went into the bathroom and was squeezed by stomach cramps, probably from all the burnt popcorn kernels I had eaten. I sat on the toilet for a long time, watching a brown spider crawl along the wall; I'd knock him down and then watch him climb back up again, toward the towels. My cramps were better but not gone, so I decided to wake my mother. My father would have been more sympathetic, but he was the heavier sleeper, and by the time he understood what I was telling him, my mother would have her bathrobe on and be massaging my stomach kindly, though without the excited concern I felt was my due as a victim of illness.

I walked down to my parents' room, turning the hall light back on. I pushed open the creaky door and saw my mother spooned up against my father's back, as she always was, and Mr DeCuervo spooned up against her, his arm over the covers, his other hand resting on the top of her head.

I stood and looked and then backed out of the bedroom. They hadn't moved, the three of them breathing deeply, in unison. What was that, I thought, what did I see? I wanted to go back and take another look, to see it again, to make it disappear, to watch them carefully, until I understood.

My cramps were gone. I went back to my own bed, staring at Lizzie and Gisela, who looked in their sleep like little girl-versions of the two men I had just seen. Just sleeping, I thought, the grown-ups were just sleeping. Maybe Mr DeCuervo's bed had collapsed, like ours did two summers ago. Or maybe it got wet in the storm. I thought I would never be able to fall asleep, but the next thing I remember is waking up to more rain and Lizzie and Gisela begging my mother to take us to the movies in town. We went to see *The Sound of Music*, which had been playing at the Bijou for about ten years.

I don't remember much else about the summer; all of the images run together. We went on swimming and fishing and taking the rowboat out for little adventures, and when the DeCuervos left I hugged Gisela but wasn't going to hug him, until he whispered in my ear, 'Next year we'll bring up a motorboat and I'll teach you to water-ski,' and then I hugged him very hard and my mother put her hand on my head lightly, giving benediction.

The next summer, I went off to camp in July and wasn't there when the DeCuervos came. Lizzie said they had a good time without me. Then they couldn't come for a couple of summers in a row, and by the time they came again, Gisela and Lizzie were at camp with me in New Hampshire; the four grown-ups spent about a week together, and later I heard my father say that another vacation with Elvira DeCuervo would kill him, or he'd kill her. My mother said she wasn't so bad.

We saw them a little less after that. They came, Gisela and Mr DeCuervo, to my high school graduation, to my mother's opening in Boston, my father's fiftieth birthday party and then Lizzie's graduation. When my mother went down to New York she'd have dinner with the three of them, she said, but sometimes her plans would change and they'd have to substitute lunch for dinner.

After all the mourners left, Mr DeCuervo gave us a sympathy note from Gisela, with a beautiful pen-and-ink of our mother inside it. The two men went into the living room and took out a bottle of Scotch and two glasses. It was like we weren't there; they put on Billie Holiday singing 'Embraceable You', and they got down to serious drinking and grieving. Lizzie and I went into the kitchen and decided to eat everything sweet that people had brought over: brownies, strudel, pfeffernuss, sweet potato pie, Mrs Ellis's chocolate cake with chocolate mousse in the middle. We laid out two plates and two mugs of milk and got to it.

Lizzie said, 'You know, when I was home in April, he called every day.' She jerked her head toward the living room.

I couldn't tell if she approved or disapproved, and I didn't know what I thought about it either.

'She called him Bolivar.'

'What? She always called him Gaucho, and so we didn't call him anything.'

'I know, but she called him Bolivar. I heard her talking to him every fucking day, El, she called him Bolivar.'

Tears were running down Lizzie's face, and I wished my mother was there to pat her soft fuzzy hair and keep her from choking on her tears. I held her hand across the table, still holding my fork in my other hand. I could feel my mother looking at me, smiling and narrowing her eyes a little, the way she did when I was balking. I dropped the fork onto my plate and went over and hugged Lizzie, who leaned into me as though her spine had collapsed.

'I asked her about it after the third call,' she said into my shoulder.

'What'd she say?' I straightened Lizzie up so I could hear her.

'She said, "Of course he calls at noon. He knows that's when I'm feeling strongest." And I told her that's not what I meant, that I hadn't known they were so close.'

'You said that?'

'Yeah. And she said, "Honey, nobody loves me more than Bolivar." And I didn't know what to say, so I just sat there feeling like "Do I really want to hear this?" and then she fell asleep.'

'So what do you think?'

'I don't know. I was getting ready to ask her again –'

'You're amazing, Lizzie,' I interrupted. She really is, she's so quiet, but she goes and has conversations I can't even imagine having.

'But I didn't have to ask because she brought it up herself, the next day after he called. She got off the phone, looking just so exhausted, she was sweating but she was smiling. She was staring out at the crab apple trees in the yard, and she said, "There were apple trees in bloom when I met Bolivar, and the trees were right where the sculpture needed to be in the courtyard, and so he offered to get rid of the trees and I said that seemed arrogant and he said that they'd replant them. So I said, 'Okay', and he said, 'What's so bad about arrogance?' And the first time he and Daddy met, the two of them drank Scotch and watched soccer while I made dinner. And then they washed up, just like at the cabin. And when the two of them are in the room together and you two girls are with us, I know that I am living in a state of grace."'

'She said that? She said "in a state of grace"? Mummy said that?'

'Yes, Ellen. Christ, what do you think, I'm making up interesting deathbed statements?' Lizzie hates to be interrupted, especially by me.

'Sorry. Go on.'

'Anyway, we were talking and I sort of asked what were we actually talking about. I mean, close friends or very close friends, and she just laughed. You know how she'd look at us like she knew exactly where we were going when we said we were going to a friend's house for the afternoon but we were really going to drink Boone's Farm and skinny-dip at the quarry? Well, she looked just like that and she took my hand. Her hand was so light, El. And she said that the three of them loved each other, each differently, and that they were both amazing men, each special, each deserving love and appreciation. She said that she thought Daddy was the most wonderful husband a woman could have and that she was very glad we had him as a father. And I asked her how she could do it, love them both, and how they could stand it. And she said, "Love is not a pie, honey. I love you and Ellen differently because you are different people, wonderful people, but not at all the same. And so who I am with each of you is different, unique to us. I don't choose between you. And it's the same way with Daddy and Bolivar. People think that it can't be that way, but it can. You just have to find the right people." And then she shut her eyes for the afternoon. Your eyes are bugging out, El.'

'Well, Jesus, I guess so. I mean, I knew . . .'

'You knew? And you didn't tell me?'

'You were eight or something, Lizzie, what was I supposed to say? I didn't even know what I knew then.'

'So, what did you know?' Lizzie was very serious. It was a real breach of our rules not to share inside dirt about our parents, especially our mother; we were always trying to figure her out.

I didn't know how to tell her about the three of them; that was even less normal than her having an affair with Mr DeCuervo with Daddy's permission. I couldn't even think of the words to describe what I had seen, so I just said, 'I saw Mummy and Mr DeCuervo kissing one night after we were in bed.'

'Really? Where was Daddy?'

'I don't know. But wherever he was, obviously he knew what was going on. I mean, that's what Mummy was telling you, right? That Daddy knew and that it was okay with him.'

'Yeah. Jesus.'

I went back to my chair and sat down. We were halfway through the strudel when the two men came in. They were drunk but not incoherent. They just weren't their normal selves, but I guess we weren't either, with our eyes puffy and red and all this destroyed food around us.

'Beautiful girls,' Mr DeCuervo said to my father. They were hanging in the doorway, one on each side.

'They are, they really are. And smart, couldn't find smarter girls.'

My father went on and on about how smart we were. Lizzie and I just looked at each other, embarrassed but not displeased.

'Ellen has Lila's mouth,' Mr DeCuervo said. 'You have your mother's mouth, with the right side going up a little more than the left. Exquisite.'

My father was nodding his head, like this was the greatest truth ever told. And Daddy turned to Lizzie and said, 'And you have your mother's eyes. Since the day you were born and I looked right into them, I thought, "My God, she's got Lila's eyes, but blue, not green." '

And Mr DeCuervo was nodding away, of course. I wondered if they were going to do a complete autopsy, but they stopped.

My father came over to the table and put one hand on each of us. 'You girls made your mother incredibly happy. There was nothing she ever created that gave her more pride and joy than you two. And she thought that you were both so special . . .' He started crying, and Mr DeCuervo put an arm around his waist.

'We're gonna lie down for a while, girls. Maybe later we'll have dinner or something.' My father kissed us both, wet and rough, and the two of them went down the hall.

Lizzie and I looked at each other again.

'Wanna get drunk?' I said.

'No, I don't think so. I guess I'll go lie down for a while too, unless you want company.' She looked like she was about to sleep standing up, so I shook my head. I was planning on calling John anyway.

Lizzie came over and hugged me, hard, and I hugged her back and brushed the chocolate crumbs out of her hair.

Sitting alone in the kitchen, I thought about John, about telling him about my mother and her affair and how the two men were sacked out in my parents' bed, probably snoring. And I could hear John's silence and I knew that he would think my father must not have really loved my mother if he'd let her go with another man; or that my mother must have been a real bitch, forcing my father to tolerate an affair 'right in his own home'. I thought I ought to call him before I got myself completely enraged over a conversation that hadn't taken place.

I called, and John was very sweet, asking how I was feeling, how the memorial service had gone, how my father was. And I told him all that and then I knew I couldn't tell him the rest and that I couldn't marry a man I couldn't tell this story to.

'I'm so sorry, Ellen,' he said. 'You must be very upset. What a difficult day for you.'

I realise that was a perfectly normal response, it just was all wrong for me. I didn't come from a normal family, I wasn't ready to get normal.

I felt terrible, hurting John, but I couldn't marry him just because I didn't want to hurt him, so I said, 'And that's not the worst of it, John. I can't marry you, I really can't. I know this is pretty hard to listen to over the phone . . .' I couldn't think what else to say.

'Ellen, let's talk about this when you get back to Boston. I know what kind of a strain you must be under. I had the feeling that you were unhappy about some of Mother's ideas. We can work something out when you get back.'

'I know you think this is because of my mother's death, and it is, but not the way you think. John, I just can't marry you. I'm not going to wear your mother's dress and I'm not going to marry you and I'm very sorry.'

He was quiet for a long time, and then he said, 'I don't understand, Ellen. We've already ordered the invitations.' And I knew that I was right. If he had said, 'Fuck this, I'm coming to see you tonight,' or even, 'I don't know what you're talking about, but I want to marry you anyway,' I'd probably have changed my mind. But as it was, I said goodbye sort of quietly and hung up.

It was like two funerals in one day. I sat at the table, poking the cake into little shapes and then knocking them over. My mother would have sent me out for a walk. I'd started clearing the stuff away when my father and Mr DeCuervo appeared, looking more together.

'How about some gin rummy, El?' my father said.

'If you're up for it,' said Mr DeCuervo.

'Okay,' I said. 'I just broke up with John Wescott.'

'Oh?'

I couldn't tell which one spoke.

'I told him that I didn't think we'd make each other happy.'

Which was what I had meant to say.

My father hugged me and said, 'I'm sorry that it's hard for you. You did the right thing.' Then he turned to Mr DeCuervo and said, 'Did she know how to call them, or what? Your mother knew that you weren't going to marry that guy.'

'She was almost always right, Dan.'

'Almost always, not quite,' said my father, and the two of them laughed at some private joke and shook hands like a pair of old boxers.

'So, you deal,' my father said, leaning back in his chair.

'Penny a point,' said Mr DeCuervo.

Elizabeth McCracken

IT'S BAD LUCK TO DIE

Maybe you wonder how a Jewish girl from Des Moines got Jesus Christ tattooed on her three times: ascending on one thigh, crucified on the other, and conducting a miniature apocalypse beneath the right shoulder. It wasn't religion that put them there; it was Tiny, my husband. I have a Buddha round the back, too. He was going to give me Moses parting the Red Sea, but I was running out of space. Besides, I told him, I was beginning to feel like a Great Figures in Religion comic book.

Tiny had been married three times before he met me, one wife right after the other. I only had him, the one, and he's been dead six months now. I met Tiny the summer I left school, 1965, when I was 18 and he was 49. My cousin Babs, who was a little wild, had a crazy boyfriend (the whole family was worried about it) and he and some of his buddies dared her to get tattooed. She called me up and told me she needed me there and that I was not to judge, squawk or faint at the sight of blood. She knew none of that was my style, anyway.

We drove to Tiny's shop over on East 14th because that's where Steve, the crazy boy, had got the panther that had a toehold on his shoulder. The shop was clean and smelled of antiseptic.

Tiny was set up on a stool at the back, smoking a cigarette, an itty-bit of a man next to a Japanese screen. He was wearing a blue dress shirt with the cuffs turned back, and his hands and arms were covered with blue-black lines: stars across the knuckles, snakes winding up under the sleeves. The wide flowered tie that spread out over his chest and stomach might've been right on a big man, but on Tiny it looked like an out-of-control garden. His trousers were white and wrinkled, and there was a bit of blue ink at the knee; a suit jacket, just as wrinkled, hung on the coat rack in back.

'So,' he said. 'Who's the one?'

'Me,' Babs said, trying to sound tough. She told him what she wanted: a little red and black bow on her bottom. He asked her if she were old enough; she got out her wallet and showed him her driver's licence.

There was something a little Southern in Tiny's voice, but I couldn't pick out what it was. He jumped off the stool, and I saw that he was about a full foot shorter than me. I'm six feet tall, have been since I was 12. I looked right down on top of his slick black hair.

He beckoned us back of the screen to a padded table, the kind you see in doctors' surgeries, only much lower. Tiny turned around politely while Babs lowered her blue jeans and clambered up. He spun back, frowned, pulled down just the top of her yellow flowered underwear like he was taking fat off a chicken, and tapped her. 'Right here's where you want it?'

'That's fine.'

'Honey, is it fine, or is it what you want?'

Babs twisted to look, careful not to catch his eye. 'That's what I want.'

He squirted her with antiseptic, got a razor and shaved the area good. I sat on a folding chair across from them.

Tiny loosened his tie, slipped it off, and hung it, still knotted, on a peg on the wall. 'Hey Stretch,' he said, looking at me. 'What's your name?'

'Lois.'

'Lois. Like Louise?' He rolled his shirtsleeves up further. Babs was holding on to the table like a drowning sailor, and Tiny hadn't even got the needle out yet.

'Lois,' I answered, and fast because I had to talk to him over Babs' hindquarters and that made me a little self-conscious, 'after my Uncle Louis. I was going to be named Natalie, after my Uncle Nathan, but then Louis died and Mum liked him better anyway.'

'My name is Tiny. No story there but the obvious.' He picked up an electric needle from a workbench and hunted for the right pot of colour.

'I'm Babs,' said Babs, reaching around for a handshake. Tiny was looking elsewhere, and he dipped the needle in some black ink and flipped it on. 'For Barbara?' he asked, setting into her skin.

'A-a-a-a-abigail. Ouch.' She gripped the table.

'Honey,' said Tiny, 'this doesn't hurt. I got you where you're good and fleshy. Might sting a little, but it doesn't hurt.'

'Okay,' said Babs, and she sounded almost convinced.

'For Abraham,' I said suddenly. 'Abigail after Abraham.'

'Pretty girls named after men,' said Tiny, taking a cloth and wiping some ink off Babs so he could see what he was doing. 'Thought that only happened in the South.'

Looking back, it seems like he took an hour working on Babs, but now I know it couldn't have been more than 10 minutes. He looked up at me from time to time, smiling or winking. I thought that he was just one of those flirty types, one of those bold little guys, and that if he had been looking at Babs in the face instead of where he was looking at her, he would've flirted with her the same. Years later he told me that he was bowled over by all those square inches of skin, how I was so big and still not fat. 'I fell for you right away,' he said.

Up until then, I'd always thought it was only sensible to fall in love with tall men so that I wouldn't look so much of a giantess. That way we could dance in public, in scale, no circus act. It didn't matter, though: I never had a date at school, couldn't dance a step. I spent my time in cinemas, because most movie stars looked pretty tall, even if it was only a trick of the camera, a crate under their feet in love scenes.

Tiny, no doubt, no tricks about it, was short, but he charmed me from the start. His charm was as quick and easy as his needle, and he could turn it on and off the same way. On the Tuesday afternoons I visited him before we got married, I saw all types jangle the bell on the front door as they pushed it open: big men, skinny kids, nervous couples gambling on love for ever. Most of them asked the same thing: 'Does it hurt?' To people who rubbed him up the wrong way, he'd say, 'If you're worried about it, I guess you don't really want one'; to those he liked, chiefly the women, he'd drawl, 'I could make you smile while I do it.' He could, too; he could tell your background by the feel of your skin, and would talk about ridiculous things –

baseball scores, recipes for homemade beer, the sorry state of music – anything but the business at hand.

He could even charm my mother, who, on meeting Tiny, this little man only two years younger than her, was aggrieved to discover she liked him.

When he was finished with Babs, he put on a bandage and handed her a little white card that said *How to Take Care of Your New Tattoo*. It had his name and address at the bottom. She read it and nodded. He turned and gave me a card, too.

'Anything for you today?' he asked me.

'No, no. I'm a chaperone, that's all.'

'Too bad. You'd tattoo great. You're pale – high contrast.'

Babs looked a little white herself now, standing up, zipping her pants. Tiny got his tie and put it back on, tightened it as we walked around to the front.

'I like to look natty,' he told me. Then he said to Steve, all business, 'Eight dollars.'

The boys crowded around Babs, who was suddenly looking pleased and jaunty, shaking her head: no, it didn't hurt; no big deal; no, not now, I'll show it to you later. I'm still the only member of the family that knows she has that tattoo.

'You wanna stick around and chat awhile?' Tiny asked me, pocketing Steve's money. 'Tuesday's my slow day.'

The boys turned and looked at me, like I was the tough one all of a sudden; I could see Babs was jealous.

'Sure,' I said.

'Careful, Lois,' said Steve. 'By the time that character gets through with you, you'll be the tattooed lady.'

But he didn't give me my first tattoo till a year later, the day after we were married: a little butterfly pooled in the small of my back. Five years later, he began referring to it as his 'early work', even though he'd been tattooing for 25 years before he met me. That didn't rankle me as much as you might think – I liked being his early body of work, work-in-progress, future. That little butterfly sat by itself for a while, but in five years' time Tiny flooded it with other designs: carnations, an apple, a bomber plane, his initials.

When I told my mother about that first tattoo, she said, 'Oh Lord. Is it pretty?' Like all good mothers, she always knew the worst was going to happen and was disappointed and relieved when it finally did. But she didn't ask to see that tattoo, or any of the ones that followed. Sunday afternoons, when I went to have lunch with her, I dressed very carefully. I covered myself whenever I left the shop, anyhow: I hated nosy women in the grocery store trying to read my arm as I reached for the peas; I suspected all waitresses of gossiping about me in the kitchen. On my visits to my mother, though, I was extra wary. Through the years, my sleeves got longer, the fabrics more opaque. I never wore white when I visited her: the colours shimmered through.

Most of Tiny's own tattoos were ancient things that he'd done when he was just starting out. He learned the art travelling with the circus in the Thirties, could only practise on himself or a grapefruit, and sometimes there wasn't a grapefruit around. The top of his left thigh was almost solid black with experiments.

When we were first married, he revealed a different tattoo every night, all of them hidden away: one night, a rose on a big toe; next, a banner that said *E Pluribus Unum* half-furled in the hinge of his armpit; the next, his own signature, crooked and ugly, on the inside of his lip. One night, he said, 'Are you ready?' and before I could answer he turned his eyelids inside out, and there was a black star floating on the back of each one, isolated, like a scientific experiment.

'Flipping them up,' he said, turning them back, 'hurts more than the needle does. I was young and drunk and crazy when I had those done, and the guy who did them was younger and drunker and crazier. I'm lucky he stopped there, didn't tattoo my eyeballs scarlet red.'

He showed me all these designs like he was performing magic tricks, and sometimes I expected him to wave his hand over his toe and the rose would disappear and end up cupped in his palm; or the banner would finish rolling out from under his arm straight into the air, and go up in a flash of fire; or his name would unwrite itself; or I would fall asleep and find, in front of my own eyes, those floating stars, as black and unruly as Tiny's hair.

It didn't take me long to get used to the feel of the needle. I learned to love it. Tiny gave me about two tattoos a year for our first four years of marriage. Little ones. The bigger ones took form over several months, or even longer. He sometimes did sketches for them on his own knee. I started sitting in the shop in a halter top and high-cut, low-slung shorts, ready to get up and turn a thigh this way or that, showing the customers how the colours went. I saw the same sorts of people I'd seen Tuesdays before I married Tiny, plus others: business-men, priests, telephone operators, school-board members. Now they started asking me, 'Does it hurt?' I told the truth. Of course it hurts, about the same as a vaccination, a slightly skinned knee, but less than a well-landed punch, a bad muscle cramp or paying the bills. And look what you get: something that can't be stolen, pawned, lost, forgotten, or outgrown.

In the late Sixties, when Tiny was still working on a small scale, every time I got a new tattoo, I'd steal a daily touch – I would feel the scab starting, covering the colours, and I'd get impatient and think about peeling it off myself. Tiny'd read my mind and bawl me out, so I'd just run my finger over the tattoo, feeling the outline raised up like it always is when fresh. Then it'd peel by itself, and one day I'd put my finger down and not be able to tell the difference in skin: it'd really be a part of me. And that's when I started wanting another one.

After we'd been married 10 years, Tiny got interested in art. Mother had given me a big book called *Masterpieces of the Renaissance* – she wanted me to latch on to something, to go to college, and she figured art history, all things considered, might appeal to me. It was a beautiful book – the gloss of the paper made all the paintings look just finished; the pages gave off the scent of brand new things. I read it the day I got it, and set it aside. The next afternoon, I picked it up and all the reproductions had been taken out with a razor blade. No Raphael, Michelangelo – just a tunnel of empty frames where they'd been, front of the book to back.

I ran down to the shop, grumbling. The plates from the book were tacked up on the wall; Tiny was eyeing an El Greco and sketching.

'What do you think you're doing?' I asked, hands on my hips, the way my mother stood when she started a fight.

'Take off your pants,' he said.

'You ruined my book.'

'I saved your mom's inscription. When I'm finished we'll tape all the pictures back in. Come on, Lois, I want to try something.'

'I don't feel like getting tattooed today, thank you very much.'

'Pen and ink, that's all. I just want to sketch something.'

'Sketch it on paper.'

'Paper doesn't curve as nice as you. It'll only take a minute. Please?'

So I gave in, and Tiny sketched something on my hip in ballpoint pen. He didn't like whatever he'd done and wiped my hip clean with rubbing alcohol. The next day he tried again. He took his time. I got a book to read while he was working (I couldn't get interested in something that wasn't permanent), but I couldn't figure out how to arrange myself. I leaned this way and that, holding my book at arm's length, and Tiny told me to stop squirming. Every night for a week he sketched and erased. He never let me see what he was doing.

One night at the end of the week, after closing, Tiny said he had achieved what he wanted. He planned to tattoo it on my hip as a surprise.

I balked; my hip was my own, and I wanted to know what was going to be there. He promised that it would be beautiful and decent and a masterpiece.

'You'll love it,' he said. 'I've got this painting racket figured out.'

'Okay,' I said.

He decided to do the work upstairs at home. I stretched out on the bed, and he put on some Bing Crosby. Tiny loved Bing Crosby and at one point wanted to tattoo his face on me, but I put my foot down on that one. He gave me a glass of wine; he often let me have a glass, maybe two, when he was working on me. Never more, because it was against his strictest principles to tattoo a drunk.

He started at eight and worked until 11. Tiny had a light touch, and by the end of the evening I had a little bit of El Greco. The colours weren't quite right, but it was mostly wonderful, the face of a Spanish monk blooming on my hip: Fray Felix Hortensio Paravacino. Tiny was good, believe it.

We went to the Art Centre every now and then and wandered through one square room after another. I tried to get Tiny to look at my favourite thing there, a little Van Gogh landscape, but he always shook his head.

'That guy,' said Tiny, 'He's not a painter, he's a sculptor.'

All those paintings and little descriptions made me sleepy; I would sprawl on a bench while Tiny practically pressed his nose to the oldest canvases.

We made the guards very nervous.

Tiny started to work bigger all the time, and put designs on my arms, down my legs. Eventually, he left only my hands, my feet, my neck and face blank – I can still get dressed and look unmarked. But look at me undressed, see how he got better over the years: his patriotic stage, his religious stage. He liked greens and reds especially, and fine single-needle outlines, which he called 'rare and elegant'. I've got George Washington on one arm and Lincoln freeing the slaves on the other; I've got a garden planted between my breasts, Japanese peonies and daisies, reds and faded yellows; I've got a little pair of arms sinking into my belly captioned *Help let me out*.

My life drove my mother crazy. All she wanted was for me to become miraculously blank. I broke her heart – that was my job. She let me know her heart was broken – that was hers. She loved me, loves me. She has had a thousand lives: as a girl, she was pretty and could dance and flirt; her mother died and she learned to take care of her father and older brother, and still she was happy, poised and courted. She worked her way through college cleaning houses; she went to law school and New York and had a practice for a while; she married the owner of a women's clothing store and moved to the Midwest; she went to Indianapolis to learn how to fit women's underwear and has her GC (Graduate Corsetière) from the Gossard School. When my father died in 1955, she took over the shop herself and ran it for 20 years. She has taught ballroom dancing, travels to foreign countries; she is a small-business consultant, the vice-president of her temple and president of the sisterhood. She used to paint, sculpt, needlepoint and knit, and there is a table in the front hall of her apartment that she made 60 years ago. My mother believes in being able to start fresh whenever life demands. Tattoos confound her.

One Sunday when I was 30 and just beginning to become the

tattooed lady (Tiny had started the Ascension the week before), my mother poured me a cup of coffee and said, 'Sweethearts carve their names on trees, not each other. Does it ever occur to you that you are not leading a normal life?'

'Yes,' I said. 'Thank you.' I adjusted my pants and peered at my ankle to see whether I had embarrassed myself, whether a tattoo had managed to come loose and slip to the floor. My cousin Babs, who had just had a baby, was coming to lunch too, and my mother and I sat on the brocade sofa waiting.

'I just feel that you're painting yourself into a corner,' Mum said to me. 'How's Tiny?'

'Doing very well,' I said. 'Business is up.' My mother winced.

The doorbell rang. Mom answered the bell and ushered in Babs, still a little thick around the middle, but elegant in her suit, stockings of just the right colour, curled hair.

Mom sat her down on the sofa.

'Honey,' she said. 'How's the darling baby?'

'A baby, all the way,' said Babs. 'No, he's fine, he's sweet.'

'Well,' said Mom. 'Look at those nice clothes.'

Babs had calmed down in the passing years; her parents had offered her a car if she stopped seeing Steve, and it was a better-than-fair deal. After college, she met and married a high school principal turned local politician and seemed to have lost every drop of wildness in her.

The sight of a well-dressed Babs never failed to surprise me. 'No one would ever suspect you had a reckless youth,' I told her.

'It's true,' said Babs. She looked at me with some regret and sighed. 'Now I'm a nice married lady who sometimes has one too many glasses of whiskey at one of my husband's parties and then tells the truth . . .' She sighed and shifted her weight on the sofa cushion. I imagined her bow tattoo pricking her skin, an old war injury kicking up.

The three of us sat there and chatted about local news, babies, recipes. We covered ourselves. Looking at my mother, I realised how little I knew of her. Recently, I had gone through her desk, trying to unearth a phone book, and found a doctor's bill for a mammogram, detailing two suspicious spots, the next appointment. My heart jumped whenever I thought of it. Did her body show what happened next? Her face didn't, and nobody – especially me – asked my mother such things. Babs, too – besides that bit of colour, what else: stretched out stomach, the zipper of a surgical scar?

I knew myself under my green trouser suit, could tap George Washington on the chin, prick a finger on the thorn of a rose, strum an apocalyptic angel's wing, trace the shape of a heart Tiny'd given me after our first fight.

Anyone could read me like a book.

When my mother took the dirty dishes to the kitchen, I leaned towards Babs.

'Watch that whiskey,' I told her, 'or sometime you'll drop your pants to show a visiting dignitary the colourful result of a misspent youth.'

She looked sad and understanding. 'Oh,' she whispered, 'I *know*.'

That night, after Babs left, my mother took me to her bedroom closet to give me some of her old clothing. She was almost as tall as I was and very fashionable, her hand-me-downs nicer than my new things.

'Here,' she said, handing me a pile of skirts and dresses. 'Try them on. Don't take what you can't use.'

I started for the bathroom to change.

She sighed, 'I'm your mother,' she said. 'I used to fit girdles on women with stranger bodies than yours. You don't have to be so modest.'

So I undressed there and tried on the clothes, and my mother looked at me and frowned. Afterwards, I sat down on her bed in my underwear and lit a cigarette.

'Wouldn't you like something to eat?' she asked me.

I did, but couldn't. I had just taken up smoking because I had put on a few pounds, and Tiny told me I better cut it out before I changed the expressions of all the tattoos. If I wasn't careful, Washington and Jesus and Fray Felix would start to look surprised or, at best, nauseated.

'No thanks,' I told her.

My mother, who only smoked in airports and hospital waiting rooms ('All that cleanliness and worry gets to me,' she'd say), slid a cigarette from my pack, took mine from my hand, and lit the end of hers. She looked at all of me stretched along the bed, started to touch my skin, but took her finger away.

'Well,' she said, blowing out smoke, 'you've finally made yourself into the freak you always thought you were.'

I looked at her sideways, not knowing what to say.

'Actually,' she said, 'you look a little like a calico cat.'

My mother was wrong. I never felt like a freak because of my height: I felt like a ghost haunting too much space, like those parents who talk about rattling around the house when the kids move out. I rattled. It's like when you move into a new place, and despite the lease and despite the rent you've paid, the place doesn't feel like home and you're not sure you want to stay. Maybe you don't unpack for a while, maybe you leave the walls blank and put off filling the fridge. Well, getting a tattoo – it's like hanging drapes, or laying carpet, or driving that first nail into the fresh plaster: it's deciding you've moved in.

When Tiny turned 70, he retired. His hands were beginning to shake a little and he hated the idea of doing sloppy work. We still had the apartment over the shop and Tiny kept the store open so that people could come in and talk. Nobody took him up on the tattooing lessons he offered; after a while he tried to convince me to learn. He said I'd attract a lot of business. I told him no, I didn't have the nerves, I wasn't brave like him.

I took a job at the public library instead, shelving books. I worked in the stacks all day, and when I came home, Tiny'd be asleep. I'd know that he'd been napping all day so that he'd be awake enough to stay up and chat. He was getting old fast, now that he wasn't working.

I pulled the dining room table into the shop's front window, because Tiny liked to see who was coming and going. He knocked on the glass and waved, even to strangers. One night, a week before his 76th birthday, his arm started hurting halfway through dinner.

'I'm calling an ambulance,' I said.

'Don't,' he told me. 'It's like saying there's something wrong. It's bad luck.'

'It's bad luck to die,' I said, and phoned.

He was surprisingly solid in that hospital bed, unlike his roommate, who looked like he had withered away to bedding. After a week, that roommate disappeared and was replaced by a huge man, a college professor with a heart problem.

One day, Tiny asked me an impossible favour. He wanted me to bring in the needle and put my initials on him.

'Ah, Tiny,' I told him, 'I'm not ready to sign you off yet.'

'You have my initials on you, but I don't have yours. It's bad luck.'

'I don't know how.'

'You've seen it a million times.'

The college professor was eavesdropping and he looked a little queasy.

'We'll get caught,' I whispered.

'We'll be quiet.'

'This is a hospital,' I said, like maybe he hadn't noticed.

'Sterile conditions,' he answered.

So I brought the needle and some black ink the next day, rolled up my sleeves, got to work. We had to bribe the professor to keep quiet, but he was easily bought.

I started with a *G*, and put an *E* on the next day. That afternoon, when I was just sitting there watching Tiny sleep, he raised his eyelids to half-mast and muttered, 'I wish I woulda finished you.'

'I thought I was finished, Tiny,' I said.

'Nope,' he said. He put a hand on my arm; his nails were rippled like old wood. 'A tree, for instance. You don't have a tree.'

'Where's room?'

'Soles of feet, earlobes. There's always room. Too late now. But you'll change anyhow, needle or no. For instance, when I put that George Washington on you, he was frowning. By the time you're my age, he'll be grinning ear to ear.' He yawned, then suddenly pulled himself onto his elbows, squeezing the one hand on my arm for support. 'I mean, tell me,' he said. 'Do you feel finished?'

'Yes,' I said, and although I was 39, it was true: it hadn't occurred to me until that minute that I'd have to exist after he was gone.

The next day I was putting a *T* on his arm when Tiny said, 'Do me a favour, Lois, huh? Don't forget me?'

The professor began to giggle in bed and ended up laughing, hard. 'Do you think she'd be able to, even if she wanted? Look at her – she's a human memo board.'

I really thought that I would keep on going, that I'd put a letter a day on him for a year, more. I hoped it would keep him going, because he seemed to be giving up a little.

By the end of the week, Tiny's arm said GET WELL in letters of all different sizes.

'Well,' he said. 'It's a little boring.'

'It's going to get more interesting.'

'It better,' he told me, smiling. 'Tomorrow you can put on a horseshoe for luck. Get fancy. Put on a heart for love.'

'Okay,' I said. But he died in the night, left without my name or love, with only my good wishes on his arm.

'What's going to happen to you now?' my mother asked me. 'What if you want to get married again? What man will want you when someone else has been scribbling all over you?'

A month after Tiny died, Mama told me she was going to start inviting nice young men to our Sunday lunches. She bought me new outfits, unrevealing ones, and told me that we should keep my figure secret – she always referred to it as my figure, as if, over the years, I had put on a few things that could easily be taken off. I go to keep her happy, and sit on one side of the sofa while the fat divorced sons of her friends flirt with her instead of me, knowing that'll get them further. Sometimes I eat fudge and don't say one word all afternoon.

'I'm sorry,' I told her. 'These are my widow's weeds.'

Three weeks ago I got a letter from a young man on the coast, a tattooist who said that Tiny was a great artist and that I was proof of it. He wanted to take my photo, see the whole gallery. I packed him a box of Tiny's things, old flash sheets and needles and pages of El Greco, and told him to study those. He called me and said I was better than any museum. I told him that I apologised, that I understood, but really: I am not a museum, not yet, I'm a love letter, a love letter.

Helen Simpson

LAST ORDERS

She was a bulbous bottle, unreliably stoppered, and any movement away from the strictest upright provoked the genie into shooting acrid slop up to her epiglottis. So she stayed vertical, and when night came propped herself against a bank of bolsters like an Anglo-Saxon afraid of death's approach during sleep.

These night hours unrolled reams of poor but heavy slumber, thick and threadbare like hessian, coarse curtains which fanned open occasionally on to thresholds of glimmering incomprehension. The dreams were of release, violent and half-baked. There was one where she was flat as a flounder with eyes on the same side of her nose, shifting along an inch above the seabed, and then she would wake into the half-light with a strong aversion to duality and everything to do with bifurcation.

This had been a bad night, spiralling down through threats of knives and stomach-globes. The easy tears streaked her cheeks, cheap as dew. She lay and languished, watching the forked radish which was Patrick pulling on his trousers in the gloom.

'Twelve days late now,' she said. 'My body doesn't work.'

'Yes it does,' said Patrick, scrabbling through a dish of loose change. 'Babies come when they're ready.'

'How would *you* know,' she said, turning her big white clumsy face into the pillow.

'The doctors say so,' he said, as usual, strapping on his watch. 'Sorry, got to rush, I'm late.'

'Good luck with the Brisbane blockbuster,' she said. 'Where's lunch?'

'Let The Good Times Roll.'

'You lucky devil.'

'Don't forget we're off to the Bengal Tiger tonight.'

She groaned.

'Worth a try,' he said. 'Whenever anybody hears you're late, they mention hot curry. If it works we'll call him Vindaloo.'

She lay in bed for an hour after he had gone, dipping back into drifts of half-sleep, trawling her memory again for more specific details of the wish-gone-sour tale which surfaced every morning now.

There was a withered old man imploring some ringleted goddess to release him. He had been granted his wish for eternal life, but had forgotten to ask for eternal youth at the same time, and now, as he hobbled across her gleaming marble halls on wrinkled feet, tears trickling down his walnut face and silvery waist-length beard, he pleaded for the ordinary power to die.

Watching the summer light strengthen at the margins of the bedroom curtains, she wondered why this story kept returning to her, since it did not concern birth, but death. When she started to worry again that her body would never work, that she would simply grow bigger and bigger, then she commenced the laborious business of getting dressed.

The telephone rang.

'*Still* nothing?' came the incredulous voice of her aunt. 'It'll have a beard and long toenails by now.'

'Any day,' she said, automatically, as she had been saying for the last month.

Now that the official hospital date, the baby's Estimated Time of Arrival, had come and gone, it was like life after death. Only she had not yet laid down her life. Perhaps this was what was meant by living on borrowed time. She had run out of credit with her waiting relatives anyway; they almost jeered at her when they telephoned now. Invalid in both senses of the word, she lumbered out into the little back garden. These days walking was like wading through sea water up to the thighs.

Bees boomed inside the freckle-throated foxgloves. From the lime trees came a rustle like stiff silk tussore and a sweet soap-and-talcum-powder smell. Already the garden was a pocket of heat. This was the hottest June for 12 years, as everybody kept saying. There was a menacing innocence, a pre-war stasis about it.

'*Still* not had it?' The old lady who lived next door appeared at the fence, her leech-black eyes peering through the trellis of honeysuckle. 'You must be very worried by now.'

'I'm all right,' she said, taking a step back towards the kitchen door. 'How are you?'

'As you know, lonely as hell since Reg died,' said Mrs Pightle. 'Sometimes I get so bored I wish even something nasty would happen.'

Wanting to avoid infection by contact with Mrs Pightle's misery, she took another step back.

'Mustn't grumble though,' said Mrs Pightle, eyeing her bulk sharply as though suspecting her of fraudulent practices, a cushion up her T-shirt. Then, unnervingly, she snapped, 'I kill each day as it comes.'

'There's the telephone,' she said, and scuttled back inside.

'*Well?*' came her mother's voice. 'Are you going to tell me you've had it?' She held the receiver at arm's length for a moment, as gingerly as if it had been a scorpion.

Twelve days ago had been the promised day. The flat was perfectly clean for the first time in its life, she had even polished the windows and mirrors; she had piled two pounds of glossy cherries into the green glass dish and had put a vase of straight-backed tulips in each of the rooms. It had felt like her birthday. Patrick had brought home a slice of Brie, almost ripe. 'I thought you might like it for your first meal after the baby,' he had said, 'since you've been complaining for nine months about how you wish you could have a little bit of soft cheese.' He had made her feel like Ben Gunn, whose first request after years of being marooned on a desert island was for some crumbs of toasted cheese. Ben Gunn, too, had had a long beard and toenails, she thought confusedly. Later that morning they had gone to the hospital for her 10-week appointment. The baby's head had not engaged, said the registrar; the absence of Braxton Hicks contractions was absolutely no cause for concern. It'll be a few days yet, he had advised, we'll have to wait for the cervix to ripen; don't look so disappointed, you've got a marvellous haemoglobin count.

A week later the tulips were swooping drunkenly, stems curving in Art Nouveau arabesques so that their splayed flower heads touched the dust-gathering surfaces at last, almost inaudibly, and fell to pieces, each petal a glamorous painted coracle. The cherries grew bruised, then rotten. She threw them away. After nine days, when it had lost in form what it had gained in odour, Patrick ate the Brie. She had to dust again, and kicked the bag she had packed for hospital six weeks ago, now standing sad and ridiculous in the corner of the bedroom like a cancelled holiday. At her 41-week appointment, they gave her a graph paper kick-chart to fill in; she ticked a square for each movement the baby made until the 10th square was attained, which was always before midday; and then she had nothing to do except field the phone calls. They told her to be patient, and she gave a wan sneer.

It was galling now to see the sunny patch of garden through the doorway and know that Mrs Pightle would get her if she put her nose outside. She hadn't been more than 500 yards from the house for more than a fortnight now, so convinced had she been that the baby would appear at its appointed time to the sound of empyreal trumpets, trailing clouds of glory. She had refused plans to meet anyone because they might have to be cancelled, and her only contact with the outside world for the last fortnight had been via the telephone wire and Patrick, or from sending out letters like messages in bottles. Prevented by Mrs Pightle from watching the grass grow, she had instead monitored the progress of her nail and hair lengths, like Rapunzel waiting for rescue from the witch's tower.

She sat down with her book, *How to Have a Baby*, and the baby inside her woke up and started its bulging movements. It, too, was a prisoner in a tower, of course. They were in a double bind. Strange, to be lounging around in this summer torpor, lazy as an aquarium, while just round the corner waited bloody scenes of violence and danger and life at its most portentous.

The telephone rang.

'Are you still in one piece? Never mind, they're bound to induce now. Make the most of your last days – this is the last time you'll ever have alone. I haven't had a minute to myself since Maisie was born.

And remember, the first six weeks are *awful*. Impossible to describe, but *you'll* see. It's *chaos*. It gets better gradually. After about a year. Have you tried sitting on a washing machine during the spin cycle?'

She went back to her book and looked up induction in the index. 'The doctor will snag a hole in the membranes which surround your baby with an instrument like a long crochet hook and the waters will then gush out,' she read.

She went to the bookcase and pulled out an old exercise book. A long time ago she had copied out a poem written in the Tower of London by a man who knew he was going to be executed the next morning. Here it was, and it was by 26-year-old Chidiock Tichbourne whose head was scythed from his trunk in 1586 before he had had time to write much at all.

My prime of youth is but a frost of cares,
My feast of joy is but a dish of pain,
My crop of corn is but a field of tares,
And all my good is but vain hope of gain;
The day is past, and yet I saw no sun,
And now I live, and now my life is done.

I'll never see Mexico, she thought, the armadillo running across the sand. I won't be able to try hang-gliding in case I leave an orphan. I haven't *done* anything yet.

My tale was heard and yet it was not told,
My fruit is fallen and yet my leaves are green,
My youth is spent and yet I am not old
I saw the world and yet I was not seen;
My thread is cut and yet it is not spun,
And now I live, and now my life is done.

The telephone rang. It was Patrick, calling from a phone box on his way to lunch.

'Do we *want* a baby?' she asked.

'Of course we do! More than anything else in the world! I'm so happy I'm almost scared.'

'I never seem to feel the right thing at the right time. I'm unnatural.'

'No you're not. But it'll be all right, you'll see. Have you any *idea* how much I love you? You're mine now.'

The pips went and she used this as an excuse to put the phone down. She heard herself swearing and cursing.

'Hormones,' she said flatly.

I sought my death and found it in my womb,
I looked for life and saw it was a shade,
I trod the earth and knew it was my tomb,
And now I die, and now I was but made;
My glass is full, and now my glass is run,
And now I live, and now my life is done.

The telephone rang again.

'It's Wendy here, *you* know, from the antenatal class. Just ringing to let you know I've had it. It's a boy, eight pounds six ounces. I know, he wasn't due for another two weeks, but he couldn't wait, could he. Funny really, even though he'll be older than yours now, when you think about it yours has actually been *alive* a whole month longer . . . What was it like? Do you *really* want to know? I don't think I should tell you. Oh, all right. It was horrible, not a bit like the classes said. At least it was quick, well, eight hours. I started getting pains about 2.45 on Saturday. Geoff wanted to go off to the gym for his circuit training and by the time he got back I said, this is it, we've got to go to hospital. Anyway I don't think I'll go into details with you in your condition – I'm so glad *I* wasn't late, I couldn't bear it – but don't believe them when they say it doesn't hurt. I was screaming my head off at the end. Then it shot out at 10.50 p.m. I remember Geoff said, just in time for last orders.'

Come pain, welcome pain, she thought as she put the phone down. I want to be cool and free again, lean and Atlantic-salted. I want to lose this fish-like full-throated extra under the chin. I wish I could run like the wind across frost-crusted grass, or lunge and bump at will in the night. I want to say goodbye to this batwing mask of pregnancy across my nose and cheeks.

The telephone rang. It was Wendy again, suggesting that she drive at 30 miles an hour over sleeping policemen since this had worked for the woman in the bed next to hers at St Mary's, and she had been two weeks overdue.

Taking up another baby book, emotional rather than technical this time, along with a handful of raisins for lunch, she read, 'When you refuse to leave your breastfed baby with a bottle and a sitter in order to go out and enjoy yourself, it isn't self-sacrifice but self-protection. While you and your baby are interlocked in this way, you can only be happy if she is happy.' She let the book rest in her lap and stared hungrily at the open door. This was what people had said before when she had voiced doubts about missing pubs, parties, dancing, travel; they always smiled as though she were odd or innocent, and said, 'You'll see; you won't *want* to.'

You will not be you any more, her ego told her id. Not only will you have produced somebody else from inside you, someone quite different and separate, but you yourself will change into somebody quite different and other, overnight – a Mother.

What if she failed to feel misery at the thought of a bottle and a sitter? What if they seemed fair exchange for a bottle and a party? *Would* she feel the necessary 'interlock' that would turn her into a stay-at-home?

Thinking back to that last outing a month ago, she realised it had been, among other things, a wake for her old self without her realising it. She had taken a valedictory taxi back to the flat, sitting upright on the high-backed seat in the purring darkness, exhausted by the baby beating away in protest since early evening, but humming and happy too.

'Enjoy yourself while you can,' said the taxi driver over his shoulder. He was the cold, light-eyed virile sort with steely grey hair and an air of grim fitness.

'Oh, that was the last party for a while,' she had said airily. 'I'm about to have a baby. Have *you* got any children?'

'I wish I'd drowned them at birth,' he had said. 'Look at it like this. Two people get together, they get on well. Out to the cinema, out to the pub, go to bed together; out to the pub. Then the little bleeder arrives. It's meant to bring you closer together, but does it? Does it ****. *You* say, let's go down the pub. *She* says, ooh no, the baby's feeding pattern, or something like that. She says, *you* go down the pub. Nah, you say. You sit around a bit. Then you think, okay, just for half an hour. So you're down there, you think, well, this is fun, it's a bit lively. Next thing you're talking to someone who's *not* the old lady. And you hear people say they bring you closer together! Still, not a lot you can do about it at this stage in the game by the look of you. Tell you what, I'll give you a tip. Give it a few spoons of Benelux – not too often – just when you really need a couple of hours' peace. Night Nurse is too strong.'

Well, she was going out tonight, wasn't she. 'Positively my last appearance,' she muttered. 'Like some old music hall star who doesn't know when to call it a day.'

Patrick brought home the Australian author whom he had taken out to lunch. They both had the withered eyelids and kamikaze air of people who have been drinking during daylight and who intend to go on against their better judgement.

'Hope you don't mind,' whispered Patrick. 'I meant to ring and warn you, but he's been like a limpet and he keeps on telling me how he doesn't know anybody in London.'

'The more the merrier,' she yawned. They shuffled off down the road to the Bengal Tiger, the men creeping along to keep her company, one on either side, like the royal escort of an ancient monarch.

Once on the threshold of the restaurant she looked around ravenously at this fresh landscape, noticing that all eyes skidded off her bulk and that she had become a visual embarrassment now she was out in public after so long. She did not care. It was somewhere different. She admired the filigree metal of the basket holding poppadoms, and watched Patrick and his author devouring stuffed paratha. They were discussing differences in national humour, comparing Australian with English.

'Ours is a bit cruder, a bit brasher,' said the Australian earnestly, popping an onion bhaji whole into his mouth. 'Our jokes are not exactly subtle. For example, would you find this funny? I do, but my humour is very antipodean.'

Patrick cocked his ear in the attitude of one about to enjoy a treat.

'Well, here's Sheila and she's standing on the edge of Sydney suspension bridge and she's about to jump off. Bruce comes running up, all concern, shouts, "Why Sheila, *why*?" "Because I'm pregnant," says Sheila. "Jeez, Sheila," says Bruce. "Not only are you a bloody good lay but you're a bloody good sport too, Sheila." Now you either find that funny or you don't.'

Patrick was looking at her uneasily, but she liked a joke, even an ideologically unsound joke, and she was sniggering into her chicken dhansak.

Relieved, Patrick laughed and crowed and said, 'Well, have you heard the one about the man who's drinking alone in a pub and he wants to go off and have a pee, but he's scared someone'll steal his pint, so he props a little note against it saying, "I have spat in this beer".'

'No,' said the Australian, grinning attentively and gulping lager.

'When he gets back from the gents his beer's still there but somebody's scribbled "So have I" on the note. Ha, ha, ha!'

The two men rocked with laughter. To her surprise, she was prickling with alarm. She heard his voice again down the telephone: 'You're *mine* now.' The baby heaved up against her ribs like a barge. She restrained herself from lifting Patrick's pint and pouring it over his head.

'Excuse me,' she said, the syllables glacial in her burning mouth; and waddled off down a spiral staircase to the ladies.

There, she locked herself into a cubicle and leant her forehead against the gleaming marble-tiled walls, and wept, and swore, and prayed for release.

Rachel Cusk

WELLBORERS AND SINKERS

Jane Bly, neither plain nor shy, came to London in search of a new life. Her old one, despite prudent care, infrequent use and the addition of new parts over the years, had been abandoned in a lay-by somewhere on the M11, soon after she had opened the car window so as to feel the wind of change in her hair, and had begun to sing to a song on the radio whose tune was catchy even if its words eluded her.

'*Bah bah!*' she sang. '*Bah-bah bah bah –*'

In her old life she had worked as a secretary for a law firm and had shared a terraced house and a small town with her boyfriend Martin. Now she worked as a secretary for a law firm and lived alone in a one-bedroom flat in Finsbury Park. She was well pleased with the change. On her way home on dark winter nights, she would walk to the tube station like an explorer through uncharted jungles: past packed, hooting pubs and murmuring bars, past natives whose beauty astounded and indifference intrigued her, on through the commotion of the canopy where taxis screeched and buses roared; so much more exciting than the quiescent order of her old route, the dark tidy streets along which erect streetlamps stood like disapproving spinster aunts.

'How's the big smoke?' Martin would say without fail every night, when equally without fail she called him; and already the countrified phrase made her flinch. He hadn't minded her going. She needed to get it out of her system, he said; like a virus or a heavy lunch.

'Fine,' she would say as a crash or a shriek from the next-door flat made her jump.

'What was that?'

'Nothing. The neighbours.'

*

She was big, Jane Bly: too big for that small town with its fingering awe and prurient ways. It seemed to her that fat people inhabited a different element, a fleshy, floating place; they danced like whales in water, they glided and capered, suspended on spindly legs with a kind of lumbering grace. She had frightened them and they had kept her like a town relic, a prehistoric monster that should have been extinct.

She had thought she would be smaller somewhere bigger, and she had been right. At night, alone in her north London room, she would try on clothes and marvel excitedly before the mirror. Then she would undress slowly in the dark, caressing her unfamiliar body; like someone delighted, like a lover.

At night there were sounds, voices mostly, a droning interchange of noise from the next-door flat which at first she had mistaken for the scripted rise and fall of a television set. She would fall asleep to its monotony until it hit an unexpected note, when she would plunge back into consciousness with a thrilling lurch, sitting up in the dark with a clear head and a pounding heart, listening. There would be thumps, crashes, sometimes the sound of something breaking. Screams and then a series of thuds, like heavy footsteps or someone falling down the stairs. Then one night a girl had shouted so loudly that she actually heard the words.

'Put down that knife!' she had screamed. 'Put it down, you bastard!'

She had pains between her legs which gripped her at unexpected moments. At work, talking to her boss, a shafting flame of agony had suddenly torn through her, illuminating red passages, the bowl of her womb black and cancerous. She had been too embarrassed to clutch her stomach and cry out, and instead had frozen in an attitude of excessive interest, grinning wildly.

'Are you all right?' he had said, staring at her.

The pain of it seemed almost to cleave her in two. She couldn't speak and instead nodded her head energetically up and down. He had walked away, apparently bemused; and she had understood then with a kind of sadness that even here such awkward moments would always follow her.

*

They haunted her like ghosts in the full moon of her loneliness. They were nocturnal and strange. Once she had been woken by the sound of breaking glass and had rushed to the window in her nightdress to view the commotion, which had erupted out into the empty street. A man in a crash helmet was mounting a motorbike, and as he started the engine he turned and waved his fist at the house from which he had recently emerged.

'Bitch!' he yelled. 'Fucking bitch!'

The roar of the engine on the quiet midnight street was like a broken law, like something ungovernable. She drew back from the window, frightened lest he should see her, and resumed her watch from a darkened corner of glass shielded by the curtain. The man shunted his bike out on to the road, and as he did so the door of the house slammed open and the girl ran out after him. Seeing her, he opened the throttle and roared away, but she ran after him and managed to grab the metal bar behind the saddle. Jane felt a rush of horrified adrenaline as she realised he wasn't going to stop. She saw the girl's thin body lifted off the ground, the peroxide shock of her hair fanning out like a fury as she was dragged after him. They roared off down the street; he hunched and fiendish, she flying, fluttering behind him like a flag, like a past life, something tenacious and ugly he wanted to escape.

Martin said he would come up for the weekend and then contracted flu. He called her at work on Friday, coughing and nasal. She was upset and they argued in low voices, at which point he forgot to be so nasal and accused her openly of not trusting him. Something thorny and suspicious took root and she clawed aside its deleterious branches all the way home. She had bought food and carried it now in heavy plastic bags with aching arms. It would grow anarchic in the fridge, bleeding swampy noxious juices and sprouting furry mould.

She approached her front door along the cold lamplit street. Something had been dumped on her doorstep. As she drew nearer she saw it was a child. It looked up at her as she stood dumbly before it and made no signs of removing itself. It was a boy, about six or seven years old. They eyed each other warily, like animals. Jane took out her keys and jangled them purposefully.

'Excuse me!' she said, moving towards him.

The boy regarded her indifferently. He wore a filthy knitted hat and his face was streaked with glittering mucus, like the sticky paths of a snail.

'Does your mummy know where you are?' she persevered. She knelt down beside him and felt a pain wrench at her abdomen. 'Hadn't you better go home? She'll be worried.'

'She ain't there,' he offered finally. His voice was small and high.

'Well, do you know where she is?'

He shrugged and opened his palms to the sky, like a showman.

'Show me which house is yours,' said Jane. She shifted awkwardly to the other leg. 'Is it that one?'

'I live there, missus,' he interrupted, pointing to the doorstep next to her own. 'And there ain't nobody home.'

So he lived next door! He lived next to her, in the charge of those mad and vociferous assailants of quiet, those community outlaws, those two terrorists of love that were her neighbours!

'Are you hungry?' she said invitingly, leaning over him and unlocking the door to the warm sanctuary of the hall.

At the office she grew lonely, unbefriended. Martin promised again to come up and this time, when he failed to arrive, Jane told him to stop promising. He agreed, sounding relieved. He had bought a season ticket at the local football club and it made weekends difficult. The pains were getting worse. Jane decided to have them seen to and she opened the Yellow Pages. She had heard of such a thing as a well-woman clinic, and considering that the last time she had taken her female problems, in the form of an unsightly genital rash, to a male doctor who had spread her legs and cried, 'Uugh!' at what he saw between them, she thought such an institution might offer a more sympathetic response. She turned to 'W' and ran a finger down the page, but the only thing she could see was a section headed *Wellborers and Sinkers*.

★

The child was on her doorstep again that night and she invited him in. She had learned that he was five years old and his name was Halen.

'It's an unusual name,' she said now, piling his plate with a second helping of chicken and mashed potatoes. 'Where does it come from?'

''s simple,' said he, evidently surmising that she was even more so. 'It's like *Van* Halen, innit? Me dad likes them. He says they're God.'

'Ah,' she replied, obscurely gleeful. 'And what does your dad do?'

He shrugged and speared a large piece of chicken, which dripped gravy on the table as he held it aloft.

'You're funny,' he said, examining her. 'You're not like my mum. You're fat, you are.'

'It's a cyst!' they said; perhaps in the same manner with which they would have said, 'It's a girl!' Jane felt sure a cyst would be female.

'Oh, good,' she said. She had been brought up to be polite.

'Don't get too attached to it,' they warned her, only half-jokingly. They evidently thought she was odd. 'It'll have to come out, you know.'

She had a dream in which she sat in a darkened room. It was completely black, as if she wasn't dreaming at all. She seemed to sit there for hours in silence. Eventually she heard the sound of footsteps approaching, but instead of calling out she found herself gripped by a desperate fear of discovery. She scrabbled into a corner, searching for something, anything she could hide behind. The footsteps grew closer and suddenly she heard the door opening. There was a small cupboard and for a moment her heart pounded with panic and despair; she would never get in there, she who was so large! But somehow, miraculously, her body seemed to shrink with sheer terror and she got inside just as the beam of a torch swung interrogatively over her. The footsteps came closer and then paused inches away from where she crouched.

'I love you!' a voice suddenly shouted. 'Let me in – I love you!'

She knew it was a trick. She tried to quieten her breathing. Her heart beat loudly. And then she was back in her room, awake in a darkness which seemed lighter than her dream. Someone was shouting in the street and she got out of bed and went to the window. The man with the motorbike was standing outside the next-door house.

'Let me in!' he shouted. 'I love you!'

She grew tired from her disturbed nights. The cyst was in her womb, the only sign of life. They removed it in hospital and she took two days off work.

'Where've you been?' demanded the boy imperiously on her return.

She let him in, hating him for a moment. She wondered if they beat him as well as each other and then stopped herself, horrified. When they sat down to supper, a volley of shouts and crashes erupted from the other side of the wall.

'What's that?' said Jane loudly, putting down her fork and cocking her head. She watched him out of the corner of her eye.

'Fuck off!' the woman shrieked. 'Just fuck off, do you hear me?'

'What? Oh, that.' The boy shrugged. 'That's them upstairs. They're nuts, they are.'

Jane stared at him, not understanding.

'But – but aren't they your parents? I mean, isn't that your house?'

He stared back at her, and for a moment she had an odd sense that he had seen through her; that with her strange words she had forfeited the right to adulthood, leaving him to take control.

'No, stupid,' he said wearily. 'We live *downstairs*. My mum says they're bonkers.'

'Where is your mother?' Jane demanded. 'I should like to speak to her.'

She saw the girl flying, thin and demonic, down the street. It occurred to her dimly, as if planning another life, that she should be happy.

'She's at work, ain't she?' he replied. 'She –'

'What about your father?' Jane was suddenly desperate to be rid of him. 'I'll talk to him instead.'

'He don't live there,' said the boy obstinately, sensing her aversion. 'Me mum takes me round his at weekends.'

'So –' Jane thought about it. 'So who looks after you while she's at work?'

They eyed each other uncertainly, the unwanted proof of one another's abandonment. The boy shrugged.

'You do, I s'pose,' he said.

She woke to find her dark room lit by flashing lights and wailing sirens. It was three o'clock in the morning. That night the noise had been the worst she had ever heard it, and eventually she had phoned Martin in tears.

'I'm coming home!' she said. 'I can't stand it!'

'Ah,' he had replied. 'Ah, I see.'

Now she leaped out of bed and stood at the window. There was an ambulance out on the street, and a police car. Her heart swelled with a kind of grim satisfaction. So, they've finally done it, she thought. Other lights were on, and people began to drift dressing-gowned out into the street.

The door of the house opened and the man with the motorbike was led out by two policemen. Jane almost pounded the window with glee.

'All right, old son,' one of them said, directing him towards the waiting police car.

Then some more men appeared from the house carrying a stretcher. On it was a very small person, like a child, the face covered with a grey blanket. Jane caught her breath wildly and pressed herself hard against the glass, straining to see. As the men came down the path, the top of the gate caught the blanket and dragged it slightly askew. From where she stood, Jane could now see a lock of hair protruding from the wrinkled cloth. It was long and limp as a dead hand, the peroxide in the moonlight the colour of untouched snow.

For a while the memory of them disturbed her more than their actual presence had, but eventually she began to forget them. She told the story to some people at work, and the conversation somehow continued until they were in one of those smart bars she had so often admired. The next day they had all acknowledged her in a different way; slightly embarrassed at first, but friendly. One of them, a man, asked her out to dinner.

'There's something you should know,' said Martin on the phone. 'If you're still coming back, that is.'

'I'm not,' said Jane.

The child came round to her house often. As the days grew longer they went to the park and kicked a ball around.

'I'm going to be a footballer, me,' said the child, directing a shot at her abdomen. 'When I grow up.'

'That's great,' Jane replied, dodging it and smiling with triumph.

'You look different,' he said then, pausing to contemplate her. 'You're all right, you are. Oi, have you seen the new neighbours?'

Barbara Gowdy

PRESBYTERIAN CROSSING

Sometimes Beth floated. Two or three feet off the ground, and not for very long, 10 seconds or so. She wasn't aware of floating when she was actually doing it, however. She had to land and feel a glowing sensation before she realised that she had just been up in the air.

The first time it happened she was on the church steps. She looked back down the walk and knew that she had floated up it. A couple of days later she floated down the outside cellar stairs of her house. She ran inside and told her grandmother, who whipped out the pen and the little pad she carried in her skirt pocket and drew a circle with a hooked nose.

Beth looked at it. 'Has Aunt Cora floated, too?' she asked.

Her grandmother nodded.

'When?'

Her grandmother held up six fingers.

'Six years ago?'

Shaking her head, her grandmother held her hand at thigh level.

'Oh,' Beth said, 'when she was six.'

When Beth was six, five years ago, her mother ran off with a man down the street who wore a toupee that curled up in humid weather. Beth's grandmother, her father's mother, came to live with her and her father. Thirty years before that, Beth's grandmother had had her tonsils taken out by a quack who ripped out her vocal cords and the underside of her tongue, with the consequence that from then on she couldn't even whisper, let alone talk.

It was a tragedy, because she and her twin sister Cora had been on the verge of stardom (or so Cora said) as a professional singing team.

They had made two long-play records: 'The Carlisle Sisters', 'Sea to Sea', and 'Christmas with the Carlisle Sisters'.

The cover of the 'Sea to Sea' album had a photograph of Beth's grandmother and Aunt Cora wearing middies and sailor hats and shielding their eyes with one hand as they peered off in different directions. Beth's grandmother still put on blue eyeshadow and red lipstick, too, every morning. And around the house she wore old, flashy, full-length stage skirts, faded now – red, orange or yellow, or flowered, or with swirls of broken-off sequins. Beth's grandmother didn't care about sloppiness or dirt. With the important exception of Beth's father's study, the house was a mess – Beth was just beginning to realise and be faintly ashamed of this.

On each of Beth's grandmother's skirts was a sewn-on pocket for her pencil and pad. Due to arthritis in her thumb she held the pencil between her middle finger and forefinger, but she still drew faster than anyone Beth had ever seen. She always referred to people with a drawing instead of by writing out their name or their initials. Beth, for instance, was a circle with tight, curly hair. Beth's friend Amy was an exclamation mark. If the phone rang and nobody was home, her grandmother answered it and tapped her pencil three times on the receiver to let whoever was on the other end know that it was her and that they should leave a message. 'Call,' she would write, and then do a drawing.

A drawing of a man's hat was Beth's father. He was a hard-working lawyer who stayed late at the office. Beth had a hazy memory of him giving her a bath once, it must have been before her mother ran off. The memory embarrassed her. She wondered if he wished that she had gone with her mother, if, in fact, she was supposed to have gone, because when he came home from work and she was still there, he seemed surprised. 'Who do we have here?' he might say. He wanted peace and quiet. When Beth got rambunctious, he narrowed his eyes as though she gave off a bright, painful light.

Beth knew that he still loved her mother. In the top drawer of his dresser, in an old wallet he never used, he had a snapshot of her mother wearing only a black slip. Beth remembered that slip, and her mother's tight black dress with the zipper down the back. And her long red fingernails that she clicked on tables. 'Your mother was too young to marry,' was her father's sole disclosure. Her grandmother disclosed nothing, pretending to be deaf if Beth asked about her mother. Beth remembered how her mother used to phone her father for money and how, if her grandmother answered and took the message, she would draw a big dollar sign and then a triangle in the middle of a line – a witch's hat.

A drawing of a triangle without a line was a church. When a Presbyterian church was built within walking distance, Beth and her mother started going to it, and her grandmother began reading the Bible and counselling Beth by way of biblical quotations. A few months later a crossing appeared at the end of the street, and for several years Beth thought it was a 'Presbyterian' instead of a 'Pedestrian' crossing and that the sign above it said, 'Watch for Presbyterians.'

Her Sunday-school teacher was an old, teary-eyed woman who started every class by singing 'When Mothers of Salem', while the children hung up their coats and sat down cross-legged on the floor in front of her. That hymn, specifically the part about Jesus wanting to hold children to His 'bosom', made Beth feel there was something not right about Jesus, and consequently it was responsible for her six months of anxiety that she would end up in hell. Every night, after saying her prayers, she would spend a few minutes chanting, 'I love Jesus, I love Jesus, I love Jesus,' the idea being that she could talk herself into it. She didn't expect to feel earthly love; she awaited the unknown feeling called 'glory'.

When she began to float, she said to herself, 'This is glory.'

She floated once, sometimes twice a week. Around Easter it began to happen less often – every 10 days to two weeks. Then it dwindled down to only about once a month. She started to chant, 'I love Jesus' again, not because she was worried any more about going to hell, she just wanted to float.

By the beginning of the summer holidays she hadn't floated in almost seven weeks. She phoned her Aunt Cora who said that, yes, floating was glory all right, but Beth should consider herself lucky it had happened even once. 'Nothing that good lasts long,' she sighed.

Beth couldn't stop hoping, though. She went to the park and climbed a tree. Her plan was to jump and have Jesus float her to the ground. But as she stood on a limb, working up her courage, she remembered God seeing the little sparrow fall and letting it fall anyway, and she climbed back down.

She felt that she had just had a close call. She lay on her back on the picnic table, gazing up in wonder at how high up she had been. It was a hot, still day. She heard heat bugs and an ambulance. Presently she went over to the swings and took a turn on each one, since there was nobody else in the park.

She was on the last swing when Helen McCormack came waddling across the lawn, calling that a boy had just been run over by a car. Beth slid off the swing. 'He's almost dead!' Helen called.

'Who?' Beth asked.

'I don't know his name. Nobody did. He's about eight. He's got red hair. The car ran over his leg and his back.'

'Where?'

Helen was panting. 'I shouldn't have walked so fast,' she said, holding her hands on either side of her enormous head. 'My cranium veins are throbbing.' Little spikes of her wispy, blonde hair stood out between her fingers.

'Where did it happen?' Beth said.

'On Glenmore. In front of the post office.'

Beth started running towards Glenmore, but Helen called, 'There's nothing there now, everything's gone!' so Beth stopped and turned, and for a moment Helen and the swings seemed to be turning, coming round and round like Helen's voice saying, 'You missed the whole thing. You missed it. You missed the whole thing.'

'He was on his bike,' Helen said, dropping on to a swing, 'and an eyewitness said that the car skidded on water and knocked him down, then ran over him twice, once with a front tyre and once with a back one. I got there before the ambulance. He probably won't live. You could tell by his eyes. His eyes were glazed.' Helen's eyes, blue, huge because of her glasses, didn't blink.

'That's awful,' Beth said.

'Yes, it really was,' Helen said, matter-of-factly. 'He's not the first person I've seen who nearly died, though. My aunt nearly drowned in the bathtub when we were staying at her house. She became a human vegetable.'

'Was the boy bleeding?' Beth asked.

'Yes, there was blood everywhere.'

Beth covered her mouth with both hands.

Helen looked thoughtful. 'I think he'll probably die,' she said. She pumped her fat legs but without enough energy to get the swing going. 'I'm going to die soon,' she said.

'You are?'

'You probably know that I have water on the brain,' Helen said.

'Yes, I know that,' Beth said. Everyone knew. It was why Helen wasn't supposed to run. It was why her head was so big.

'Well, more and more water keeps dripping in all the time, and one day there will be so much that my brain will literally drown in it.'

'Who said?'

'The doctors, who else?'

'They said you're going to die?'

Helen threw her an ironic look. 'Not exactly. What they tell you is, you're not going to live.' She squinted up at a plane going by. 'The boy, he had . . . I think it was a rib, sticking out of his back.'

'Really?'

'I *think* it was a rib. It was hard to tell because of all the blood.' With the toe of her shoe, Helen began to jab a hole in the sand under her swing. 'A man from the post office hosed the blood down the sewer, but some of it was already caked from the sun.'

Beth turned and walked towards the shade of the picnic table. The air was so thick and still. Her arms and legs, cutting through it, seemed to produce a thousand soft clashes.

'The driver was an old man,' Helen said, 'and he was crying uncontrollably.'

'Anybody *would* cry,' Beth said hotly. Her eyes filled with tears.

Helen squirmed off her swing and came over to the table. Grunting with effort, she climbed on to the seat across from Beth and began to roll her head. 'At least *I'll* die in one piece,' she said.

'Are you really going to?' Beth asked.

'Yep.' Helen rotated her head three times one way, then three times the other. Then she propped it up with her hands cupped under her chin.

'But can't they do anything to stop the water dripping in?' Beth asked.

'Nope,' Helen said distantly, as if she were thinking about something more interesting.

'You know what?' Beth said, swiping at her tears. 'If every night, you closed your eyes and chanted over and over, "Water go away, water go away, water go away," maybe it would start to, and then your head would shrink down.'

Helen smirked. 'Somehow,' she said, 'I doubt it.'

From the edge of the picnic table Beth tore a long sliver of wood like the boy's rib. She pictured the boy riding his bike no-hands, zigzagging down the street the way boys did. She imagined bursting Helen's head with the splinter to let the water gush out.

'I'm thirsty,' Helen sighed. 'I've had a big shock today. I'm going home for some lemonade.'

Beth went with her. It was like walking with her grandmother, who, because of arthritis in her hips, also rocked from side to side and took up the whole sidewalk. Beth asked Helen where she lived.

'I can't talk,' Helen panted. 'I'm trying to breathe.'

Beth thought that Helen lived in the apartments where the immigrants, crazy people and bums were, but Helen went past those apartments and up the hill to the new Regal Heights subdivision, which had once been a landfill site. Her house was a split-level with a little turret above the garage. On the door was an engraved wooden sign, the kind that Beth had seen nailed to posts in front of cottages. No solictors, it said.

'My father is a solicitor,' Beth said.

Helen was concentrating on opening the door. 'Darn thing's always stuck,' she muttered, as she shoved it open with her shoulder. 'I'm home!' she hollered, then sat heavily on a small mauve suitcase next to the door.

Across the hallway a beautiful woman was dusting the ceiling with a mop. She had dark, curly hair tied up in a red ribbon, and long, slim legs in white short shorts.

To Beth's amazement she was Helen's mother. 'You can call me Joyce,' she said, smiling at Beth as though she loved her. 'Who's this lump of potatoes?' she laughed, pointing the mop at Helen.

Helen stood up: 'A boy got run over on Glenmore,' she said.

Joyce's eyes widened, and she looked at Beth. 'I didn't see it,' Beth told her.

'We're dying of thirst,' Helen said. 'We want lemonade in my room.'

While Joyce made lemonade from a can, Helen sat at the kitchen table, resting her head on her folded arms. Joyce's questions about the accident seemed to bore her. 'We don't need ice,' she said impatiently when Joyce went to open the freezer. She demanded cookies, and Joyce poured some Oreos on to the tray with their coffee mugs of lemonade, then handed the tray to Beth, saying with a little laugh that, sure as shooting, Helen would tip it over.

'I'm always spilling things,' Helen agreed.

Beth carried the tray through the kitchen to the hallway. 'Why is that there?' she asked, nodding at the suitcase beside the front door.

'That's my hospital suitcase,' Helen said. 'It's all packed for an emergency.' She pushed open her bedroom door so that it banged against the wall. The walls were the same mauve colour as the suitcase, and there was a smell of paint. Everything was put away – no clothes lying around, no games or toys on the floor. The dolls and books, lined up on white bookshelves, looked as if they were for sale. Beth thought contritely of her own dolls, their tangled hair and dirty dresses, half of them naked, some of them missing legs and hands, she could never remember why, she could never figure out how a hand got in with her Scrabble letters.

She set the tray down on Helen's desk. Above the desk was a chart that said Heart Rate, Blood Pressure and Bowel Movements down the side. 'What's that?' she asked.

'My bodily functions chart.' Helen grabbed a handful of cookies. 'We're keeping track of every week to see how much things change before they completely stop. We're conducting an experiment.'

Beth stared at the neatly stencilled numbers and the gently waving red lines. She had the feeling that she was missing something as stunning and obvious as the fact that her mother was gone for good. For years after her mother left she asked her father, 'When is she coming back?' Her father, looking confused, always answered, 'Never,' but Beth just couldn't understand what he meant by that, not until she finally thought to ask, 'When is she coming back for the rest of her life?'

She turned to Helen. 'When are you going to die?'

Helen shrugged. 'There's no exact date,' she said with her mouth full.

'Aren't you afraid?'

'Why should I be? Dying the way I'm going to doesn't hurt, you know.'

Beth sat on the bed. There was the hard feel of plastic under the spread and blankets; she recognised it from when she'd had her tonsils out and they'd put plastic under her sheets then. 'I hope that boy hasn't died,' she said, suddenly thinking of him again.

'He probably has,' Helen said, running a finger along the lowest line on the chart.

The lines were one above the other, not intersecting. When Beth's grandmother drew one wavy line, that was water. Beth closed her eyes. Water go away, she said to herself. Water go away, water go away . . .

'What are you doing?' The bed bounced, splashing lemonade out of Beth's mug as Helen sat down.

'I was conducting an experiment,' Beth said.

'What experiment?'

More lemonade, this time from Helen's mug, poured on to Beth's leg and her shorts. 'Look what you're doing!' Beth cried. She used the corner of the bedspread to dry herself. 'You're so stupid sometimes,' she muttered.

Helen drank down what was left in her mug. 'For your information,' she said, wiping her mouth on her arm, 'it's not stupidity. It's deterioration of the part of my brain lobe that tells my muscles what to do.'

Beth looked up at her. 'Oh, from the water,' she said softly.

'Water is one of the most destructive forces known to mankind,' Helen said.

'I'm sorry,' Beth murmured. 'I didn't mean it.'

'So what did you mean you were trying an experiment?' Helen asked, pushing her glasses up on her nose.

'You know what?' Beth said. 'We could both do it.' She felt a thrill of virtuous resolve. 'Remember what I said about chanting "water go away, water go away"? We could both chant it and see what happens.'

'Brother,' Helen sighed.

Putting her lemonade on the table, Beth jumped off the bed and went over to Helen's desk. 'We'll make a chart,' she said, fishing around in the drawer for a pen and some paper. She found a red coloured pencil. 'Do you have any paper?' she asked. 'We need paper and a measuring tape.'

'Brother,' Helen said again, but she left the room and came back a few minutes later with a pad of foolscap and her mother's sewing basket.

Beth wrote Date and Size at the top of the page and underlined it twice. Under Date she wrote June 30, then she unwound the measuring tape and measured Helen's head – the circumference above her eyebrows – and wrote 27½. Then she and Helen sat cross-legged on the floor, closed their eyes, held each other's hands and said, 'Water go away,' starting out in almost a whisper, but Helen kept speeding up, and Beth had to raise her voice to slow her down. After a few moments both of them were shouting, and Helen was digging her nails into Beth's fingers.

'Stop!' Beth cried. She yanked her hands free. 'It's supposed to be slow and quiet!' she cried. 'Like praying!'

'We don't go to church,' Helen said, pressing her hands on either side of her head. 'Whew,' she breathed. 'For a minute there I thought that my cranium veins were throbbing again.'

'We did it wrong,' Beth said crossly. Helen leaned over to get the measuring tape. 'You should chant tonight before you go to bed,' Beth said, watching as Helen pulled on the bedpost to hoist herself to her feet. 'Chant slowly and softly. I'll come back tomorrow after lunch and we'll do it together again. We'll just keep doing it every afternoon for the whole summer, if that's what it takes. Okay?'

Helen was measuring her hips, her wide, womanly hips in their dark green Bermuda shorts.

'*Okay?*' Beth repeated.

Helen bent over to read the tape. 'Sure,' she said indifferently.

When Beth got back to her own place, her grandmother was playing her *Sea to Sea* record and making black bean soup and dinner rolls. Talking loudly to be heard over the music, Beth told her about the car accident and Helen. Her grandmother knew about Helen's condition but thought that she was retarded – in the flour sprinkled on the table she traced a circle with a triangle sitting on it, which was a 'dunce', and a question mark. 'No,' Beth said, surprised. 'She gets all As.'

Her grandmother pulled out her pad and pencil and wrote, 'Don't get her hopes up.'

'But when you *pray*, that's getting your hopes up,' Beth argued.

Her grandmother looked impressed. 'We walk by faith,' she wrote.

There was a sudden silence. 'Do you want to hear side two?' Beth asked. Her grandmother made a cross with her fingers. 'Oh, okay,' Beth said and went into the living room and put on her grandmother's other record, the Christmas one. The first song was 'Hark! The Herald Angels Sing'. Beth's father's name was Harold. The black bean soup, his favourite, meant he'd be home for supper. Beth wandered down the hall to his den and sat in his green leather chair and swivelled for a moment to the music – 'Offspring of a Virgin's womb . . .'

After a few minutes she got off the chair and began searching through his wastepaper basket. Whenever she was in here and noticed that the basket hadn't been emptied, she looked at what was in it. Usually just pencil shavings and long, handwritten business letters with lots of crossed-out sentences and notes in the margin. Sometimes there were phone messages from his office, where he was called Hal, by Sue, the woman who wrote the messages out.

'PDQ!' Sue wrote. 'ASAP!'

Today there were several envelopes addressed to her father, a couple of fliers, an empty cigarette packet and a crumpled, pink note from her grandmother's pad. Beth opened the note up.

'Call,' it said, and then there was a triangle. Underneath the triangle was a telephone number.

Beth thought it was a message for her father to call the church. Her mother hadn't called in over four years, so it took a moment of wondering why the phone number didn't start with two fives like every other phone number in the neighbourhood did, and why her father, who didn't go to church, should get a message from the church, before Beth remembered that a line under a triangle meant not 'church' but 'witch's hat'.

In the kitchen Beth's grandmother was shaking the bean jars to 'Here We Come a-Wassailing'. Beth felt the rhythm as a pounding between her ears. 'My cranium veins are throbbing,' she thought in revelation, and putting down the message she pressed her palms to her temples and remembered when her mother used to phone for money. Because of those phone calls Beth had always pictured her mother and the man with the toupee living in some poor place, a rundown apartment, or one of the insulbrick bungalows north of the city. 'I'll bet they're broke again,' Beth told herself, working up scorn. 'I'll bet they're down to their last penny.' She picked up the message and crumpled it back into a ball, then, changing her mind, opened it up again, folded it in half and slipped it into the pocket of her shorts.

Sticking to her promise, she went over to Helen's every afternoon. It took her 20 minutes, a little longer than that if she left the road to go through the park, which she often did out of a superstitious feeling that the next time she floated, it would be there. The park made her think of the boy who was run over. On the radio it said that his foot had been amputated and that he was in desperate need of a liver transplant. 'Remember him in your prayers,' the announcer said, and Beth and her grandmother did. The boy's name was Kevin Legg.

'Kevin *Legg* and he lost his *foot!*' Beth pointed out to Joyce.

Joyce laughed, although Beth hadn't meant it as a joke. A few minutes later, in the bedroom, Beth asked Helen, 'Why isn't your mother worried about us getting your hopes up?'

'She's just glad that I finally have a friend,' Helen answered. 'When I'm by myself, I get in the way of her cleaning.'

Beth looked out the window. It hadn't occurred to her that she and Helen were friends.

Beth's best friend, Christine, was at a cottage for the summer. Amy, her other friend, she played with in the mornings and when she returned from Helen's. Amy was half Chinese; small and thin. She was on pills for hyperactivity. 'Just think what I'd be like if I *wasn't* on them!' she cried, spinning around and slamming into the wall. Amy was the friend that Beth's grandmother represented with an exclamation mark because of her high, excited voice. Whatever they were playing, Amy got tired of it after five minutes, but she usually had another idea. She was fun, although not very nice. When Beth told her about Helen dying, she cried, 'That's a lie!'

'Ask her mother,' Beth said.

'No way I'm going to that fat-head's place!' Amy cried.

Amy didn't believe the story about the doctor ripping out Beth's grandmother's tonsils, either, not even after Beth's grandmother opened her mouth and showed her her mutilated tongue.

So Beth knew better than to confide in Amy about floating. She knew better than to confide in anybody, aside from her grandmother and her Aunt Cora, since it wasn't something she could prove and since she found it hard to believe herself. At the same time she was passionately certain that she *had* floated, and might again if she kept up her nightly 'I love Jesus' chants.

She confided in Helen about floating, though, on the fifteenth day of *their* chanting, because that day, instead of sitting on the floor and holding Beth's hands, Helen curled up on her side facing the wall and said, 'I wish we were playing draughts,' and Beth thought how trusting Helen had been so far, chanting twice a day without any reason to believe that it worked.

The next day, the sixteenth day, Helen's head had measured 27 inches.

'Are you sure you aren't pulling the tape tighter?' Helen asked.

'No,' Beth said. 'I always pull it this tight.'

Helen pushed the tape off her head and waddled to the bedroom door. 'Twenty-seven inches!' she called.

'Let's go show her,' Beth said, and they hurried to the living room, where Joyce was using a nail to clean between the floor boards.

'Aren't you guys smart!' Joyce said, sitting back on her heels and wiping specks of dirt from her slim legs and little pink shorts.

'Come on,' Helen said, tugging Beth back to the bedroom. Breathlessly she went to the desk and wrote down the measurement on the chart.

Beth sat on the bed. 'I can't believe it,' she said, falling on to her back. 'It's working. I mean I *thought* it would, I *hoped* it would, but I wasn't absolutely positively, 100 per cent sure.'

Helen came and sat beside her and began to roll her head. Beth pictured the water sloshing from side to side. 'Why do you do that?' she asked.

'I get neck cramps,' Helen said. 'One thing I won't miss are these darn neck cramps.'

The next day her head lost another half inch. The day after that it lost an entire inch, so that it was now down to 25½. Beth and Helen demonstrated the measurements to Joyce, who acted amazed, but Beth could tell that for some reason she really wasn't.

'We're not making it up,' Beth told her.

'Well, who said you were?' Joyce asked, pretending to be insulted.

'Don't you think her head *looks* smaller,' Beth said, and both she and Joyce considered Helen's head, which *had* looked smaller in the bedroom, but now Beth wasn't so sure. In fact, she was impressed, the way she used to be when she only saw Helen once in a while, by just how big Helen's head was. And by her lumpy, grown-up woman's body, which at this moment was collapsing on to a chair.

'You know, I think maybe it *does* look smaller,' Joyce said brightly.

'Wait'll Doctor Dobbs sees me,' Helen said in a tired voice, folding her arms on the table and laying her head down.

Joyce gave Helen's shoulder a little punch. 'You all right, kiddo?'

Helen ignored her. 'I'll show him our chart,' she said to Beth.

'Hey,' said Joyce. 'You all right?'

Helen closed her eyes. 'I need a nap,' she murmured.

*

When Beth returned home there was another message from her mother in her father's wastepaper basket.

This time, before she could help herself, she thought, 'She wants to come back, she's left that man,' and she instantly believed it with righteous certainty. 'I *told* you,' she said out loud, addressing her father. Her eyes burned with righteousness. She threw the message back in the wastepaper basket and went out to the back yard, where her grandmother was tying up the tomato plants. Her grandmother had on her red blouse with the short, puffy sleeves and her blue skirt that was splattered with what had once been red music notes but which were now faded and broken pink sticks. Her plait was wrapped around her head. 'She looks like an immigrant,' Beth thought coldly, comparing her to Joyce. For several moments Beth stood there looking at her grandmother and feeling entitled to a few answers.

The instant her grandmother glanced up, however, she didn't want to know. If, right at that moment, her grandmother had decided to tell her what the messages were about, Beth would have run away. As it was, she ran around to the front of the house and down the street. 'I love Jesus, I love Jesus,' she said, holding her arms out. She was so light on her feet! Any day now she would float, she could feel it.

Her father came home early that evening. It seemed significant to Beth that he did not change into casual pants and a sports shirt *before* supper, as he normally did. Other than that, however, nothing out of the ordinary happened. Her father talked about work, her grandmother nodded and signalled and wrote out a few conversational notes, which Beth leaned over to read.

After supper her father got around to changing his clothes, then went outside to cut the grass while Beth and her grandmother did the dishes. Beth, carrying too many dishes to the sink, dropped and smashed a saucer and a dinner plate. Her grandmother waved her hands – 'Don't worry, it doesn't matter!' – and to prove it she got the Sears catalogue out of the cupboard and showed Beth the new set of dinnerware she intended to buy anyway.

It wasn't until Beth was eating breakfast the next morning that it dawned on her that if her mother was coming back, her grandmother would be leaving, and if her grandmother was leaving, she wouldn't be buying new dinnerware. This thought left Beth feeling as if she had just woken up with no idea yet what day it was or what she'd just been dreaming. Then the radio blared '. . . Liver . . .' and she jumped and turned to see her grandmother with one hand on the volume knob, and the other held up for silence. 'Doctors report that the transplant was a success,' the announcer blared, 'and that Kevin is in a serious but stable condition.'

'Did they find a donor?' Beth cried as the announcer said, 'The donor, an 11-year-old girl, died in St Andrew's Hospital late last night. Her name is being withheld at her family's request.'

Her grandmother turned the volume back down.

'Gee, that's great,' Beth said. 'Everybody was praying for him.'

Her grandmother tore a note off her pad. 'Ask and it shall be given you,' she wrote.

'I know!' Beth said exultantly. 'I know!'

Nobody was at home at Helen's that afternoon. Peering in the window beside the door, Beth saw that the mauve suitcase was gone, and the next thing she knew, she floated from Helen's door to the end of her driveway. Or at least she thought she floated, because she couldn't remember how she got from the house to the road, but the strange thing was, she didn't have the glowing sensation – the feeling of glory. She drifted home, holding herself as if she were a soap bubble.

At her own house there was a note on the kitchen counter . . . a drawing of an apple, which meant that her grandmother was out grocery shopping. The phone rang, but when Beth said hello, the person hung up. She went into her bedroom, opened the drawer of her bedside table and took out the message with her mother's number on it. She returned to the kitchen and dialled it. After four rings, an impatient sounding woman said, 'Hello?' This time Beth said nothing. 'Yes, hello?' the woman said.

Beth hung up. She dialled Helen's number and immediately hung up. She stood there for a few minutes, biting her knuckles.

She wandered down to her bedroom and looked out the window. Two back yards away, Amy was jumping off her porch. She was climbing on to the porch railing, leaping like a long jumper, tumbling on the grass, springing to her feet, running up the stairs and doing it again. It made Beth's head spin.

About a quarter of an hour later her grandmother returned. She dropped the groceries against a cupboard door that slammed shut. She opened and shut the fridge. Turned on the tap. Beth, now lying on the bed, didn't move. She sat bolt upright when the phone rang, though. Five rings before her grandmother answered it.

Beth got up and went over to the window again. Amy was throwing a ball up into the air. Through the closed window Beth couldn't hear a thing, but she knew from the way Amy clapped and twirled her hands between catches that she was singing, 'Ordinary moving, laughing, talking . . .'

She knew from hearing the chair scrape that her grandmother was pulling it back to sit down. She knew from hearing the faucet still run that her grandmother was caught up in what the caller was saying. Several times her grandmother tapped her pencil on the mouthpiece to say to the caller, 'I'm still listening. I'm taking it all down.'

Pam Houston

COWBOYS ARE MY WEAKNESS

I have a picture in my mind of a tiny ranch on the edge of a stand of pine trees with some horses in the yard. There's a woman standing in the doorway in cut-offs and a blue chambray work shirt and she's just kissed her tall, bearded and soft-spoken husband goodbye. There's laundry hanging outside and the morning sun is filtering through the tree branches like spiderwebs. It's the morning after a full moon, and behind the house the deer have eaten everything that was left in the garden.

If I were a painter, I'd paint that picture just to see if the girl in the doorway would turn out to be me. I've been out west 10 years now, long enough to call it my home, long enough to know I'll be here for ever, but I still don't know where that ranch is. And even though I've had plenty of men here, some of them tall and nearly all of them bearded, I still haven't met the man who has just walked out of the painting, who has just started his pick-up truck, whose tyre marks I can still see in the sandy soil of the drive.

The west isn't a place that gives itself up easily. Newcomers have to sink into it slowly, to descend through its layers, and I'm still descending. Like most easterners, I started out in the transitional zones, the big cities and the ski towns that outsiders have set up for their own comfort, the places so often referred to as 'the best of both worlds'. But I was bound to work my way back, through the land, into the small towns and beyond them. That's half the reason I wound up on a ranch near Grass Range, Montana; the other half is Homer.

I've always had this thing about cowboys, maybe because I was born in New Jersey. But a real cowboy is hard to find these days, even in the west. I thought I'd found one on several occasions, I even at one time thought Homer was a cowboy, and though I loved him like crazy for a while and in some ways always will, somewhere along the line I had to face the fact that even though Homer looked like a cowboy, he was just a capitalist with a Texas accent who owned a horse.

Homer's a wildlife specialist in charge of a whitetail deer management project on the ranch. He goes there every year to observe the deer from the start of the mating season in late October until its peak in mid-November. It's the time when the deer are most visible, when the bucks get so lusty they lose their normal caution, when the does run around in the middle of the day with their white tails in the air. When Homer talked me into coming with him, he said I'd love the ranch, and I did. It was 60 miles from the nearest paved road. All of the buildings were whitewashed and plain. One of them had been ordered from a 1916 Sears catalogue. The ranch hands still rode horses, and when the late afternoon light swept the grainfields across from headquarters, I would watch them move the cattle in rows that looked like waves.

Homer has gone to the ranch every year for the last six, and he has a long history of stirring up trouble there. The ranch hands watch him sit on the hillside and hate him for the money he makes. He's slept with more than one or two of their wives and girlfriends. There was even some talk that he was the reason the ranch owner got divorced.

When he asked me to come with him I knew it would be me or somebody else and I'd heard good things about Montana so I went. There was a time when I was sure Homer was the man who belonged in my painting and I would have sold my soul to be his wife, or even his only girlfriend. I'd come close, in the spring, to losing my mind because of it, but I had finally learnt that Homer would always be separate, even from himself, and by the time we got to Montana I was almost immune to him.

Homer and I live in Fort Collins, Colorado, most of the year, in houses that are exactly one mile apart. He's out of town as often as not, keeping track of 15 whitetail deer herds all across the west. I go with him when he lets me, which is lately more and more. The herds Homer studies are isolated by geography, given plenty of food in bad winters, and protected from hunters and wolves. Homer is working on reproduction and genetics, trying to create, in the wild, superbucks bigger and tougher than elk. The Montana herd has been his most successful, so he spends the long mating season there. Under his care the bucks have shown incredible increases in antler mass, in body weight and in fertility.

The other scientists at the university that sponsors Homer respect him, not only for his success with the deer, but for his commitment to observation, for his relentless dedication to his hours in the field. They also think he is eccentric and a bit overzealous.

At first I thought he just liked to be outdoors, but when we got to the ranch his obsession with the deer made him even more like a stranger. He was gone every day from way before sunrise till long after dark. He would dress all in camouflage, even his gloves and socks, and sit on the hillsides above where the deer fed and watch, making notes a few times an hour, changing position every hour or two. If I went with him I wasn't allowed to move except when he did, and I was never allowed to talk. I'd try to save things up for later that I thought of during the day, but by the time we got back to our cabin they seemed unimportant and Homer liked to eat his dinner in front of the TV. By the time we got the dishes done it was way past Homer's bedtime. We were making love less and less, and when we did, it was always from behind.

The ranch owner's name was David, and he wasn't what you'd think a Montana ranch owner would be. He was a poet, and a vegetarian. He listened to Andreas Vollenweider and drank hot beverages with names like Suma and Morning Rain. He wouldn't let the ranch hands use pesticides or chemicals, he wouldn't hire them if they smoked cigarettes. He undergrazed the ranch by about 50 per cent, so the organic grain was belly-high to a horse almost everywhere.

David had an idea about recreating on his 40,000 acres the Great Plains that only the Indians and the first settlers had seen. He wasn't making a lot of money ranching, but he was producing the fattest, healthiest, most organic Black Angus cattle in North America. He was sensitive, thoughtful, and kind. He was the kind of man I always knew I should fall in love with, but never did.

Homer and David ate exactly one dinner a week together, which I always volunteered to cook. Homer was always polite and full of incidental conversation and much too quick to laugh. David was quiet and sullen and so restrained that he was hard to recognise.

The irreconcilable differences between Homer and me had been revealing themselves one at a time since late summer. In early November I asked him what he wanted to do on Thanksgiving, and he said he'd like most of all to stay on the ranch and watch the does in heat.

Homer was only contracted to work on the ranch until the Sunday before Thanksgiving. When he asked me to come with him he told me we would leave the ranch in plenty of time to have the holidays at home.

I was the only child in a family that never did a lot of celebrating because my parents couldn't plan ahead. They were sun worshippers, and we spent every Thanksgiving in a plane on the way to Puerto Rico, every Christmas in a car on Highway 95, heading for Florida. What I remember most from those days is Casey Casom's Christmas shows, the long-distance dedications, 'I'll be home for Christmas' from Bobby D in Spokane to Linda S in Decatur. We never had hotel reservations and the places we wound up in had no phones and plastic mattress covers and triple locks on the doors. Once we spent Christmas night parked under a fluorescent street light, sleeping in the car.

I've spent most of the holidays in my adult life making up for those road trips. I spend lots of money on hand-painted ornaments. I always cook a roast 10 pounds bigger than anything we could possibly eat.

Homer thinks my enthusiasm about holidays is childish and self-serving. To prove it to me, last Christmas morning he set the alarm for six-thirty and went back to his house to stain a door. This year I wanted Thanksgiving in my own house. I wanted to cook a turkey we'd be eating for weeks.

I said, 'Homer, you've been watching the deer for five weeks now. What else do you think they're gonna do?'

'You don't know anything about it,' he said. 'Thanksgiving is the premium time. Thanksgiving,' he shook one finger in the air, 'is the height of the rut.'

★

David and I drank tea together, and every day took walks up into the canyon behind ranch headquarters. He talked about his ex-wife, Carmen, about the red flowers that covered the canyon walls in June, about imaging away nuclear weapons. He told me about the woman Homer was sleeping with on the ranch the year before, when I was back in Colorado counting days till he got home. She was the woman who took care of the chickens, and David said that when Homer left the ranch she wrote a hundred love songs and made David listen while she sang them all.

'She sent them on a tape to Homer,' David said, 'and when he didn't call or write, she went a little nuts. I finally told her to leave the ranch. I'm not a doctor, and we're a long way from anywhere out here.'

From the top of the canyon we could see Homer's form blending with the trees on the ridge above the garden, where the deer ate organic potatoes by the hundreds of pounds.

'I understand if he wasn't interested any more,' David said. 'But I can't believe even he could ignore a gesture that huge.'

We watched Homer crawl along the ridge from tree to tree. I could barely distinguish his movements from what the wind did to the tall grass. None of the deer below him even turned their heads.

'What is it about him?' David said, and I knew he was looking for an explanation about Carmen, but I'd never even met her and I didn't want to talk about myself.

'Homer's always wearing camouflage,' I said. 'Even when he's not.'

The wind went suddenly still and we could hear, from headquarters, the sounds of cats fighting, a hen's frantic scream, and then, again, the cats.

David put his arm around me. 'We're such good people,' he said. 'Why aren't we happy?'

One day when we got back from my walk with David, Homer was in the cabin in the middle of the day. He had on normal clothes and I could tell he'd shaved and showered. He took me into the bedroom and climbed on top of me frontwards, the way he did when we first met and I didn't even know what he did for a living.

Afterwards he said, 'We didn't need a condom, did we?' I counted the days forward and backward and forward again. Homer always kept track of birth control and groceries and gas mileage and all the other things I couldn't keep my mind on. Still, it appeared to be exactly 10 days before my next period.

'Yes,' I said. 'I think we did.'

Homer has never done an uncalculated thing in his life, and for a moment I let myself entertain the possibility that his mistake meant that somewhere inside he wanted to have a baby with me, that he really wanted a family and love and security and the things I thought everybody wanted before I met Homer. On the other hand, I knew that one of the ways I had gotten in trouble with Homer, and with other men before him, was by inventing thoughts for them that they'd never had.

'Well,' he said. 'In that case we better get back to Colorado before they change the abortion laws.'

Sometimes the most significant moments of your life reveal themselves to you even as they are happening, and I knew in that moment that I would never love Homer the same way again. It wasn't so much that not six months before, when I had asked Homer what we'd do if I got pregnant, he said we'd get married and have a family. It wasn't even that I was sure I wanted a baby. It wasn't even that I thought there was going to be a baby to want.

It all went back to the girl in the log cabin, and how the soft-spoken man would react if she thought she was going to have a baby. It would be winter now, and snowing outside the windows warm with yellow light. He might dance with the sheepdog on the living room floor, he might sing the theme song from *Father Knows Best*, he might go out and do a swan dive into the snow.

I've been to a lot of school and read a lot of thick books, but at my very core there's a made-for-TV-movie mentality I don't think I'll ever shake. And although there's a lot of doubt in my mind about whether or not an ending as simple and happy as I want is possible any more in the world, it was clear to me that afternoon that it wasn't possible with Homer.

★

Five o'clock the next morning was the first time I saw the real cowboy. He was sitting in the cookhouse eating cereal and I couldn't make myself sleep next to Homer so I'd been up all night wandering around.

He was tall and thin and bearded. His hat was white and ratty and you could tell by looking at his stampede strap that it had been made around a campfire after lots of Jack Daniels. I'd had my fingers in my hair for 12 hours and my face was breaking out from too much stress and too little sleep and I felt like such a grease ball that I didn't say hello. I poured myself some orange juice, drank it, rinsed the glass, and put it in the dish drainer. I took one more look at the cowboy, and walked back out the door, and went to find Homer in the field.

Homer's truck was parked by a culvert on the South Fork road, which meant he was walking the brush line below the cliffs that used to be the Blackfeet buffalo jumps. It was a boneyard down there, and the place where hundreds of buffalo, chased by the Indians, had jumped 500 feet to their death, and the soil was extremely fertile. The grass was thicker and sweeter there than anywhere on the ranch, and Homer said the deer sucked calcium out of the buffalo bones. I saw Homer crouched at the edge of a meadow I couldn't get to without being seen, so I went back and fell asleep in the bed of his truck.

It was hunting season, and later that morning Homer and I found a deer by the side of the road that had been poached but not taken. The poacher must have seen headlights or heard a truck engine and gotten scared.

I lifted the back end of the animal into the truck while Homer picked up the antlers. It was a young buck, two and a half at the oldest, but it would have been a monster in a few years, and I knew Homer was taking the loss pretty hard.

We took it down to the performance centre, where they weigh the organic calves. Homer attached a meat hook to its antlers and hauled it into the air above the pick-up.

'Try and keep it from swinging,' he said. And I did my best considering I wasn't quite tall enough to get a good hold, and its blood was bubbling out of the bullet hole and dripping down on me.

That's when the tall cowboy, the one from that morning, walked out of the holding pen behind me, took a long slow look at me trying to steady the back end of the dead deer, and settled himself against the fence across the driveway. I stepped back from the deer and pushed the hair out of my eyes. He raised one finger to call me over. I walked slow and didn't look back at Homer.

'Nice buck,' he said. 'Did you shoot it?'

'It's a baby,' I said. 'I don't shoot animals. A poacher got it last night.'

'Who was the poacher?' he said, and tipped his hat just past my shoulder towards Homer.

'You're wrong,' I said. 'You can say a lot of things about him, but he wouldn't poach a deer.'

'My name's Montrose T. Coty,' he said. 'Everyone calls me Monte.'

I shook his hand. 'Everyone calls you Homer's girlfriend,' he said, 'but I bet that's not your name.'

'You're right,' I said, 'it's not.'

I turned to look at Homer. He was taking measurements off the hanging deer: antler length, body length, width at its girth.

'Tonight's the Stockgrowers' Ball in Grass Range,' Monte said. 'I thought you might want to go with me.'

Homer was looking into the deer's hardened eyeballs. He had its mouth open, and was pulling on its tongue.

'I have to cook dinner for Homer and David,' I said. 'I'm sorry. It sounds like fun.'

In the car on the way back to the cabin, Homer said, 'What was that all about?'

I said, 'Nothing,' and then I said, 'Monte asked me to the Stockgrowers' Ball.'

'The Stockgrowers' Ball?' he said. 'Sounds like a great time. What do stockgrowers do at a ball?' he said. 'Do they dance?'

I almost laughed with him until I remembered how much I loved to dance. I'd been with Homer chasing whitetail so long that I'd forgotten that dancing, like holidays, was something I loved. And I started to wonder just then what else being with Homer had made me forget. Hadn't I, at one time, spent whole days listening to music? And didn't

I love to be able to go outdoors and walk anywhere I wanted, and to make, if I wanted, all kinds of noise?

I wanted to blame Homer, but I realised then it was more my fault than his. Because even though I'd never let the woman in the chambray work shirt out of my mind I'd let her, in the last few years, become someone different, and she wasn't living, anymore, in my painting. The painting she was living in, I saw, belonged to somebody else.

'So what did you tell him?' Homer said.

'I told him I'd see if you'd cook dinner,' I said.

I tried to talk to Homer before I left. First I told him that it wasn't a real date; that I didn't even know Monte, and that really I was only going because I didn't know if I'd ever have another chance to go to a Stockgrowers' Ball. When he didn't answer at all I worked up to saying that maybe it was a good idea for me to start seeing other people. That maybe we'd had two different ideas all along and we needed to find two other people who would better meet our needs. I told him that if he had any opinions I wish he'd express them to me, and he thought for a few minutes and then he said, 'Well, I guess we have Jimmy Carter to thank for all the trouble in Panama.'

I spent the rest of the day getting ready for the Stockgrowers' Ball. All I'd brought with me was some of Homer's camouflage and blue jeans, so I wound up borrowing a skirt that David's ex-wife had left behind, some of the chicken woman's dress shoes that looked ridiculous and made my feet huge, and a vest that David's grandfather had been shot at in by the Plains Indians.

Monte had to go into town early to pick up ranch supplies, so I rode in with his friends Buck and Dawn, who spent the whole drive telling me what a great guy Monte was, how he quit the rodeo circuit to make a decent living for himself and his wife, how she'd left without saying goodbye not six months before.

They told me that he'd made two thousand dollars in one afternoon doing a Wrangler commercial. That he'd been in a laundromat on his day off and the director had seen him through the window, had gone in and said, 'Hey, cowboy, you got an hour? You want to make two thousand bucks?'

'Ole Monte,' Buck said. 'He's the real thing.'

After an hour and a half of washboard road we pulled into the dance hall just on our edge of town. I had debated about wearing the cowboy hat I'd bought especially for my trip to Montana, and was thankful I'd decided against it. It was clear, once inside, that only the men wore hats, and only dress hats at that. The women wore high heels and stockings and in almost every case hair curled away from their faces in great airy rolls.

We found Monte at a table in the corner, and the first thing he did was give me a corsage, a pink one, mostly roses that couldn't have clashed more with my rust-coloured blouse. Dawn pinned it on me, and I blushed, I suppose, over my first corsage in 10 years, and a little old woman in spike heels leaned over and said, 'Somebody loves you!' just loud enough for Monte and Buck and Dawn to hear.

During dinner they showed a movie about a cattle drive. After dinner a young enthusiastic couple danced and sang for over an hour about cattle and ranch life and the Big Sky, a phrase which since I'd been in Montana had seemed perpetually on the tip of everybody's tongue.

After dinner the dancing started, and Monte asked me if I knew how to do the Montana two-step. He was more than a foot taller than me, and his hat added another several inches to that. When we stood on the dance floor my eyes came right to the place where his silk scarf disappeared into the shirt buttons on his chest. His big hands were strangely light on me and my feet went the right direction even though my mind couldn't remember the two-step's simple form.

That's it,' he said into the part in my hair. 'Don't think. Just let yourself move with me.'

And we were moving together, in turns that got tighter and tighter each time we circled the dance floor. The songs got faster and so did our motion until there wasn't time for anything but the picking up and putting down of feet, for the swirling colours of Carmen's ugly skirt, for breath and sweat and rhythm.

I was farther west than I'd ever imagined, and in the strange, nearly flawless synchronisation on the dance floor I knew I could be a

Montana ranch woman, and I knew I could make Monte my man. It had taken me 10 years, and an incredible sequence of accidents, but that night I thought I'd finally gotten where I'd set out to go.

The band played till two and we danced till three to the jukebox. Then there was nothing left to do but get in the car and begin the two-hour drive home.

First we talked about our horses. It was the logical choice, the only thing we really had in common, but it only lasted 20 minutes.

I tried to get his opinion on music and sailing, but just like a cowboy, he was too polite for me to tell anything for sure.

Then we talked about the hole in my vest that the Indians shot, which I was counting on, and half the reason I wore it.

The rest of the time we just looked at the stars.

I had spent a good portion of the night worrying about what I was going to say when Monte asked me to go to bed with him. When he pulled up between our two cabins he looked at me sideways and said, 'I'd love to give you a great big kiss, but I've got a mouthful of chew.'

I could hear Homer snoring before I got past the kitchen.

Partly because I didn't like the way Monte and Homer eyed each other, but mostly because I couldn't bear to spend Thanksgiving watching does in heat, I loaded my gear in my truck and got ready to go back to Colorado.

On the morning I left, Homer told me that he had decided that I was the woman he wanted to spend the rest of his life with after all, and that he had planned to go to town and buy a ring just as soon as the rut ended.

He was sweet on my last morning on the ranch, generous and attentive in a way I'd never seen. He packed me a sack lunch of chicken salad he mixed himself, and he went out to my car and dusted off the inch of snow that had fallen in our first brush with winter, overnight. He told me to call when I got to Fort Collins, he even said to call collect, but I suppose one of life's big tricks is to give us precisely the thing we want, two weeks after we've stopped wanting it, and I couldn't take Homer seriously, even when I tried.

★

When I went to say goodbye to David he hugged me hard, said I was welcome back on the ranch any time. He said he enjoyed my company and appreciated my insight. Then he said he liked my perfume and I wondered where my taste in men had come from, I wondered whoever taught me to be so stupid about men.

I knew Monte was out riding the range, so I left a note on his car thanking him again for the dancing and saying I'd be back one day and we could dance again. I put my hat on, that Monte had never got to see, and rolled out of headquarters. It was the middle of the day, but I saw seven bucks in the first five miles, a couple of them giants, and when I slowed down they just stood and stared at the truck. It was the height of the rut and Homer said that's how they'd be, love-crazed and fearless as bears.

About a mile before the edge of ranch property, I saw something that looked like a lone antelope running across the skyline, but antelope are almost never alone, so I stopped the car to watch. As the figure came closer I saw it was a horse, a big chestnut, and it was carrying a rider at full gallop, and it was coming right for the car.

I knew it could have been any one of 50 cowboys employed on the ranch, and yet I've learned to expect more from life than that, and so in my heart I knew it was Monte. I got out of the car and waited, pleased that he'd see my hat most of all, wondering what he'd say when I said I was leaving.

He didn't get off his horse, which was sweating and shaking so hard I thought it might die while we talked.

'You on your way?' he said.

I smiled and nodded. His chaps were sweat-soaked, his leather gloves worn white.

'Will you write me a letter?' he said.

'Sure,' I said.

'Think you'll be back this way?' he asked.

'If I come back,' I said, 'will you take me dancing?'

'Damn right,' he said, and a smile that seemed like the smile I'd been waiting for my whole life spread wide across his face.

'Then it'll be sooner than later,' I said.

He winked and touched the horse's flank with his spurs and it hopped a little on the take-off and then there was just dirt flying while the high grass swallowed the horse's legs. I leaned against the door of my pick-up truck watching my new cowboy riding off toward where the sun was already low in the sky and the grass shimmering like nothing I'd ever seen in the mountains.

And for a minute I thought we were living inside my painting, but he was riding away too fast to tell. And I wondered then why I always imagined my cowboy's truck as it was leaving. I wondered why I hadn't turned the truck around and painted my cowboy coming home.

There's a story – that isn't true – that I tell about myself when I first meet someone, about riding a mechanical bull in a bar. In the story, I stay on through the first eight levels of difficulty, getting thrown on level nine only after dislocating my thumb and winning my boyfriend, who was betting on me, a big pile of money. It was something I said in a bar one night, and I liked the way it sounded so much I kept telling it. I've been telling it for so many years now, and in such scrupulous detail, that it has become a memory and it's hard for me to remember that it isn't true. I can smell the smoke and beer-soaked carpets, I can hear the cheers of all the men. I can see the bar lights blur and spin, and I can feel the cold iron buck between my thighs, the painted saddle slam against my tailbone, the surprise and pain when my thumb extends too far and I let go. It's a good story, a story that holds my listeners' attention, and although I consider myself almost pathologically honest, I have somehow allowed myself this one small lie.

And watching Monte ride off through the long grains, I thought about the way we invent ourselves through our stories, and in a similar way, how the stories we tell put walls around our lives. And I think that may be true about cowboys. That there really isn't much truth in my saying cowboys are my weakness; maybe, after all this time, it's just something I've learned how to say.

I felt the hoofbeats in the ground long after Monte's white shirt and ratty hat melded with the sun. When I couldn't even pretend to feel them any more, I got in the car and headed for the hard road.

I listened to country music the whole way to Cody, Wyoming. The men in the songs were all either brutal or inexpressive and always sorry later. The women were victims, every one. I started to think about coming back to the ranch to visit Monte, about another night dancing, about another night wanting the impossible love of a country song, and I thought:

This is not my happy ending.

This is not my story.

Margaret Atwood

THE BOG MAN

Julie broke up with Connor in the middle of a swamp.

Julie silently revises: not exactly in the middle, not knee-deep in rotting leaves and dubious brown water. More or less on the edge; sort of within striking distance. Well, in an inn, to be precise. Or not even an inn. A room in a pub. What was available.

And not in a swamp anyway. In a bog. *Swamp* is when the water goes in one end and out the other, *bog* is when it goes in and stays in. How many times did Connor have to explain the difference? Quite a few. But Julie prefers the sound of *swamp*. It is mistier, more haunted. *Bog* is a slang word for toilet, and when you hear *bog* you know the toilet will be a battered and smelly one, and that there will be no toilet paper.

So Julie always says: *I broke up with Connor in the middle of a swamp*.

There are other things she revises as well. She revises Connor. She revises herself. Connor's wife stays approximately the same, but she was an invention of Julie's in the first place, since Julie never met her. Sometimes she used to wonder whether the wife really existed at all, or was just a fiction of Connor's, useful for keeping Julie at arm's length. But, no, the wife existed all right. She was solid, and she became more and more solid as time went on.

Connor mentioned the wife, and the three children and the dog, fairly soon after he and Julie met. Well, not met. Slept together. It was almost the same thing.

Julie supposes, now, that he didn't want to scare her off by bringing up the subject too soon. She herself was only 20, and too naive to even think of looking for clues, such as the white circle on the ring finger.

By the time he did get around to making a sheepish avowal or confession, Julie was in no position to be scared off. She was already lying in a motel room, wound loosely in a sheet. She was too tired to be scared off and also too amazed, and also too grateful. Connor was not her first lover but he was her first grown-up one, he was the first who did not treat sex as some kind of panty-raid. He took her body seriously, which impressed her no end.

At the time – what was the time? It was 20 years ago, or 25. More like 30. It was the early Sixties; the precise year had to do with bubble-cut hairdos, with white lipstick, with dark rings pencilled around the eyes. Also purple was big as a colour, although Julie herself favoured the more rebellious black. She thought of herself as a sort of pirate. A dark-eyed, hawk-faced, shaggy-haired raider, making daring inroads on the borders of smug domestic settlements. Setting fire to the roofs, getting away with the loot, suiting herself. She studied modern philosophy, read Sartre on the side, smoked Gitanes, and cultivated a look of bored contempt. Inwardly she was seething with unfocused excitement, and looking for someone to worship.

Connor was it. Julie was in her last year of university, in Toronto, and Connor was her professor for Archaeology – a one-hour-a-week course you could take instead of Religious Knowledge. Julie fell in love with his voice, rich and rough-edged, persuasive and abraded, rising and falling in the darkness like a stroking, insistent hand while he showed them slides of Celtic tombs. Then she got tangled up with him in his office, where she'd gone intentionally late in the day to discuss her final term paper. Then they'd ended up in the motel. In that era such things happened more easily between students and their professors, without any fear on the part of the professors that they would be accused of sexual harassment and lose their jobs. There was no such phrase as 'sexual harassment', even. There was no such thought.

At the time, Julie did not think the wife and the three kids and the dog had anything to do with her and Connor. She was too young to make such connections: the wife was as old as her own mother, almost, and women like that did not really have lives. She could not picture Connor in any context other than the motel rooms they would sneak into, or the apartments of Julie's friends, shambling, cheap apartments furnished with mattresses and decorated with egg cartons painted black nailed to the ceiling and with chianti-bottle candleholders. She did not think of him as having an existence apart from her: the wife and kids were just boring subsistence details, like brushing your teeth. Instead she saw him in glorious and noble isolation, a man singled out, like an astronaut, like a diver in a bell jar, like a saint in a medieval painting, surrounded by a golden atmosphere of his own, a total-body halo. She wanted to be in there with him, participating in his radiance, basking in his light.

Because of her original awe of Connor – he was very smart, he knew a lot about ancient bones, about foreign travel, about how to mix drinks – she did not drive nearly as hard a bargain with him as she could have driven. But then, she had not been conscious of driving a bargain at all. She had been possessed by some notion of self-sacrifice; she had asked nothing for herself, except that Connor should continue to be superhuman.

The first motel was two months ago. Julie feels she has aged a great deal since then. She sits in the uncomfortable maroon plush armchair in her room in the Scottish pub in the small town near the bog, beside the window with its grubby white curtains and the clear northern light coming in, smoking Gitanes and drinking from a cold cup of tea she's brought up from her spectacularly awful breakfast with its limp underdone bacon and its burnt grilled tomatoes. She sits and she smokes, and she knits.

Knitting is something she has just taken up again, having learnt it as a child from a mother who believed in the female domestic virtues. She was also taught to crochet, to set in zippers, to polish silverware, to produce a gleaming toilet. This was baggage she'd discarded as soon as she hit Spinoza: two years, a year ago, she would have despised knitting. But there is not a lot to do in this town when Connor is not here. Julie has been up and down the main street several times; she has been drizzled on by the weather, she has been scowled at by the tweed-covered inhabitants. She has sat in the one café and drunk vile coffee and eaten bland and lard-flavoured scones. She has inspected the ancient church: not a lot to see there. The stained-glass windows must have gone when the Presbyterians took over. Dead soldiers' names on the wall, as if God was interested.

The knitting is a last resort. Whatever else tiny Scottish towns like this one may lack, they all have wool stores. Julie went into the wool store, fended off enquiries as to her marital status and general mode of existence, and bought a pattern for a sweater – jumper, they call it here – and some big needles, and a number of skeins of dark grey wool. She wound the skeins into balls, and then she went back to the wool store and bought an ugly tapestry bag with wooden handles to put them in. Knitting is not really very soothing but it gives her something to do with her hands while she broods and waits for Connor.

What she's knitting is a sweater for Connor. She's doing the first sleeve. After a while she realises that she's knitted the sleeve eight inches longer than it should be. It will make Connor look like an orang-utan. Let him complain, she thinks. She leaves it that way and begins on the other sleeve. She intends to make it equally as long.

While Julie knits, Connor is off inspecting the bog man. The bog man is why they are here.

When the bog man find was announced, they were on the island of Orkney. Connor was looking at standing stone ring sites and Julie was pretending to be his assistant. This was Connor's bright idea. It has allowed him to write off Julie as part of the expense of this particular expedition, but it has fooled nobody for long; at least not the barmen, at least not the maids in the various inns where they've been staying, who sneer at Julie in a dour, self-righteous way, despite the fact that Julie and Connor have taken care to book separate rooms. Maybe Julie should look more industrious; maybe she should carry notebooks and bustle around more.

Despite the sneers of the maids and the innuendos of the barmen, Julie enjoyed herself quite a lot in Orkney. Not even the breakfasts dismayed her, not even the congealed oatmeal and the dry toast. Not even the dinners. It would have taken a good many rock-hard lamb chops, a great deal of over-fried fish, to dampen her spirits. It was her first trip across the Atlantic Ocean; she wanted things to be old and picturesque. More importantly, it was the first time she and Connor had been alone together for any length of time. She felt almost marooned with him. He felt it too; he was more uninhibited, less nervous about footsteps outside the door; and although he still had to get up and sneak out in the middle of the night, it was comforting to know that he only snuck next door.

It was July, the fields were green, the sun shone, the stone circles were suitably mysterious. If Julie stood in the centres of them and closed her eyes and kept still, she thought she could hear a sort of hum. Connor's theory was that these rings were not merely large harmless primitive calendars, erected for the purpose of determining the solstices. He thought they were the sites of ritual human sacrifices. This should have made them more sinister for Julie, but it did not. Instead she felt a connection with her ancestors. Her mother's family had come from this part of the world, more or less; from somewhere in the north of Scotland. She liked to sit among the standing stones and picture her ancestors running around naked and covered with blue tattoos, offering cups of blood to the gods, or whatever they did. Some bloodthirsty, indecipherable Pictish thing. The blood made them authentic, as authentic as the Mayans; or at least more authentic than all that clan and tartan and bagpipe stuff, which Julie found tedious and sentimental. There had been enough of it at her university, enough to last her for a while.

But then the bog man had been discovered and they'd had to pack and take the ferry to the mainland, where it was rainier. Julie would have liked to stay on Orkney but Connor was hot on the trail. He wanted to get there before the bog man had been completely, as he said, ruined. He wanted to get there before everyone else.

This particular bog man was unearthed by a peat-digger, who'd cut into it accidentally with the sharp blade of his shovel, severing the feet. He'd thought it was a recent murder victim. It was hard for him to believe the bog man was 2,000 years old: it was so perfectly preserved.

Some of the previously uncovered bog people aren't much to look at, judging by the pictures of them Connor has showed her. The bog water has tanned their skins and preserved their hair, but often their bones have been dissolved and the weight of the peat has squashed them flat, so that they resemble extremely sick items of leather gear.

Julie does not feel the same connection with them that she felt with the standing stones. The idea of human sacrifice is one thing, but the leftovers are something else again.

Before this trip, Julie didn't know much about bog people, but now she does. For instance, this bog man died by being strangled with a twisted leather noose and sunk in the bog, probably as a sacrifice to the Great Goddess Nerthus, or someone like her, to ensure the fertility of the crops. 'After a sexual orgy of some kind,' said Connor hopefully. 'Those nature goddesses were voracious.'

He proceeded to give examples of other things that had been sacrificed to the nature goddesses. Necklaces were a feature, and pots. Many pots and cauldrons had been dug up out of the bogs, here and there around Northern Europe. Connor has a map, with the sites marked and a list of what has been found at each one. He seems to think Julie ought to have memorised this list, that she ought to have its details at her fingertips, and acts surprised when it turns out she doesn't. Among his other virtues, or defects – Julie is just beginning to find it hard to tell the difference – Connor is very pedagogical. Julie has started to suspect him of trying to mould her mind. Into what, is the question.

As she knits, she makes a mental list of other things that get moulded. Steamed Christmas puddings, poured concrete lawn dwarfs, gelatin desserts, wobbly and bright pink and dotted with baby marshmallows. Thinking of these reminds Julie of her own mother, and then of Connor's wife.

It's astounding to her, the way this invisible wife has put on flesh, has gradually acquired solidity and presence. At the beginning of her two months with Connor the wife was merely a negligible shadow. Julie wasn't even that interested in going through Connor's wallet to look for family photos while he was out of the way in the shower.

She didn't bother then, but she's bothered since. Tucked behind the driver's licence there's the whole family group, in colour, taken on the lawn in summer: the wife, huge in a flowered dress and squinting; the three boys with Connor's red hair, squinting also; the dog, a black Labrador which knew better than to look at the sun, its tongue out and drooling. The ordinariness, the plainness of this picture offends

Julie deeply. It interferes with her idea of Connor, with his status as romantic isolate; it diminishes him, and it has made Julie feel, for the first time, cheap and furtive. Extraneous, auxiliary. If they were all on a troika and the wolves were gaining, she has no doubt – looking at the dog, the red-headed kids, the suburban lawn – that she herself would be the first to be hurled off. Compared to those upper arms emerging from the short sleeves of the wife's florid dress – those laundry-toting, child-whacking arms – Julie herself, with her long dark pirate's hair and her 24-inch waist, is a frill.

It's all very well for Connor to say that his wife doesn't understand him. This hefty, squinting woman looks as if she already understands a great deal too much. If she and Julie were to meet, she would not take Julie seriously. She would glance at Julie, merely glance, and then she would chuckle, and Julie would shrivel away to nothing.

Homely is the word. That is the wife's ace up the sleeve, her insurance policy. Even though she looks like a truck tyre, she has the territory staked out. She has the home. She has the house, she has the garage, she has the doghouse and the dog to put into it. She has Connor's children, forming together with them one single invincible monster with four heads and 16 arms and legs. She has the cupboard where Connor hangs his clothes and the washing machine where his socks whirl on washdays, ridding themselves of the lint they've picked up from the bathmats in the motel rooms he's shared with Julie. Motels are a no-man's land: they are not a territory, they cannot be defended. Julie has Connor's sexual attention, but the wife has Connor.

Julie has knitted enough for one day; she rolls the newly begun second sleeve around the needles and tucks it into her tapestry bag. She decides to walk out to the bog, to find Connor. She has not seen the bog before; she has not seen the bog man. She has picked up the impression from Connor that she would be in the way. Even he has dropped the pretence that she is an assistant in any real sense. She runs the risk of being treated as an interruption, but it's a risk she is now willing to take. Boredom is the mother of invention.

She picks up her over-the-shoulder bag from the chipped dressing table, peers at herself in the decaying mirror, pushing her hair back off her face. She is getting that sunless look. She ferrets in the closet for her raincoat, stuffs her Gitanes into her pocket, closes and locks the door and descends the stairs, skirting the cleaning woman, who gave her a baleful glare, and heads out into the mist.

She knows where the bog is: everyone knows. It takes her half an hour to walk there, along the road that is so old it has cut itself into the land like a rut. Connor goes there in a car which has been rented in Edinburgh by one of the other archaeologists. No hope of renting a car in this town.

The bog does not look much like a bog. It looks more like a damp field; tall grasses grow on it, small shrubs. The chocolate-brown scars of the peat-cuttings open into it here and there. It would have been more watery in the days of the bog man; more like a lake. More convenient for drowning.

Connor is over by a roughly constructed tarpaulin shelter. There's another man with him, and several others out on the bog surface, fooling around in the peat-cutting, Julie supposes, to see what other buried treasures may come to light. Julie says hello but does not otherwise account for her presence. Let Connor explain it. Connor gives her a quick annoyed glance.

'How did you get here?' he says, as if she's dropped from the sky.

'Walked,' says Julie.

'Ah, the vigour of youth,' says the other man, with a smile. He's fairly young himself, or anyway younger than Connor, a tall blond Norwegian. Another archaeologist. He looks like something out of a Viking movie. The metallic scent of rivalry is in the air.

'Julie is my assistant,' Connor says. The Norwegian knows better.

'Ah yes,' he says mockingly. He gives Julie a bone-crushing handshake, gazing into her eyes while she flinches. 'Did I hurt you?' he asks tenderly.

'Can I see the bog man?' Julie says. The Norwegian expresses mock surprise that she has not done so already, an assistant like her. With a proprietary air – he was in the area, he got there right after the Scots, he beat Connor to it – he ushers Julie into the tent.

The bog man is lying on a piece of canvas, curled on his side. His hands have deft, slender fingers, each fingerprint intact. His face is a little sunken in but perfectly preserved; you can see every pore. His skin is dark brown, the bristles of his beard and the wisps of hair that escape from under his leather helmet are an alarming bright red. The colours are the effects of the tannic acid in the bog. Julie knows that. But still it is hard to picture him as any other colour. His eyes are closed. He does not look dead or even asleep, however. Instead he seems to be meditating, concentrating: his lips are slightly pursed, a furrow of deep thought runs between his eyes. Around his neck is the twisted double cord used to strangle him. His two cut-off feet have been placed neatly beside him, like bedroom slippers waiting to be put on.

For a moment, Julie feels this digging-up, this unearthing of him, as a desecration. Surely there should be boundaries set upon the wish to know, on knowledge merely for its own sake. This man is being invaded. But the moment passes, and Julie goes out of the tent. Maybe she looks a little green in the face: after all, she's just seen a dead body. When she lights a cigarette her hands are shaky. The Norwegian gives her a solicitous look and places a hand underneath her elbow. Connor does not like this.

The three men who have been out at the peat-cutting return: one Scottish physical anthropologist and two workmen with peat-cutting spades. Lunch is proposed. The workmen have brought their own, and stay to guard the tent. The archaeologists and Julie get into the Norwegian's rented car. There's no place to eat except the pub, so that is where they go.

For lunch, Julie has bread and cheese, which is the safest thing, a lot safer than the flabby Scotch eggs and the barely warmed, fat-saturated meat pasties. The three men talk about the bog man. That he was a sacrifice is beyond doubt. The question is, to which goddess? And at which solstice? Was he bumped off at the winter solstice, to make the sun return, or at the summer solstice, to make the crops prosper? Or perhaps in spring or fall? An examination of the stomach – which they intend to remove, not here and now but later and in Edinburgh – will reveal clues. Seeds, grains and the like. This has been done with all the other bog people that have been found, those who still had stomachs. Julie is just as glad she has stuck to the bread and cheese.

'Some have said the dead cannot talk,' says the Norwegian, twinkling at Julie. Many of his remarks have been addressed to Connor, but aimed at her. Under the table he lays a hand, briefly, upon her knee. 'But these bog men have many wonderful secrets to tell us. However, they are shy, like other men. They don't know how to convey their message. They must have a little help. Some encouragement. Don't you agree?'

Julie doesn't answer. There's no way she can answer without participating, beneath Connor's very nose, in what amounts to a flagrant proposition. It's a possibility; or would be, if she weren't in love with Connor.

'Perhaps such things as stomachs disgust you?' says the Norwegian. 'Things of the flesh. My wife does not like them either.' He gives her a hyena grin.

Julie smiles, and lights a Gitane. 'Oh, do you have a wife?' she says brightly. 'So does Connor. Maybe the two of you can discuss your wives.'

She doesn't know why she has just said this. She doesn't look at Connor, but she can feel his anger coming at her like heat from a stove. She gathers up her purse and coat, still smiling, and walks out of the room. What's running through her head is one of the first axioms from Logic: *A thing cannot be both self and non-self at the same time.* She has never been convinced by this, and now she is even less so.

Connor does not follow her to her room. He doesn't reappear all afternoon. Julie knits and reads, knits and smokes. She's waiting. Something has changed, she has changed something, but she doesn't yet know what.

When Connor does show up, after sundown, he's morose. He says nothing about her piece of rudeness. He says nothing much at all. They have dinner with the Norwegian and the Scot, and the three of them talk about the bog man's feet. In some of these cases the feet have been tied together, to keep the dead from walking, returning to the land of the living, for revenge or some other reason. But not in this instance; or they think not. The cutting off of the feet may have interfered with something of course. Ropes, thongs.

The Norwegian is no longer flirting; the looks he gives her are speculative, as if there is more to her than he'd thought and he'd like to know what. Julie doesn't care. She eats her ossified lamb chop and says nothing. She thinks of the bog man, out there under his tarpaulin. Of all of them at this moment, she would rather be with him. He is of more interest.

She excuses herself before dessert. Connor, she thinks, will stay down there, drinking beer in the pub, and he does.

Around 10.30 he knocks at Julie's door as usual, then comes in. Julie is already in bed, propped upon the pillows, knitting. She's been sure he will come, but also not sure. She shoves the wool and needles into her tapestry bag and waits to see what he will do.

Connor does not say anything. He takes off his sweater, drapes it over the back of the chair, undoes deliberately the buttons of his shirt. He is not looking at Julie, but into the wavering patchy glass of the dressing-table mirror. His reflection there has a watery look, as if a lake bottom with decaying leaves on it is visible in glimpses beneath him, beneath his face and the whiter skin of his torso. In this light his red hair has faded. 'I'm getting love-handles,' he says, slapping his belly. This room flattens his beautiful voice, muffles it. 'The curse of the middle-aged.' It's a signal: if he's angry with her he's not going to mention it. They will go on as if nothing has happened. Maybe nothing has.

That's fine with her. She smiles. 'No you aren't,' she says. She doesn't like him doing this. He's not supposed to examine himself in mirrors or think about his appearance. Men are not supposed to.

Connor gives her a reproachful glance. 'One of these days,' he says, 'you're going to run off with some young stud.'

He has said such things before, about Julie's future lovers. Julie has not paid much attention. Now she does. Is this about the Norwegian, is he looking for reassurance? Does he want to hear from her that he is still young? Or is he telling her something real? Julie has never before thought of him as middle-aged, but now she can see that there might be a difference between her idea of him and his own idea of himself.

He climbs into the sagging bed with something like a sigh of resignation. He smells of beer and pub smoke. 'You're wearing me out,' he says. He has said this before also, and Julie has taken it as a sexual compliment. But he means it.

Julie turns out the bedside lamp. Once she wouldn't have bothered; once she wouldn't have had time. Once Connor would have turned it back on. Now he does not. He does not need to see her, she has been seen enough.

Meditatively and without ardour, he begins to run his hand along her: knee to thigh to hip, hip to knee. Julie lies stiffly, eyes wide open. The wind gusts through the cracks around the window, handfuls of rain are thrown against the glass. Light seeps in from under the door, and from the few streetlamps outside: in it the dressing-table mirror gleams like dark oil. Connor is a bulk beside her. His stroking does not excite her. It irritates her, like sandpaper, like the kneading paws of a cat. She feels that she's been demoted, against her will. What to her has been self-abandonment, to him has been merely sin. Grubby sin, sin of a small order. Cheating. Now he feels trapped by it. She is no longer a desire for him, she is a duty.

'I think we should get married,' says Julie. She has no idea where these words have come from. But yes, this is what she thinks.

Connor's hand stops. Then it's withdrawn suddenly, as if Julie's body is hot, hot as coals, or else cold; as if Connor has found himself in bed with a mermaid, all scales and fishy slime from the waist down.

'What?' he says, in a shocked voice. An offended voice, as if she's insulted him.

'Forget it,' says Julie. But Connor will not be able to forget it. She has said the unforgettable thing, and from now on it will be hopeless. But it's been hopeless anyway. Connor's unseen wife is in the bed with them, where she's been all along. Now she is materialising, taking on flesh. The springs creak with her added weight.

'Let's talk about it tomorrow,' says Connor. He's recovered himself, he's plotting. 'I love you,' he adds. He kisses her. His mouth feels separate from him: soft, moist, coolish. It feels like uncooked bacon.

'I could use a drink,' Julie says. Connor keeps a flask of Scotch in his room. Grateful that she's given him something to do, some small thing he can offer her instead of what she really wants, he clambers out of bed, pulls on his sweater and cords and goes in search of it.

As soon as he's out of the room, Julie locks the door. Connor comes back. He shakes the doorknob; he whispers and taps, but she does not answer. She lies in her bed, shivering with grief and anger, waiting to see whether Connor loves her enough to kick at the door, to shout. Whether she's important enough. He does not. She is not. After a while he goes away.

Julie hunches up under the mound of damp coverings and tries without success to go to sleep. When at last she manages it she dreams of the bog man, climbing in through her window, a dark tender shape, a shape of baffled longing, slippery with rain.

In the morning Connor makes another attempt. 'If you don't answer me,' he says through the keyhole, 'I'll get them to break down the door. I'll tell them you've committed suicide.'

'Don't flatter yourself,' says Julie. This morning she's no longer sad. She's furious, and determined.

'Julie, what did I do?' says Connor. 'I thought we were getting along so well.' He sounds truly perplexed.

'We were,' says Julie. 'Go away.'

She knows he will try to ambush her in the breakfast room. She waits him out, her stomach growling. Instead of eating she packs her bag, glancing from time to time out the window. At last she sees him leaving for the bog, in the Norwegian's car. There's a noon bus that will get her to another bus, that will get her to a train for Edinburgh. She leaves behind her the tapestry bag and the unfinished sweater. It's as good as a note.

Back in Toronto, Julie pins her hair into a brisk but demure French roll. She buys herself a beige cotton twill suit and a white blouse, and deludes the Bell Telephone Company into hiring her as a personnel trainee. She's supposed to learn how to train other women in the job of complaint management. She doesn't intend to stay with this for long, but it's good money. She rents herself a large, empty apartment on the top floor of a house. She has no long-term plans. Although she was the one who left Connor, she feels deserted by him. At night she listens to the radio and cooks subsistence meals, and cries on to her plate.

After a while she resumes her black clothing, at night, and goes to folk clubs. She no longer smokes Gitanes, because they frighten men. She picks up a boy she knew slightly from her Spinoza course. He makes a crack about windowless monads and buys her a beer, and tells her he used to be terrified of her. They end up in bed.

For Julie, this is like a romp with an entire litter of puppies. There's the same effect of gangly enthusiasm, of wriggling, of uncontrolled tongues. It's not passionate or even sensuous, but it's invigorating. Julie tells herself she's enjoying it, and she is. Or she would be, except for Connor. She wants him to know about it. Then she would really enjoy it. Even better would be the Norwegian. She should've taken advantage of that while she had the chance.

Connor returns at the end of August. It doesn't take long for him to track her down.

'I've missed you,' he says. 'I think we should talk.'

'What about?' says Julie warily. She thought she was over him, but it isn't true.

'Why can't we go back the way we were?' he says.

'Where were we?' says Julie.

Connor sighs. 'Maybe we should get married, after all. I'll divorce her.' He says this as if it's being torn out of him.

Julie starts to cry. She's crying because she no longer wants to marry Connor. She no longer wants him. The divinity is going out of him, like air. He is no longer a glorious blimp, larger than life and free in the heavens. Soon he will be just a damp piece of flabby rubber. She is mourning his collapse.

'I'll come right over,' says Connor, in a pleased, consoling voice. Tears mean he's made headway.

'No,' says Julie, and hangs up.

She puts on her black clothes, eats quickly, finds her cigarettes. She phones her boyish lover. She wants to pull him over her like a blanket, hug him to her like a stuffed animal. She wants comfort.

She goes out of the door of her building and there is Connor, waiting for her. She's imagined him so much that she's forgotten what he looks like. He's shorter than she thought, he's saggier. His eyes look sunken and also too bright, a little wild. Is this what she's changed him into, or was he always like that?

'Julie,' he says.

'No,' says Julie. The knees of his brown cords are baggy. This is the only detail Julie finds actually repulsive. The rest just leaves her cold.

He reaches out a hand towards her. 'I need you,' he says. It's a trite line, a line from a mushy song, but he does need her. It's in his eyes. This is the worst thing yet. It was always supposed to be her that needed him; he was supposed to be well above such a weak thing as need.

'I can't help it,' says Julie. She means she can't help it that things are the way they are, that she herself is without feeling for him; but it comes out more flippant, more pitiless, than she intended.

'Jesus Christ,' says Connor. He moves as if to grab her. She ducks around him and begins to run down the street. She's got her black pants on, and her flat black shoes. Now that she's cut down on her smoking she's a decent runner.

What does she expect, now that she's in full flight? That he will go away finally, that he'll never be able to catch up? But he hasn't gone away, he is catching up. She can hear the thudding of his feet, the gasping of his breath. Her own breath is rasping in her throat: she's losing speed.

She's come to a cross-street, there's a phone booth. She ducks into it, slams the folding glass door shut, pushes against it with both of her feet, leaning her back against the phone-book shelf for leverage. The smell of ancient pee surrounds her. Then Connor is right there, outside, pushing at the door, pounding at it.

'Let me in!' he says.

Her heart pounds in panic. 'No! No!' she yells. Her voice is tiny, as if she's in a soundproof booth. He presses his whole body against the glass door, wraps his arms as far around the phone booth as they will go.

'I love you!' he shouts. 'God damn it, can't you hear me? I said I love you!' Julie covers her ears. She is truly frightened of him now, she's whimpering with fright. He's no longer anyone she knows; he's the universal child's nightmare, the evil violent thing, fanged and monstrous, trying to get in at the door. He mashes his face frontways into the glass, in a gesture of desperation or a parody of a kiss. She can see the squashed tip of his nose, his mouth deformed, the lips shoved back from the teeth.

Julie remembers that she's in a phone booth. Without taking her eyes off him, she fumbles in her purse for change. 'I'll call the police,' she screams. And she does.

It took them some time to come. By the time they did, Connor was gone. Whatever else he wanted, he did not want to be caught in the act of sexually attacking a phone booth. Or this is how Julie puts it, when she tells the story these days.

At first she did not tell it all. It was too painful for her, in too complicated a way. Also she did not know what it was about. Was it about the way she had been taken advantage of, by someone older and more experienced and superior to her in power? Or was it about how she had saved herself from an ogre in the nick of time? But Connor was not an ogre. She had loved him, uselessly. This was the painful thing: that she had been so wrong about him. That she was capable, once, of such abject self-deception. Or still is, because in some way she still misses him; him, or her own mistaken adoration.

Then, after she was married, after she was divorced, she began to tell the story of Connor once in a while. She told it late at night, after the kids were in bed and after a few drinks, always to women. It became part of an exchange, the price she was willing to pay for hearing other, similar stories. These were mystery stories. The mysterious objects in them were the men, them and their obscure behaviour. Clues were discovered and examined, points of view exchanged. No definite solutions were found.

Now that she was married again, she tells it more frequently. By this time she concentrates on the atmosphere – the Scottish rain, the awful food in the pub, the scowling inhabitants of the town, the bog itself. She puts in the more comic elements: her own obsessive knitting, the long dangling sleeves, the lumpiness of the bed.

As for Connor, how can she explain him, him and his once-golden aura? She no longer tries. She skims over the worshipping love she once felt for him, which would be mawkish out loud. She skims over the wife, who is no longer the menacing rival of the piece: Julie has now been a wife herself, and feels a sneaking sympathy.

She skims over the grief.

She leaves out entirely any damage she may have caused to Connor. She knows the damage was done, was severe, at least at the time, but how can it be acknowledged without sounding like a form of gloating? It was unintentional on her part; more or less. At any rate it does not really fit into the story.

Julie eases forward in her chair, leans her arms on the table, lights a cigarette. She still smokes, though not as much. Over the years she's put on weight around the face, and her waist has solidified. Also she's cut her hair; it's no longer a mane, it's fashionably short at the back and sides, with a wispy, puckish mop on the top. She wears silver earrings in the shape of starfish, an eccentric touch, the last vestige of her days of piracy. Except for these earrings, she looks like any woman of that age you might see, walking a dog or shopping, in one of the newly renovated neighbourhoods.

'God knows,' she says, 'what I thought I was doing.' She laughs, a rueful, puzzled laugh which is also indulgent.

The story has now become a story about her own stupidity, or call it innocence, which shines at this distance with a soft and mellowing light. The story is now like an artefact from a vanished civilisation, the customs of which have become obscure. And yet every one of its physical details is clear to her: she can see the ruined mirror in the room, the slabs of dry toast at breakfast, the grasses moving on the surface of the bog. For all of this she has total recall. With each retelling, she feels herself more present in it.

Connor, however, loses in substance every time she forms him in words. He becomes fatter and more leathery, more life goes out of him, he becomes more dead. By this time he's almost an anecdote, and Julie is almost old.

Joseph O'Connor

MOTHERS WERE ALL THE SAME

I met Catriona again on the train in from Luton. I had noticed her on the plane, just before we came in to land, leafing through the lousy in-flight magazine – 'a great big top o'the morning from Delaney's Irish Cabaret' – while the old lady beside her worried about air disasters. The hostess told her to calm down and held her bony little hand. The old lady's hand, that is. Not Catriona's. Catriona's hands weren't bony at all. They were cute.

She said that it was statistically impossible. She said you had more chance of being kicked to death by a mule than dying in an air crash. The old lady said to tell that to Yuri Gagarin, but the hostess just giggled and said, 'Who's he when he's at home? Something to do with *glasnost*, is it?' Catriona looked over at me. She grinned, and she rolled her beautiful eyes.

The plane screeched in, bucked, as the wheels skimmed the ground, and shuddered to a halt outside the arrivals terminal. Catriona was ahead of me as we shuffled in off the tarmac, collars raised in the cold. Two police cars emptied. The plain-clothes men stared and scribbled like crazy on their clipboards as we filed past them.

I told the customs guy I'd just arrived from Dublin, and I didn't know how long I'd be staying. That was true all right. He glared under his peaked cap, making me feel guilty. He had a face like the *Spitting Image* puppet of Norman Tebbit, but without the charm. I mean, I hadn't done anything, but the way he looked at me made me feel like some kind of terrorist, just the same. Then he asked me to write down my full name, and he slouched off into a back room. That's it, I thought, I'm finished now. I gazed around the baggage lounge, full of wailing babies and neon signs. Luton: Gateway to the

South East. Ryanair to the Republic of Ireland. Loadza luvverly lolly in the sizzling soaraway *Sun*. Then I saw her staring at me. I smiled back, but she turned away to look for her bags. I made up my mind to ask her later, if I got the chance.

'Right,' said the customs man, and he told me to report my address to the local police as soon as I had one. I was going to ask why. But you don't bother, do you? You're so relieved that your name hasn't somehow crept into their bloody computer that you just smile politely and say thanks very much. He said he hoped I had a nice trip, and he was sorry for holding me up. But it was for everyone's good, if I knew what he meant. I knew what he meant.

I only had my rucksack, so I caught up with her on the other side of customs. I saw her immediately, looking in the window of the Sock Shop.

A troop of Boy Scouts was lined up at the burger counter, screaming curses and waving banknotes. Three football fans were drunk and singing in the corner, beer all over their England shirts. Soldiers walked up and down with machine guns in their hands. Actually, there were uniforms everywhere, now that I think of it. That's one thing I noticed straightaway, everybody seemed to be wearing a uniform. Customs, police, pilots, cleaners, waitresses, delivery boys, hostesses, all rushing around the hall. Above it all was the sound of the loudspeaker, announcing late flights and missing passengers.

I said, 'Excuse me,' and she turned around, looking a little surprised.

'Yeah?' she said.

I asked if I had seen her somewhere before. I was hoping she wouldn't think this was some big corny pick-up line, but I really did think I had seen her somewhere before and I couldn't remember where. I said I couldn't help noticing her on the plane and she looked familiar. She said she really didn't think so, and she looked away. I said I was sure. She turned again and scrutinised me. Then she asked if I was a friend of Johnny Reilly, by any chance. I said, yeah, I was. Used to be anyway. Recognition dawned on her face. That party he had – last Christmas? I was there with a blonde-haired girl. Susan. Yes. She remembered me now. I was pretty flattered, actually, until she pointed out the reason she remembered me. I was the one who had puked over the aspidistra in the hall.

I grinned. She pursed her lips and looked at her watch. I said it was a small world. She said, yeah, it was a small world, but she wouldn't like to have to paint it. There didn't seem to be much else to say. She'd just come over for the weekend. What about me? I was here looking for a job. Who wasn't? I told her I didn't know how long I'd stick it. She just kept staring at that watch so eventually I just said bye, and she wished me luck and dragged her case outside to the bus stop for Luton station.

I waited for the next bus. Well, if she wanted to be like that, fine, I didn't really feel like being friendly anyway. Too many things on my mind. I didn't feel like some big conversation. Okay, okay, so I had Aunt Martha's place, but that was only good for a few weeks at most, the old bat. I'd have to get a job soon. Then my own place. I never knew the folks would be so upset about me going, either. When I told them first they were delighted. But the morning I left it was a different story. Tears and scribbled addresses and folded-up tenners in the suit pocket. The whole emigrant bit. You'd have sworn I was going to the moon, the way they went on. The whole thing was like some bloody Christy Moore song come to life in our front room. On the way out to the airport I actually thought my father was going to tell me the facts of life. It was that bad.

At least the suit wasn't too hick. Still fitted me, anyway. Just about. Though I'd really have to go on a diet. All the drinking I'd done in the weeks I was saying my goodbyes was catching up fast. I must have put on eight pounds. But everyone insists on buying you pints, so what can you do? Everyone except Johnny Reilly, of course, the tight shit. My father got me the suit the week I started college. It was hanging over the back of my door when I reeled in that night. He said I'd need a good suit. I wore it twice in three years. Once for Granny's funeral and once for my graduation. He said to bring it with me to London anyway. He said I'd need it for all the interviews.

On the bus I thought about Una Murray. I'd never known she was into me until it was too late. But after our farewell drink she lunged at me on Capel Street Bridge, with the wind from the Liffey blowing through her hair like in a movie or something. Shit. If only I'd known before. Well, it wouldn't have made any difference. Still, would have been nice to know. Susan would have been jealous as hell.

When I got to Luton station, the London train was just pulling in, and the scramble of passengers was milling around the doorways. I fought my way on, dragging the rucksack behind, and I made a rush for the one spare seat. There were posters everywhere, saying that unattended luggage would be removed by the cops and blown up.

There she was, sitting opposite me as I squeezed in. Catriona. She was reading a book. *The Ultimate Good Luck* by Richard Ford. She looked up and smiled again. She said we must stop meeting like this. I tried to think of something smart but nothing came. I just grinned back like an idiot and I think I blushed as I offered her a duty-free cigarette. She shook her head and took off her glasses and pointed to another sign. *No smoking*. An old man with a moustache glared at me.

'Haven't you heard of King's Cross?' he said.

We got talking again. She asked me where I was staying in London. Strange, but I said I didn't know. I don't know why I said that. Because I did know. But, as Johnny Reilly says, I can't give anyone a straight answer, and I must admit that much is true. I suppose I was afraid she'd have nowhere to stay and want to come to Aunt Martha's with me. Look, I know it's stupid, but I'm funny like that. I like my space. Crazy, I know, but what can you do? I think it's because everyone at home asks so many bloody questions. Where were you? Until when? Who were you with? And the great bloody existential conundrum of course: just who do you think you are? All that stuff is enough to make anyone defensive. I'm not saying it's right. I'm just saying that's the way it is.

I needn't have worried. She was fixed up already, staying in some hotel near the station. It was a small place, she said, but it was hunky-dory. I couldn't remember the last time I'd heard that expression. Hunky-dory. As the train pulled in I asked if she needed any help with her bags. I knew she didn't, but I thought I'd ask anyway. She said she could manage on her own. So I shook hands with her on the platform and said goodbye again. Her hand was cold. She smiled, because I was being so formal, I suppose, with the handshake and everything. She said she might see me around. I shrugged and said I hoped so. She told me she hoped I'd find somewhere to stay, and I said good luck, see you, and walked off.

'Eddie,' she shouted, as I walked through the ticket barrier. I turned and saw her trotting towards me, dragging her case, panting. She said she was sorry, that I must have thought she was really rude. I wondered what she meant. She said if I really had nowhere to stay why didn't I come with her? She said that was the obvious thing. She was sure they'd have another room. It was a really cheap place too, and if I needed a place to sleep for a few nights, until I found somewhere else, it was probably okay. I hesitated. I knew I couldn't afford to stay in any hotel, no matter how cheap, not even for one night. Three nights would nearly clean me out. But then I thought, to hell with it. Why not? Nothing ventured, all of that. I just felt like doing something different. I don't know why. Something spontaneous after all the weeks of planning every last moment. That's what I wanted. And I suppose I have to admit I thought she was pretty cute, too. I asked whether she was sure she wouldn't mind. She said of course not. She'd love the company. I could come with her now, and maybe she could show me some of the sights over the weekend. All right. I said I would.

She was amazed that I'd never been to London before. She'd come over every summer for three years. She had a job over here whenever she wanted it, in some trendy lefty bookshop on Charing Cross Road. She might come over for good next year she said. But she knew what it was like to be in London on your own. It was such an overwhelming place. So huge and anonymous and impersonal. So different to Dublin. Yeah, I told her, that's why I came over.

Then she wanted to know what Johnny Reilly was doing these days. I said I didn't know. I was going to tell her about our big falling out, but I didn't bother. I just said I hadn't seen him for a while, and I hadn't a clue what he was up to, but it was probably either illegal or a waste of time.

'That sounds like Johnny all right,' she said.

So we went over together to the El Dorado Hotel and we signed in. The Greek guy behind the counter told us he rented rooms by the hour. You didn't have to have them for the whole night. There were no questions asked here, not blooming likely. I blushed like a sap and she made some joke. The Greek laughed out loud and apologised. Then he said he did have separate rooms to spare and he'd show us the way. Creaking up the stairs I whispered that I wasn't so crazy about this kip. But she told me not to be so silly, that old Zorba was only joking about the hourly rate. I said I thought he was pretty serious, and she sighed and said she knew, but for seven-fifty a night you couldn't expect The Ritz. I coughed knowledgeably and said I supposed she was right.

While she changed and unpacked, I slipped downstairs and outside and phoned Aunt Martha. The phone box was plastered with stickers advertising masseuses and prostitutes and kinky nuns and 'corporal punishment specialists'. I thought it must be great to be a specialist at something. Aunt Martha's businesslike voice buzzed down the line. I was to come over immediately. She had the dinner on and my cousins were just dying to meet me again. I imagined Uncle Frank and her and Alvin and Sharon sitting around the table. I could just see them all – waiting for me. I reconsidered, just for a second.

But I just couldn't face it. I told Aunt Martha I was sorry but I was still in Dublin airport and I couldn't make it until Monday. It was the fog, I said. Everything was screwed up because of the fog. I felt bad about lying, but what can you do? She sounded so disappointed though. Soon as I'd said it, I regretted it, but it was too late then. She said they'd just have to wait. I said I was really sorry. She said she should think so too. All the trouble she'd gone to, not to mention the expense. I noticed her weird accent. She nearly didn't sound Irish at all.

The funny thing was, though, as soon as I put the phone down I knew in my heart that this whole thing was a big mistake. I really did. I just had this feeling, you know? Like God was going to get me for lying to Aunt Martha. Not that I believe in God. But still. You never know.

Back at the El Dorado things were looking up. My room was fine. It was small, but you could see Tower Bridge in the distance, and there was a television in the corner. I flicked the switch but nothing happened. You had to put a pound coin in the slot to make it work. Well, it looked good. And although I didn't want to watch anything, it made me feel good knowing that I could, if I wanted to, if I had a pound to spare.

I sat down and bounced on the bed. Gently. Yeah, this was great. God, I thought, if my mother could only see me now. Holed up with a strange woman in a King's Cross knocking shop. I felt like a Harold Robbins hero.

I said this to Catriona on the Tube up to Leicester Square that night. She said she wasn't familiar with the Harold Robbins oeuvre – she was a little sarcastic really – but she knew what I meant about the El Dorado. It hadn't been quite as sleazy last time she was here. Still, never mind. It was all part of our little adventure, she said. We walked around the square for a while, looking at the lights and the posters in the cinema windows.

I bought her an ice cream in a little place in Soho. She said this was a really trendy area now, and the shops were way too expensive. I said she didn't have to tell me, the ice creams had cost six-fifty. She smiled and said she'd give me the money. I told her not to be so silly, but she insisted, so I took it. I gave the waiter a two-quid tip. Well, I didn't want her to think I was mean. She said, 'You only did that because you don't want me to think you're mean.' I tried to be as offended as possible but she just slipped her arm through mine and laughed again, and there was something about her made me want to be happy. So I admitted it and she sighed with mock desperation that men were so transparent.

Catriona was beautiful when she sighed. Wearing jeans and Doc Martens and a Public Enemy T-shirt, she was far more elegant than any of the women we watched swanning out of the Opera House in pearls and fur. Her eyes were kind of soft and sparkling, the kind you read about in books. Her face was lightly freckled. She had a way of talking fast and avoiding my eyes that was just irresistible. And she was funny, too. In the wine bar she made sarcastic comments about the poseurs and yuppies in the corners.

I told her about home and Susan and everything. It's funny how much you can trust and say to a total stranger. And I told her I wasn't really sure what kind of job I was looking for, just something a bit more interesting than sitting in Dublin on the old rock and roll. She said she still had a year to go in art school, then she'd probably come over here and do some course or another. She had lots of friends over here already. In fact, she knew more people over here than she did in Dublin. Lots of people. Bucket-loads of them. She'd never be stuck in London, she said.

The thing that got me was this. When we were talking about gigs and holidays and stuff I noticed she said 'we' all the time. We did this. We saw that. Some lucky bastard was obviously going out with her back home, and I suppose she kept dropping this 'we' shit to let me know that. Halfway through the second bottle of wine I plucked up the courage to ask her. She said he was a brilliant guy, Damien, they were really happy together and all that. A really wonderful pass-the-sickbag relationship.

'So, what's happening?' I asked her, pretending not to be jealous as hell. 'I mean, are we talking wedding bells or what?'

'Maybe,' she admitted, 'when he qualifies.'

'And kids and everything?'

'Yeah,' she said. 'I'm sure we'll have children. I mean, why wouldn't we?'

'I don't know,' I said. 'Why would you? I mean, why?'

'What is this,' she said, 'twenty fucking questions?'

I suppose I shouldn't have been so pushy and everything. It's not good to pry. I know that, but you know, it was just the booze really. Booze makes some people happy or sad or horny. It makes me curious. Always has. Outside in the rain I felt uneasy and confused. She seemed very quiet now, like there was something on her mind. The mood of things had changed. The feel of the night was suddenly weird and different now. Maybe this hadn't been such a great idea. I told her I was sorry for asking so many personal questions. She just stood there outside the Hippodrome chewing her fingernails and saying nothing.

'Do you want me to go away?' I said.

She smiled then. She slipped her hand into mine. She said she was sorry too. She didn't know what had come over her. She had things on her mind. She couldn't say. Maybe she'd tell me some other time. She was really sorry, though. Here she was spoiling my first night in London. I told her that was rubbish, and if it wasn't for her I'd be having an awful time. I said come on, here I was in London with a gorgeous woman and not a care in the world. She smiled and looked up at me then. She asked me if I meant the gorgeous bit.

'Yeah,' I said. I did. She said she'd been called beautiful before, but never gorgeous. 'They're not the same thing,' I said, 'not the same thing at all.'

'Charmer,' she said, in a sad voice, 'you're just like Damien.' I said I was sure I wasn't. She said I was, but for one night it didn't matter.

That night Catriona and I made love in the El Dorado Hotel. I had no condoms but she said it was safe. We held each other tight as the bedsprings gave us away. I didn't care. I didn't think about anything except her. I couldn't. Afterwards we lay in each other's arms. I asked her was she sure it was safe. She said yes. Her voice sounded weird. Like she was about to shout. Then I touched her face and she softened. She held my hand very hard.

When I woke up I didn't know where I was. My head hurt and my mouth was numb. She was sitting at the dressing table, putting her earrings in. She said she was going out for the day and wouldn't be back until tea time. She had to see this friend of hers. I asked if it was a guy. She laughed and said no. But she wouldn't let me come. It was just girl talk, she said.

'I'll probably tell her all about you,' she smiled, 'all about how I seduced you.' She kissed me before she slipped out of the room. She said she'd see me back here at eight.

'Yeah,' I said, 'mind yourself.' She said she would.

Down in the breakfast room the Greek grinned lasciviously as he ladled a large sausage on to my plate.

'Eat it all up,' he said. 'You will need all your strength, yes?'

I spent the day dossing around. On Oxford Street the shop windows were full of cheap suits and grim-looking dummies. A guy in sunglasses was selling gold chains from a cardboard box outside the HMV Megastore. 'Any shop in the West End, ladies and gents, they'd costya two hundred nicker straight up but here it's not two hundred, it's not one hundred fifty, it's not seventy-five or fifty or even twenty-five. A pony, ladies and gents. First twenty pounds down gets it.' Nobody moved. 'Come on now, loves,' he said, 'before Mister Plod comes back, who'll give me twenty for one of these lovely items?' I walked away and bought a postcard of Princess Diana for my mother. I wrote it over coffee in a little place on Russell Street. I told her I'd arrived safely, and that I was fine, and already making friends. I smiled when I wrote that. I couldn't find a post office open anywhere so I put the card in my pocket and forgot all about it. I never sent it. I still have it in my pocket somewhere, all crumpled up and torn. I've always kept it.

When Catriona came back that night she had an upset stomach. She was bleary-eyed and pale. She told me she'd eaten some awful burger or something, and it hadn't agreed with her at all. I told her to watch it. I told her catching salmonella is the national fucking sport over here. But when she tried to laugh it really creased her up. She had to lie down. She had to get some sleep. Soon as she said that she leaned over and vomited on the floor. I was worried. She walked into the room and flopped on to the bed, shivering and clutching her stomach. She really was in a bad way. When I put my arms around her she started all of a sudden – I mean for absolutely no reason – to cry. I asked her to tell me what was wrong. Had she had some row with her friend? She said, no, she hadn't even seen her. Why not? She snapped at me then. I mean, she nearly bit my fucking head off. She really got weird on me, started saying she had no friends and she was on her own. I said I was her friend and she laughed and said, yeah, things were that bad. Then she said she was sorry. I held her hand as she eased painfully under the sheets, with all her clothes still on. I asked if it was something to do with her period.

'Oh my God,' she sighed, 'spare me the new man bit.' She laughed out loud then, really laughed the bloody roof down. No, she said, if there was one thing it had nothing to do with, it was that. Then she told me she just had to get some sleep. I was to come back and see her later on.

In my room I walked up and down, chain-smoking and flicking ash all over the carpet. I didn't care. Then I lay on my bed and stared out at the lights on the street. What the hell was wrong? Would she be all right? Jesus, say if she bloody died or something. I got up and poured myself a glass of duty free. The tumbler was dirty and it tasted like toothpaste. But I drank it anyway. Then I had another one. Then I had a double. She'd probably be okay. Just some bug or something, that was all. In fact I wasn't feeling so terrific myself. I fed a pound into the television. I watched a documentary about a tribe in the Amazon that eat monkeys.

The bed was wet when I woke up. The stench of the whisky was everywhere. The clock on the wall said ten past eleven. Shit. I must have dozed off holding the bottle. It was nearly all spilt. My jeans stuck to my legs. I splashed water over my face. I stared in the mirror. I looked awful. My face was pale and my tongue felt all furry. Maybe it was that ice cream we'd had the night before. I don't know. Six-quid-fifty for strawberry-flavoured botulism. Or too much cheap red wine. Yeah. That was probably what was wrong with her. Just a hangover.

When I stumbled in she was sitting up in bed and wearing my pyjama top. I sat down beside her and asked how she was. She had been crying again. She wrapped her arms around me. The smell of drink filled my head. I told her not to worry. I said everything would be all right. She said my name a few times while I tried to kiss her. She was so beautiful. I couldn't help it.

'Please,' she said, taking my hands off her. She couldn't. It wasn't that she didn't want to. She just couldn't. 'Don't you understand anything?' she said, with tears in her eyes. 'I mean, do I have to paint you a picture?'

I said if she wanted to be like that she could stay on her own. It wasn't my bloody fault she was sick. I told her I bet old Damien wouldn't have stood for this bloody prima donna crap. Who the hell did she think she was, anyway? She told me to get out. I said I was sorry. She started screaming, 'Get out, you shit. Get out of my room.' She picked up a glass and pitched it at me; it smashed on the wall.

When I came back later and knocked on her door there was no answer. I stood in the corridor, apologising through the keyhole. No sound came from the room. The Greek came by and saw me on my knees.

'The ladies, my friend,' he shrugged, 'what can you do with them?' I said nothing.

Next morning Catriona was gone. She'd checked out at seven-thirty, taken all her stuff, ordered a cab for Luton airport. The Greek said he was terribly sorry. I said I hadn't known her that well anyway.

'Still,' he said, 'a very sad situation.' I asked him what he meant. He said no offence, but it was just very sad, a young girl like her.

Breathless, I stood in Catriona's room, staring at the made-up bed and the open windows. My pyjama top lay on the chair by the window. There was a brown bloodstain on it. The Greek's wife came in with an armful of clean white towels.

The young lady had been very ill in the night, she said. They were going to call me but Catriona had insisted that they shouldn't. She begged them not to. She couldn't let anyone find out. If her parents discovered, they would kill her. She explained everything and said it was nothing to worry about. The nurses had told her all this would happen. What she needed now was rest. No worry, and plenty of sleep. It was all over now. But a little discomfort was only to be expected.

The Greek's wife told me she was terribly sorry. She'd thought I would have been aware of things. If only she'd known, she would have broken it more gently. I felt like my whole body was turning to water. She asked me if I wanted a drink. I said no, I still had some duty free left.

I arrived at Aunt Martha's place at lunchtime on Sunday. The door opened and I fell in. She was furious with me. What did I mean, turning up in this drunken state? Did I think this was some kind of boarding house? And where had I been, anyway? She'd phoned Dublin on Friday night to see whether the fog had lifted. My mother had been worried sick about me. I'd better have a good explanation. They were just about to call the police. My father was searching the house for a photo to give them for *The News*. The only one he could find was the one they took the day of my graduation. They didn't know what kind of trouble I was in. Out in the hall I rang home. I said I'd bumped into Johnny Reilly, a guy I once knew in college, who was living over here now. I decided to stay a few nights with him. My mother said she wanted me back home on the next plane.

She said it was patently obvious that I couldn't be trusted to look after myself.

Alvin and Sharon said it was good to see me. Sharon had purple hair now, and Alvin had a ring through his nose. I managed to croak that I was sorry for all the trouble I'd caused. They shrugged and said not to worry. They said London was all about enjoying yourself. They said I shouldn't let my mother guilt-trip me. In the kitchen someone made me a cup of strong coffee. Alvin said not to pay any attention to Aunt Martha either. He said mothers were all the same. Then Sharon put her arms around me and told me to stop crying. She was sure it would all blow over soon. We'd be laughing about it, she said, in a few weeks.

I went to bed and stared at the ceiling. I wrapped the blanket tight around me. Really tight. Over my head. So tight that it felt like a second skin. And the whole world was shut out now, on the other side of the darkness.

Carol Shields

MRS TURNER CUTTING THE GRASS

Oh, Mrs Turner is a sight cutting the grass on a hot afternoon in June! She climbs into an ancient pair of shorts and ties on her halter top and wedges her feet into crepe-soled sandals and covers her red-grey frizz with Gord's old golf cap – Gord is dead now, 10 years ago, a seizure on a Saturday night while winding the mantel clock.

The grass flies up around Mrs Turner's knees. Why doesn't she use a catcher, the Saschers next door wonder. Everyone knows that leaving the clippings like that is bad for the lawn. Each fallen blade of grass throws a minute shadow which impedes growth and repair. The Saschers themselves use their clippings to make compost which they hope one day will be ripe as the good manure that Sally Sascher's father used to spread on his fields down near Emerson Township.

Mrs Turner's carelessness over the clippings plucks away at Sally, but her husband Roy is far more concerned about the Killex that Mrs Turner dumps on her dandelions. It's true that in Winnipeg the dandelion roots go right to the middle of the earth, but Roy is patient and persistent in pulling them out, knowing exactly how to grasp the coarse leaves in his hand and how much pressure to apply. Mostly they come up like corks with their roots intact. And he and Sally are experimenting with new ways to cook dandelion greens, believing as they do that the components of nature are arranged for a specific purpose – if only that purpose can be divined.

In the early summer Mrs Turner is out every morning by 10 with her sprinkling can of chemical killer, and Roy, watching from his front porch, imagines how this poison will enter the ecosystem and move by quick capillary surges into his fenced vegetable plot, newly seeded now with green beans and lettuce. His children, his two little girls aged two and four – that they should be touched by such poison makes him morose and angry. But he and Sally so far have said nothing to Mrs Turner about her abuse of the planet because they're hoping she'll go into an old-folks' home soon or maybe die, and then all will proceed as it should.

High-school girls on their way home in the afternoon see Mrs Turner cutting her grass and are mildly, momentarily repelled by the lapped, striated flesh on her upper thighs. At her age. Doesn't she realise? Every last one of them is intimate with the vocabulary of skincare and knows that what has claimed Mrs Turner's thighs is the enemy called cellulite, but they can't understand why she doesn't take the trouble to hide it. It makes them queasy; it makes them fear for the future.

The things Mrs Turner doesn't know would fill the Saschers' new compost pit, would sink a ship, would set off a tidal wave, would make her want to kill herself. Back and forth, back and forth she goes with the electric lawn mower, the grass flying out sideways like whiskers. Oh, the things she doesn't know! She has never heard, for example, of the folk-rock recording star Neil Young, though the high school just around the corner from her house happens to be the very school Neil Young attended as a lad. His initials can actually be seen carved on one of the desks, and a few of the teachers say they remember him, a quiet fellow of neat appearance and always very polite in class. The desk with the initials NY is kept in a corner of Mr Pring's homeroom, and it's considered lucky – despite the fact that the renowned singer wasn't a great scholar – to touch the incised letters just before an exam. Since it's exam time now, the second week of June, the girls walking past Mrs Turner's front yard (and shuddering over her display of cellulite) are carrying on their fingertips the spiritual scent, the essence, the fragrance, the aura of Neil Young, but Mrs Turner is as ignorant of that fact as the girls are that she, Mrs Turner, possesses a first name – which is Geraldine.

Not that she's ever been called Geraldine. Where she grew up in Boissevain, Manitoba, she was known always – the Lord knows why – as Girlie Fergus, the youngest of the three Fergus girls and the one who got herself in hot water. Her sister Em went to normal school and her sister Muriel went to Brandon to work at Eatons, but Girlie got caught one night – she was 19 – in a Boissevain hotel room with a local farmer, married, named Gus MacGregor. It was her father who got wind of where she might be and came banging on the door, shouting and weeping, 'Girlie, Girlie, what have you done to me?'

Girlie had been working in the Boissevain Dairy since she'd left school at 16 and had a bit of money saved up, and so, a week after the humiliation in the local hotel, she wrote a farewell note to the family, crept out of the house at midnight and caught the bus to Winnipeg. From there she got another bus down to Minneapolis, then to Chicago and finally New York City. The journey was endless and wretched, and on the way across Indiana and Ohio and Pennsylvania she saw hundreds of towns whose unpaved streets and narrow, blinded houses made her fear some conspiratorial, punishing power had carried her back to Boissevain. Her father's soppy-stern voice sang and sang in her ears as the wooden bus rattled its way eastward. It was summer, 1930.

New York was immense and wonderful, dirty, perilous and puzzling. She found herself longing for a sight of real earth which she assumed must lie somewhere beneath the tough pavement. On the other hand, the brown flat-roofed factories with their little windows tilted skywards pumped her full of happiness, as did the dusty trees, when she finally discovered them, lining the long avenues. Every last person in the world seemed to be outside walking, filling the streets, and every corner breezed with noise and sunlight. She had to pinch herself to believe this was the same sunlight that filtered its way into the rooms of the house back in Boissevain, fading the curtains but nourishing her mother's ferns. She sent postcards to Em and Muriel which said, 'Don't worry about me. I've got a job in the theatre business.'

It was true. For eight-and-a-half months she was an usherette in the Lamar Movie Palace in Brooklyn. She loved her perky maroon uniform, the way it fitted on her shoulders, the way the strips of crinkly, gold braid outlined her figure. With a little flashlight in hand she was able to send streams of light across the furry darkness of the theatre and on to the plum-coloured aisle carpet. The voices from the screen talked on and on. She felt after a time that their resonant declarations and tender replies belonged to her.

She met a man named Kiki in her first month in New York and moved in with him. His skin was as black as ebony. *As black as ebony* – that was the phrase that hung like a ribbon on the end of his name, and it's also the phrase she uses, infrequently, when she wants to call up his memory, though she's more than a little doubtful about what *ebony* is. It may be a kind of stone, she thinks, something round and polished that comes out of a deep mine.

Kiki was a good-hearted man, though she didn't like the beer he drank, and he stayed with her, willingly for several months after she had to stop working because of the baby. It was the baby itself that frightened him off, the way it cried probably. Leaving 50 dollars on the table, he slipped out one July afternoon when Girlie was shopping, and went back to Troy, New York, where he'd been raised.

Her first thought was to take the baby and get on a bus and go find him, but there wasn't enough money, and the thought of the baby crying all the way on the hot bus made her feel tired. She was worried about the rent and about the little red sores in the baby's ears – it was a boy, rather sweetly formed, with wonderful smooth feet and hands. On a murderously hot night, a night when the humidity was especially bad, she wrapped him in a clean piece of sheeting and carried him all the way to Brooklyn Heights where the houses were large and solid and surrounded by grass. There was a house on a corner she particularly liked because it had a wide front porch (like those in Boissevain) with a curved railing – and parked on the porch, its brake on, was a beautiful wicker baby carriage. It was here she placed her baby, giving one last look to his sleeping face, as round and calm as the moon. She walked home, taking her time, swinging her legs. If she had known the word *foundling* – which she didn't – she would have bounded along on its rhythmic back, so airy and wide did the world seem that night.

Most of these secrets she keeps locked away inside her mottled thighs or in the curled pinkness of her genital flesh. She has no idea what happened to Kiki, whether he ever went off to Alaska as he wanted to or whether he fell down a flight of stone steps in the silverware factory in Troy, New York, and died of head injuries before his 30th birthday. Or what happened to her son – whether he was bitten that night in the baby carriage by a rabid cat or whether he was discovered the next morning and adopted by the large, loving family who lived in the house. As a rule, Girlie tries not to think about the things she can't even guess at. All she thinks is that she did the best she could under the circumstances.

In a year she saved enough money to take the train home to Boissevain. She took with her all her belongings, and also gifts for Em and Muriel, boxes of hose, bottles of apple blossom cologne, phonograph records. For her mother she took an embroidered apron and for her father a pipe made of curious gnarled wood. 'Girlie, my Girlie,' her father said, embracing her at the station. Then he said, 'Don't ever leave us again,' in a way that frightened her and made her resolve to leave as quickly as possible.

But she didn't go far the second time around. She and Gordon Turner – he was, for all his life, a tongue-tied man, though he did manage a proper proposal – settled down in Winnipeg, first in St Boniface where the rents were cheap and then Fort Rouge and finally the little house in River Heights just around the corner from the high school. It was her husband Gord who planted the grass that Mrs Turner now shaves in the summertime. It was Gord who trimmed and shaped the caragana hedge and Gord who painted the little shutters with the cut-out hearts. He was a man who loved every inch of his house, the wide wooden steps, the oak door with its glass inset, the radiators and the baseboards and the snug sash windows. And he loved every inch of his wife, Girlie, too, saying to her once, and only once, that he knew about her past (meaning Gus MacGregor and the incident in the Boissevain Hotel), and that as far as he was concerned the slate had been wiped clean. Once he came home with a little package in his pocket: inside was a diamond ring, delicate and glittering. Once he took Girlie on a picnic all the way up to Steep Rock, and in the woods he took off her dress and underthings and kissed every part of her body.

After he died, Girlie began to travel. She was far from rich, as she liked to say, but with care she could manage one trip every spring.

She has never known such ease. She and Em and Muriel have been to Disneyland as well as Disney World. They've been to Europe, taking a 16-day trip through seven countries. The three of them have visited the South and seen the famous antebellum houses of Georgia, Alabama and Mississippi, after which they spent a week in the city of New Orleans. They went to Mexico one year and took pictures of Mayan ruins and queer, shadowy gods cut squarely from stone. And three years ago they did what they swore they'd never have the nerve to do: they got on an airplane and went to Japan.

The package tour started in Tokyo where Mrs Turner ate, on her first night there, a chrysanthemum fried in hot oil. She saw a village where everyone earned a living by making dolls and another village where everyone made pottery. Members of the tour group, each holding up a green flag so their tour leader could keep track of them, climbed on a little train, zoomed off to Osaka where they visited an electronics factory, and then went to a restaurant to eat uncooked fish. They visited more temples and shrines than Mrs Turner could keep track of. Once they stayed the night in a Japanese hotel where she and Em and Muriel bedded down on floor mats and little pillows stuffed with cracked wheat, and woke up, laughing, with backaches and shooting pains in their legs. That was the same day they visited the Golden Pavilion in Kyoto. The three-storey temple was made of wood and had a roof like a set of wings and was painted a soft old flaky gold. Everybody in the group took pictures – Em took a whole roll – and bought postcards; everybody, that is, except a single tour member, the one they all referred to as the Professor. The Professor travelled without a camera, but jotted notes almost continuously into a little pocket scribbler. He was bald, had a trim body and wore Bermuda shorts, sandals and black nylon socks. Those who asked him learned that he really was a professor, a teacher of English poetry in a small college in Massachusetts. He was also a poet who, at the time of the Japanese trip, had published two small chapbooks based mainly on the breakdown of his marriage. The poems, sadly, had not caused much of a stir.

It grieved him to think of that paltry, guarded nut-like thing that was his artistic reputation. His domestic life had been too cluttered; there had been too many professional demands; the political situation in America had drained him of energy – these were the thoughts that buzzed in his skull as he scribbled and scribbled, like a man with a fever, in the back seat of a tour bus travelling through Japan.

Here in this crowded, confused country he discovered simplicity and order and something spiritual, too, which he recognised as being authentic. He felt as though a flower, something like a lily, only smaller and tougher, had unfurled in his hand and was nudging along his fountain pen. He wrote and wrote, shaken by catharsis, but lulled into a new sense of his powers.

Not surprisingly, a solid little book of poems came out of his experience. It was published soon afterwards by a well-thought-of Boston publisher who, as soon as possible, sent him around the United States to give poetry readings.

Mostly the Professor read his poems in universities and colleges where his book was already listed on the Contemporary Poetry course. He read in faculty clubs, student centres, classrooms, gymnasiums and auditoriums, and usually, part way through a reading, someone or other would call from the back of the room, 'Give us your Golden Pavilion poem.'

He would have preferred to read his Fuji meditation or the tone poem of the Inner Sea, but he was happy to oblige his audiences, though he felt *A Day at the Golden Pavilion* was a somewhat light piece, even what is sometimes known on the circuit as a 'crowd pleaser'. People (admittedly they were mostly undergraduates) laughed out loud when they heard it; he read it well, too, in a moist, avuncular, amateur actor's voice, reminding himself to pause frequently, to look upwards and raise an ironic eyebrow. The poem was not really about the Golden Pavilion at all, but about three Midwestern lady tourists who, while viewing the temple and madly snapping photos, had talked incessantly and in loud, flat-bottomed voices about knitting patterns, indigestion, sore feet, breast lumps, the cost of plastic raincoats and a previous trip they'd made together to Mexico. They had wondered, these three – noisily, repeatedly – who back home in Manitoba should receive a postcard, what they'd give for an honest cup of tea, if there was an easy way to remove stains from an electric coffee maker, and where they would go the following year, Hawaii?

They were the three Furies, the three witches, who for vulgarity and tastelessness formed a shattering counterpoint to the Professor's own state of transcendence. He had been affronted, angered, half-crazed.

One of the sisters, a little pug of a woman, particularly stirred his contempt, she of the pink pantsuit, the red toenails, the grapefruity buttocks, the overly bright souvenirs, the garish Mexican straw bag containing Dentyne chewing gum, aspirin, breath mints, sun goggles, envelopes of saccharine, and photos of her dead husband standing in front of a squat, ugly house in Winnipeg. This defilement she had spread before the ancient and exquisitely proportioned Golden Pavilion of Kyoto, proving – and here the Professor's tone became grave – proving that sublime beauty can be brought to the very doorway of human eyes, ears and lips and remain unperceived. When he comes to the end of *A Day at the Golden Pavilion* there is generally a thoughtful half-second of silence, then laughter and applause. Students turn in their seats and exchange looks with their fellows. They have seen such unspeakable tourists themselves. There was old Auntie Marigold or Auntie Flossie. There was that tacky Mrs Shannon with her rouge and her jewellery. They know – despite their youth, they know – the irreconcilable distance between taste and banality. Or perhaps that's too harsh; perhaps it's only the difference between those who know about the world and those who don't.

It's true Mrs Turner remembers little about her travels. She's never had much of a head for history or dates; she never did learn, for instance, the difference between a Buddhist temple and a Shinto shrine. She gets on a tour bus and goes and goes, and that's all there is to it. She doesn't know if she's going north or south or east or west. What does it matter? She's having a grand time. And she's reassured, always, by the sameness of the world. She's never heard the word *commonality*, but is nevertheless fused with its sense. In Japan she was made as happy to see carrots and lettuce growing in the fields as she was to see sunlight, years earlier, pouring into the streets of New York City. Everywhere she's been she's seen people eating and sleeping and working and making things with their hands and urging things to grow. There have been cats and dogs, fences and bicycles and telephone poles, and objects to buy and take care of; it is amazing, she thinks, that she can understand so much of the world and that it comes to her as easily as bars of music floating out of a radio.

Her sisters have long forgotten about her wild days. Now the three of them love to sit on tour buses and chatter away about old friends and family members, their stern father and their mother who never once took their part against him. Muriel carries on about her children (a son in California and a daughter in Toronto) and she brings along snaps of her grandchildren to pass round. Em has retired from school teaching and is a volunteer in the Boissevain Local History Museum, to which she has donated several family mementos; her father's old carved pipe and her mother's wedding veil and, in a separate case, for all the world to see, a white cotton garment labelled 'Girlie Fergus Underdrawers, handmade, trimmed with lace, circa 1918'. If Mrs Turner knew the word irony she would relish this. Even without knowing the word irony, she relishes it.

The professor from Massachusetts has won an important international award for his books of poems; translation rights have been sold to a number of foreign publishers; and recently his picture appeared in *The New York Times*, along with a lengthy quotation from *A Day at the Golden Pavilion*. How providential, some will think, that Mrs Turner doesn't read *The New York Times* or attend poetry readings, for it might injure her deeply to know how she appears in certain people's eyes, but then there are so many things she doesn't know.

In the summer, as she cuts the grass, to and fro, to and fro, she waves to everyone she sees. She waves to the high-school girls who timidly wave back. She hollers hello to Sally and Roy Sascher and asks them how their garden is coming on. She cannot imagine that anyone would wish her harm. All she's done is live her life. The green grass flies up in the air, a buoyant cloud swirling about her head. Oh, what a sight is Mrs Turner cutting her grass and how, like an ornament, she shines.

David Mamet

A FAMILY VACATION

My people have always been anxious about travelling. I think this dates back to the Babylonian Exile. In any case, when I was growing up, the smallest move was attended by fear, puttering, and various manifestations of nerves. My father and mother would fight, we would invariably get lost, we would miss meals, bedtimes and destinations entirely.

My parents' fears took many convenient forms: fear of polio, of contamination from drinking fountains, of drowning from swimming too close on the heels of eating . . . all of these were just handy guises for the severest xenophobia, which I saw all around me as a child, in my home and my friends' homes.

Looking back, the fear of the strange that I saw around me is understandable, and I am only half kidding in referring to it as a cultural trait. My parents and the parents of my friends were one short generation removed from The Pale of Settlement in Russo-Poland; and to *their* parents the shortest trip away from home offered real possibilities of real trouble: difficulty of obtaining food acceptable to their religious laws, of confusion as to the local customs, of persecution and murder itself.

So this was the jolly burden which my parents inherited from their parents and passed down to me; and 70 years removed from the Cossacks I was still unable to take a vacation.

On our honeymoon, my wife and I went to Paris and I spent two days curled up on the bed. Yes, you will say, correctly, that probably had something to do with getting married – but isn't that a journey of a sort as well?

The above specious observation to the contrary notwithstanding, in eight years of marriage, and based on our informative experiences on the honeymoon, we have not really had a vacation.

But this year it occurred to both of us that we were not going to live for ever, that our daughter was not forever going to stay a fascinating, loving, three-year-old, and that on our respective deathbeds we were going to be unlikely to say, 'I'm glad I advanced my career in 1986.'

So my wife, speaking not for herself, but for the Group, signed us up to take a vacation. A model husband, I, of course, agreed and congratulated her on her decision, knowing that as the time came to leave, I would find some pull of work that kept me at home, or at the very best, feign sickness and, failing that, I could actually *become* sick.

The last being a tactic I'd employed before and to advantage: '*You* girls go away, don't worry about me, go and refresh yourselves,' and then they'd go, and I could stretch out over the whole bed and smoke cigars in the living room.

But this time it was not to be. And, as the day set for departure drew near, I told my wife that I was heartbroken, but I could not accompany them; to which she replied that she had checked my datebook, and I had nothing scheduled for the week in question save a haircut appointment, which she had cancelled for me; and that she had already told the kid how Daddy was going to come down for a week and 'not work'.

Well, I fought a holding action on the rectitude of her having unilaterally cancelled my haircut appointment, and on the collateral issue of my well-known inability to enjoy myself when my hair is too long. To which arguments my wife responded, 'Tough,' and off we went to fun and frolic in the Caribbean surf.

On the way to the airport, the cabbie asked us why we were going to vacation on an island which was currently being decimated by a hurricane. I thought, Aha! The cavalry arrives. But my wife said, 'We're going down there to find out, and if it has not passed we'll just come home, and that's what we're going to do.' We prepared to get on the plane.

I explained to my wife that on the plane going down I was going to have to do research and she said, 'Fine.' My research consisted of reading the galleys of a detective novel someone wanted to make into a movie, and my enjoyment of it would have been increased if she had resisted, but she did not. So I struggled through the book. My daughter watched *Romancing the Stone*, and my wife coloured in the kid's colouring book for three and a half hours.

At the island we found that the hurricane had indeed passed, so I scowled and we went off to our hotel. We got to the hotel, and I braced for what the Semitic Traveller will of course recognise as the interlude of: I am here, I am paying good money, everything is wrong. Change everything immediately and make it different or I am going to die.

The bellman put the bags in the room, I opened the doors to the patio beyond which was the sand beach and the Caribbean, and a football landed with a huge 'plop' in the water outside.

Fine, I thought, here I'm paying good money for some peace and quiet, and some overly American jock who can't leave home without his props is going to ruin my vacation.

Then as I watched, the football opened its wings and revealed itself to be a pelican which had just dived for a fish.

Okay, I thought, I'll try. And I did try. I changed into my suit and sat on the beach. I thought about Somerset Maugham and his sea stories. I thought about Joseph Conrad. I picked up a seashell and thought how very Victorian it looked, and wondered at the Multiplicity of Nature.

The sun went down, we put the baby to bed, and my wife and I went to dinner. We sat in a beautiful restaurant, hanging out on a cliff over the beach. There was a 'popping' sound below, like far off fireworks. I looked and saw the sound was made by the undertow, dragging the stones behind it. I said, 'The stones being dragged on the beach sound like far off fireworks.' My wife said nothing. I said, 'It occurs to me that the teaching of literature is completely *wrong*. Now: here we have a lovely simile – but the point is not the *simile* . . . the point is not the writer's knack at making a *comparison* – the point is the *stone*!'

My wife said, 'Why don't you take a vacation?'

Well, I had another drink, then I had *another* drink, then we went back to our room and we fell asleep, and I slept for 18 hours on each of the next two days, and on the third day I wasn't thinking about Joseph Conrad any more.

My daughter asked me to come out and make 'flour', and rather than responding, 'Just a minute,' I went out and made flour. Making flour consisted of pouring sand into a palm leaf, and I was surprised to find it just as enjoyable as (and certainly more productive than) a business lunch at the Russian Tea Room.

The punch line was that we had a grand old time. We swam and went waterskiing, we had breakfast on the patio. The baby went naked on the beach for a week with a strand of beads around her neck, and her hair got bleached and streaked.

Some good friends were vacationing on a neighbouring island, and they came over for a day and we all got drunk and went skinny-dipping in the moonlight; my daughter and I bounded on a trampoline a couple of hours every day; and, all in all, it was the trip of a lifetime.

I thought: we are Urban people, and the Urban solution to most any problem is to do more: to find something new to eat in order to lose weight; to add a sound in order to relax; to upgrade your living arrangements in order to be comfortable; to buy more, to eat more, to do more business. Here, on the island, we had nothing to do. Everything had been taken away but the purely natural.

We got tired as the sun went down, and active when it rose; we were treated to the rhythm of the surf all day: the heat and the salt renewed our bodies.

We found that, rather than achieving peace by the addition of a new idea, quality time, marital togetherness, responsibility, we naturally removed the noise and distractions of a too-busy life, and so had *no need* of a new idea. We found that a more basic idea sufficed: the unity of the family.

I did leave the island two days earlier than they, as I had to be in Los Angeles on business. As I got on the plane, I harboured a small secret joy at my forthcoming return to the addiction of busy life: I would have meetings and talk on the phone and lounge across the bed and smoke cigars in the hotel room.

I waved from the plane window and put my writer hat back on, and several thoughts occurred to me. The first was of Thorstein Veblen, who said that nobody travelling on a business trip would ever have been missed if he did not arrive. And I said to myself, You know, that's true.

And I thought of Hippocrates, and his hospital on the island of Cos, where the sick were treated to a peaceful view, and warm winds, and the regenerative rhythm of the surf – to a place where man could be healed because the natural order was allowed to reassert itself; and I missed my family, and was very grateful for the week that we spent with each other on the beach.

Tatyana Tolstaya

THE POET AND THE MUSE

Nina was a marvellous woman, an ordinary woman, a doctor, and it goes without saying that she had her right to personal happiness like everyone else. Of this she was well aware. Nearing the age of 35 after a lengthy period of joyless trial and error – not even worth talking about – she knew precisely what she needed: a wild, true love, with tears, bouquets, midnight phone vigils, nocturnal taxi chases, fateful obstacles, betrayals, and forgiveness. She needed a – you know – an animal passion, dark windy nights with street lamps aglow. She needed to perform a heroine's classical feat as if it were a mere trifle; to wear out seven pairs of iron boots, break seven iron staffs in two, devour seven loaves of iron bread, and receive in supreme reward not some golden rose or snow-white pedestal but a burned-out match or a crumpled ball of a bus ticket – a crumb from the banquet table where the radiant king, her heart's desire, had feasted. Well, of course, quite a few women need pretty much the same thing, so in this sense Nina was, as has already been said, a perfectly ordinary woman, a marvellous woman, a doctor.

She had been married: it was as if she'd done an interminable, boring stretch on a transcontinental train and emerged – tired, dispirited and yawning uncontrollably – into the starless night of a strange city, where the only kindred soul was her suitcase.

Then she lived the life of a recluse for a while: she took up washing and polishing the floors in her spotless little Moscow apartment, developed an interest in patterns and sewing, and once again grew bored. An affair with the dermatologist Arkady Borisovich, who had two families not counting Nina, smouldered sluggishly along. After work she would drop by his office to see him. There was nothing the least bit romantic about it; the cleaning lady would be emptying out the trash cans and slopping a wet mop across the linoleum while Arkady Borisovich washed his hands over and over, scrubbing them with a brush, suspiciously inspecting his pink nails and examining himself in the mirror with disgust. He would stand there, pink, well-fed and stiff, egg-shaped, and take no notice of Nina, though she was already in her coat on her way out the door. Then he would stick out his triangular tongue and twist it this way and that – he was afraid of infection. A fine Prince Charming! What sort of passion could she find with Arkady Borisovich? None, of course.

Yet she'd certainly earned the right to happiness, she was entitled to a place in the line where it was being handed out: her face was white and pretty and her eyebrows broad, her smooth black hair grew low from her temples and was gathered at the back in a bun. And her eyes were black, so that out in public men took her for a Moldavian Gypsy, and once, in the metro, in the passageway to the Kirovskaya station, a fellow had even pestered her, claiming that he was a sculptor and she must come along with him immediately, supposedly to sit for the head of a houri – right away, his clay was drying out! Of course she didn't go with him; she had a natural mistrust of people in the creative professions, since she had already been through the sorry experience of going for a cup of coffee with an alleged film director and barely escaping in one piece; the fellow had a large apartment with Chinese vases and a slanted garret ceiling in an old building.

But time was marching on, and at the thought that out of the approximately 125 million men in the USSR fate in all its generosity had managed to dribble out only Arkady Borisovich for her, Nina sometimes got upset. She could have found someone else, but the other men who came her way weren't right either. After all, her soul was growing richer as the years passed, she experienced and understood her own being with ever greater subtlety, and on autumn evenings she felt more and more self-pity: there was no one to whom she could give herself – she, so slim and black-browed.

Occasionally Nina would visit some married girlfriend and, having stopped off to buy chocolates at the nearest sweet shop for someone else's big-eared child, would drink tea and talk for a long time, eyeing herself all the while in the dark glass of the kitchen door, where her reflection was even more enigmatic, and more alluring in comparison with her friend's spreading silhouette. Justice demanded that someone sing her praises. Having finally heard her friend out – what had been bought, what had been burned, what ailments the big-eared child had survived – and having examined someone else's standard-issue husband (a receding hairline, sweatpants stretched at the knees – no, she didn't need one like that), she left feeling dismayed. She carried her elegant self out the door, on to the landing, and down the staircase into the refreshing night: these weren't the right sort of people, she should never have come, in vain had she given of herself and left her perfumed trace in the drab kitchen, she had pointlessly treated someone else's child to exquisite bittersweet chocolate – the child just gobbled it down with no appreciation; oh, well, let the little beast break out in an allergic rash from head to toe.

She yawned.

And then came the epidemic of Japanese flu. All the doctors were pulled out of the district clinics for house calls, and Arkady Borisovich went too, putting on a gauze face mask and rubber gloves to keep the virus from getting a hold on him, but he couldn't protect himself and came down with it, and his patients were assigned to Nina. And there, as it turned out, was where fate lay in wait for her – in the person of Grisha, stretched out completely unconscious on a bench in a custodian's lodge, under knit blankets, his beard sticking up. That was where it all happened. The near-corpse quickly abducted Nina's weary heart: the mournful shadows on his porcelain brow, the darkness around his sunken eyes, and the tender beard, wispy as a springtime forest – all this made for a magical scene. Invisible violins played a wedding waltz, and the trap sprang shut. Well, everybody knows how it usually happens.

A sickeningly beautiful woman with tragically undisciplined hair was wringing her hands over the dying man. (Later on, to be sure, it turned out that she was no one special, just Agniya, a schoolfriend of Grisha's, an unsuccessful actress who sang a little to a guitar, nothing to worry about, that wasn't where the threat lay.) Yes, yes, she said, she was the one who'd called the doctor – you must save him! She had just, you know, dropped in by chance; after all he doesn't lock his door, and he'd never call for help himself, not Grisha – custodian, poet, genius, saint! Nina unglued her gaze from the demonically handsome custodian and proceeded to look the place over: a large room, beer bottles under the table, dusty moulding on the ceiling, the bluish light of snowdrifts from the windows, an abandoned fireplace stuffed with rags and rubbish.

'He's a poet, a poet – he works as a custodian so he can have the apartment,' mumbled Agniya.

Nina kicked Agniya out, lifted her bag from her shoulder and hung it on a nail, carefully took her heart from Grishunya's hands and nailed it to the bedstead. Grishunya muttered deliriously, in rhyme. Arkady Borisovich melted away like sugar in hot tea. The thorny path lay ahead.

On recovering the use of his eyes and ears, Grishunya learned that the joyous Nina meant to stay with him to the bitter end. At first he was a bit taken aback, and suggested deferring this unexpected happiness, or – if that wasn't possible – hastening his meeting with that end; later, though, soft-hearted fellow that he was, he became more complaisant, and asked only that he not be parted from his friends. Nina compromised for the time being, while he regained his strength. This, of course, was a mistake; he was soon back on his feet, and he resumed his senseless socialising with the entire, endless horde. There were a few young people of indeterminate profession; an old man with a guitar; teenage poets; actors who turned out to be chauffeurs and chauffeurs who turned out to be actors; a demobilised ballerina who was always crying, 'Hey, I'll call our gang over, too'; ladies in diamonds; unlicensed jewellers; unattached girls with spiritual aspirations in their eyes; philosophers with unfinished dissertations; a deacon from Novorossiysk who always brought a suitcase full of salted fish; and a Tungus from eastern Siberia, who'd got stuck in Moscow – he was afraid the capital's cuisine would spoil his digestion and so would ingest only some kind of fat, which he ate out of a jar with his fingers.

All of them – some one evening, some the next – crammed into the custodian's lodge; the little three-storey outbuilding creaked, the upstairs neighbours came in, people strummed guitars, sang, read poems of their own and others, but mainly listened to those of their host. They all considered Grishunya a genius; a collection of his verse had been on the verge of publication for years, but a certain pernicious Makushkin, on whom everything depended, was blocking it – Makushkin, who had sworn that only over his dead body . . . They cursed Makushkin, extolled Grishunya, the women asked him to read more, more. Flushed, self-conscious, Grisha read on – thick, significant poems that recalled expensive, custom-made cakes covered with ornamental inscriptions and triumphant meringue towers, poems slathered with sticky linguistic icing, poems containing abrupt, nut-like crunches of clustered sounds and excruciating, indigestible caramel confections of rhyme. 'Eh-eh-eh,' said the Tungus, shaking his head; apparently he didn't understand a word of Russian. 'What's wrong? Doesn't he like it?' murmured the other guests. 'No, no – I'm told that's the way they express praise,' said Agniya, fluffing her hair nervously, afraid that the Tungus would jinx her. The guests couldn't take their eyes off Agniya, and invited her to continue the evening with them elsewhere.

Naturally, this abundance of people was unpleasant for Nina. But most unpleasant of all was that every time she dropped by, whether during the day or in the evening after her shift, there was this wretched creature sitting in the custodian's lodge – no fatter than a fork, wearing a black skirt down to her heels and a plastic comb in her lacklustre hair, drinking tea and openly admiring Grisha's soft beard: a person name Lizaveta. Of course, there wouldn't possibly be any affair going on between Grishunya and this doleful aphid. You had only to watch her extricate a red, bony hand from her sleeve and reach timidly for an ancient, rock-hard piece of gingerbread – as if she expected any moment to be slapped and the gingerbread snatched away. She had rather less cheek than a human being needs, and rather more jowl; her nose was gristly; in fact, there was something of the fish about her – a dark, colourless deepwater fish that slinks through the impenetrable gloom on the ocean floor, never rising to the sun-streaked shallows where azure and crimson creatures sport and play.

No, no love affair, there couldn't be. Nonetheless, Grishunya, the beautiful little soul, would gaze with pleasure at that human hull; he read poems to her, wailing and dipping on the rhymes, and afterward, deeply moved by his own verse, he would blink hard and turn his eyes up towards the ceiling as if to staunch his tears, and Lizaveta would shake her head to show the shock to her entire organism, blow her nose and imitate a child's sporadic whimpers, as if she, too, had just been sobbing copiously.

No, this was all extremely unpleasant for Nina. Lizaveta had to be gotten rid of. Grishunya liked this brazen worship, but then, he wasn't picky; he liked everything on earth. He liked swishing a shovel about in the loose snow in the morning, living in a room with a fireplace full of trash, being on the ground floor with the door open so anyone could drop in; he liked the crowd and the aimless comings and goings, the puddle of melted snow in the vestibule, all those girls and boys, actors and old men; he liked the ownerless Agniya, supposedly the kindest creature in the world, and the Tungus, who came for who knows what reason; he liked all the eccentrics, licensed and unlicensed, the geniuses and the outcasts; he liked raw-boned Lizaveta, and – to round things out – he liked Nina as well.

Among the little outbuilding's visitors, Lizaveta was considered an artist, and indeed she did exhibit in second-rate shows. Grishunya found inspiration in her dark daubings, and composed a corresponding cycle of poems. In order to concoct her pictures, Lizaveta had to work herself into an unbridled frenzy, like some African shaman; a flame would light up in her dim eyes, and with shouts, wheezes and a sort of grubby fury she would attack the canvas, kneading blue, black and yellow paint with her fists, and scratching the wet, oily mush with her fingernails. The style was called 'nailism' – it was a terrible sight to behold. True, the resulting images looked rather like underwater plants and stars and castles hanging in the sky – something that seemed to crawl and fly simultaneously.

'Does she have to get so excited?' Nina whispered to Grishunya once as they observed a session of nailism.

'Well, I guess it just doesn't happen otherwise,' dear Grishunya whispered back, exhaling sweet toffee breath. 'It's inspiration, the spirit, what can you do, it goes its own way.' And his eyes shone with affection and respect for the possessed scrabbler.

Lizaveta's bony hands bloomed with sores from caustic paints, and similar sores soon covered Nina's jealous heart, still nailed to Grisha's bedstead. She did not want to share Grisha; the handsome custodian's blue eyes and wispy beard should belong to her and her alone. Oh, if only she could become the fully empowered mistress of the house once and for all, instead of just a casual, precarious girlfriend; if only she could put Grisha in a trunk, pack him in mothballs, cover him with a canvas cloth, bang the lid shut and sit on it, tugging at the locks to check: Are they secure?

Oh, if only . . . Yes, then he could have whatever he wanted – even Lizaveta. Let Lizaveta live and scratch out her paintings, let her grind them out with her teeth if she wanted, let her stand on her head and stay that way, trembling like a nervous pillar beside her barbaric canvases at her annual exhibitions, her dull hair decked out with an orange ribbon, red-handed, sweaty and ready to cry from hurt or happiness, while over in the corner various citizens sit at a rickety table cupping their palms to shield against inquisitive eyes as they write their unknown comments in the gallery's luxurious red album: 'Revolting', perhaps; or 'Fabulous'; or 'What *does* the arts administration think it's doing?'; or else something maudlin and mannered, signed by a group of provincial librarians, about how sacred and eternal art had supposedly pierced them to the core.

Oh, to wrest Grisha from that noxious milieu! To scrape away the extraneous women who'd stuck to him like barnacles to the bottom of a boat; to pull him from the stormy sea, turn him upside down, tar and caulk him and set him in dry dock in some calm, quiet place!

But he – a carefree spirit ready to embrace any street mongrel, shelter any unsanitary vagrant – went on squandering himself on the crowd, giving himself out by the handful. This simple soul took a shopping bag, loaded it with yogurt and sour cream, and went to visit Lizaveta, who had fallen ill. And of course Nina had to go with him – and my God, what a hovel! what a place! yellow, frightful, filthy, a dark little closet, not a single window! There lay Lizaveta, barely discernible on an iron cot under an army blanket, blissfully filling her black mouth with white sour cream. Bent over school notebooks at a table was Lizaveta's fat, frightened daughter, who bore no resemblance to her mother but looked as though Lizaveta had once upon a time bred with a St Bernard.

'Well, how are you doing here?' asked Grishunya.

Lizaveta stirred beside the dingy wall: 'All right.'

'Do you need anything?' Grishunya insisted.

The iron cot creaked. 'Nastya will take care of everything.'

'Well then, study hard.' The poet shuffled about and stroked fat Nastya on the head; he backed into the hallway, but the enfeebled Lizaveta was already dozing, a stagnant lake of unswallowed yogurt apparently frozen in her half-open mouth.

'She and I should really, er, hook up or something,' Grishunya said to Nina, gesturing vaguely and looking the other way. 'You see what problems she has getting an apartment. She's from way up north, from Totma, she can only rent this storeroom, but what talent, no? And her daughter's very drawn to art, too. She sculpts, she's good – and who can she study with in Totma?'

'You and I are getting married. I'm all yours,' Nina reminded him sternly.

'Yes, of course, I forgot,' Grishunya apologised. He was a gentle man; it was just that his head was full of a lot of nonsense.

Destroying Lizaveta turned out to be as hard as cutting a tough apple worm in half. When they came to fine her for violating the residence permit in her passport, she was already holed up in a different place, and Nina sent the troops over there. Lizaveta hid out in basements and Nina flooded basements; she spent the night in sheds and Nina tore them down; finally, Lizaveta evaporated to a mere shadow.

Seven pairs of iron boots had Nina worn out tramping across passport desks and through police stations, seven iron staffs had she broken on Lizaveta's back, seven kilos of iron gingerbread had she devoured in the hated custodian's lodge: it was time for the wedding.

The motley crowd had already thinned out, a pleasant quiet reigned in the little house in the evenings, and now it was with due respect that the occasional daredevil knocked at the door, carefully wiping his feet under Nina's watchful gaze and immediately regretting that he had ever come by. Soon Grishunya would no longer be slaving with a shovel and burying his talent in the snowdrifts; he would be moving to Nina's, where a sturdy, spacious glass-topped desk awaited him, with two willow switches in a vase on the left, and, on the right, from one of those frames that lean on a tail, Nina's photo smiled at him. And her smile promised that everything would be fine, that he'd be well fed and warm and clean, that Nina herself would go to see Comrade Makushkin and finally resolve the long-drawn-out question of the poetry collection: she would ask Comrade Makushkin to look over the material carefully, to give his advice, fix a few things and cut up the thick, sticky layer cake of Grisha's verse into edible slices.

Nina allowed Grishunya a final goodbye to his friends, and the innumerable horde poured in for the farewell supper – girls and freaks, old men and jewellers. Three balletic youths with women's eyes arrived prancing on turned-out toes, a lame man limped in on crutches, someone brought a blind boy, and Lizabeta's now nearly fleshless shadow flitted about. The crowd kept coming; it buzzed and blew around like trash from a vacuum cleaner hooked up backward; bearded types scurried past; the walls of the little house bulged under the human pressure; and there were shouts, sobs and hysterics. Dishes were broken. The balletic youths made off with the hysterical Agniya, catching her hair in the door; Lizaveta's shadow gnawed her hands to shreds and thrashed on the floor, demanding to be walked all over (the request was honoured); the deacon led the Tungus into a corner and questioned him in sign language on the faith of his people, and the Tungus answered, also by signs, that their faith was the best of all faiths.

Grisha beat his porcelain brow against the wall and cried out that fine, all right, he was prepared to die, but after his death – you'll see – he'd come back to his friends and never be parted from them again. The deacon didn't approve of such proclamations. Neither did Nina.

By morning all the scum had vanished, and, packing Grishunya into a taxi, Nina carried him off to her crystal palace.

Ah, who could possibly paint the portrait of the beloved when, rubbing his sleep-filled blue eyes and freeing a young, hairy leg from beneath the blankets, he yawns with all his might? Entranced, you gaze at him: everything about him is yours, yours! The gap between his teeth, and the bald spot, and that marvellous wart!

You feel you're a queen, and people make way for you on the street, and your colleagues nod respectfully, and Arkady Borosovich politely offers you his hand, wrapped in sterilised paper.

How fine it was to doctor trusting patients, to bring home bags full of goodies, to check in the evenings, like a solicitous sister, to see what Grishunya had written during the day.

Only he was a frail thing: he cried a lot and didn't want to eat, and he didn't want to write neatly on clean paper but, out of habit, kept on picking up scraps and cigarette packs, and doodling or else just drawing flourishes and curlicues. And he wrote about a yellow, yellow road, on and on about a yellow road, and high above the road hung a white star. Nina shook her head: 'Think about it, sweetheart. You can't show poems like that to Comrade Makushkin, and you should be thinking about your book. We live in the real world.' But he didn't listen, and kept on writing about the road and the star, and Nina shouted, 'Did you understand me, sweetheart? Don't you dare write things like that!' And he was frightened and jerked his head about, and Nina, softening, said, 'Now, now, now,' and put him to bed. She fed him mint and lime blossom tea, infusions of adonis and motherwort, but the ungrateful man whimpered and made up poems that offended Nina, about how motherwort had sprouted in his heart, his garden had gone to seed, the forests had burned to the ground, and some sort of crow was plucking, so to speak, the last star from the now silent horizon, and how he, Grishunya, seemed to be inside some hut, pushing and pushing at the frozen door, but there was no way out, there was only the pounding of red heels in the distance . . . 'Whose heels are those?' demanded Nina, waving the piece of paper. 'I'm just interested – whose heels are they?'

'You don't understand anything,' Grishunya snatched the paper.

'No, I understand everything perfectly well,' answered Nina bitterly. 'I just want to know whose heels they are and where it is they're pounding!'

'Aaa-agh!!! They're pounding in my head!!!' screamed Grishunya, covering his head with the blanket, and Nina went into the bathroom, tore up the poems, and scattered them into the watery netherworld, the little domestic Niagara.

Men are men; you have to keep an eye on them.

Once a week she checked his desk and threw out the poems that were indecent for a married man to compose. And once in a while she would rouse him at night for interrogation: Was he writing for Comrade Makushkin, or was he shirking? And he would cover his head with his hands, lacking the strength to withstand the bright light of her merciless truth.

They managed this way for two years, but Grishunya, though surrounded by every care and concern, did not appreciate her love, and stopped making an effort. He roamed the apartment and muttered – muttered that he would soon die, and the earth would be heaped over him in clayey, cemeterial layers, and the slender gold of birch coins would drift over his grave mound like alms, and the wooden cross or pyramid marker (whichever they didn't begrudge him) would rot beneath the autumn rains, and everyone would forget him, and no one would visit, only the idle passer-by would struggle for a moment to read the four-digit dates. He strayed from poetry into ponderous free verse as damp as pine kindling, or into rhythmic lugubrious prose, and instead of a pure flame a sort of white, suffocating smoke poured from his malignant lines, so that Nina coughed and hacked, waved her hands about, and, choking, screamed, 'For heaven's sake, stop writing!'

Then some kind-hearted people told her that Grishunya wanted to return to his little house, that he had gone to see the custodian hired in his place – a fat woman – and bargained to see how much she would ask for handing him back his former life, and the woman had actually entered into negotiations. Nina had connections in the Municipal Health Department, and she dropped hints that there was a wonderful three-storey building in the centre of town, it could be taken over by an institution, hadn't they been looking for something? Municipal Health thanked her, it did suit them, and very soon the little building was no longer a custodian's lodge: the fireplace was torn out, and one of the medical institutes settled its faculty there.

Grisha fell silent, and for about two weeks he was quiet and obedient. Then he actually cheered up, took to singing in the bath and laughing – but he completely stopped eating, and he kept going up to the mirror and pinching himself. 'What are you so cheerful about?' Nina interrogated him. He opened his identity card and showed her the blue margins freshly stamped with fat lilac letters reading 'Not Subject to Burial'. 'What does that mean?' asked Nina, frightened. Grishunya laughed again and told her that he had sold his skeleton for 60 rubles to the Academy of Sciences, that 'his ashes he would outlast, the worms elude', that he would never lie in the damp ground, as he had feared, but would stand among lots of people in a clean, warm room, laced together and inventoried, and students – a fun crowd – would slap him on the shoulder, flick his forehead and treat him to cigarettes; he'd figured it all out perfectly. And he wouldn't say another word in answer to Nina's shouts; he simply proposed that they go to bed. But she should keep in mind that from now on she was embracing government property and thus was materially responsible before the law for the sum of 60 rubles and 25 kopecks.

And from that moment on, as Nina said later, their love seemed to go awry, because how could she burn with full-fledged passion for public property, or kiss academic inventory? Nothing about him belonged to her anymore.

And just think what she must have gone through – she, a marvellous, ordinary woman, a doctor, who had indisputably earned her piece of the pie like everyone else, a woman who had fought for her personal happiness, as we were all taught to do, and had won her right in battle.

Despite all the grief he'd caused her, she was still left with pure, radiant feelings, she said. And if love didn't turn out quite the way she had dreamed, well, Nina was hardly to blame. Life was to blame. And after his death she suffered a good deal, and her girlfriends sympathised with her, and at work they were kind and gave her 10 unpaid days off. And when all the red tape was done with, Nina made the rounds of her friends and told them that Grisha now stood in the little house as a teaching aid, tagged with an inventory number they'd given him, and she'd already gone to have a look. And everything was actually just as he had wanted: the students joke with him, they tug on his wrist to make him dance about, and they put a white cap on his head. The place is well heated, at night he's locked up in the closet, but otherwise he's always around people.

And Nina also said that at first she was very upset about everything, but then it was all right, she calmed down after a woman she knew – also a lovely woman, whose husband had also died – told her that she, for one, was even rather pleased. The thing was that this woman had a two-room apartment and she'd always wanted to decorate one room Russian style, just a table in the middle, nothing else, and benches, benches all around the sides, very simple ones, rough wood. And the walls would be covered with all kinds of peasant shoes, icons, sickles, spinning wheels – that kind of thing. And so now that one of her rooms was free, this woman had apparently gone and done it, and it's her dining room, and she always gets a lot of compliments from visitors.

Mary Gaitskill

TINY, SMILING DADDY

The phone rang five times before he got up to answer it. It was his friend Norm. They greeted each other and then Norm, his voice strangely weighted, said, 'I saw the issue of *Self* with Kitty in it.'

He waited for an explanation. None came so he said, 'What issue of *Self*? What's *Self*?'

'Good grief Stew, I thought for sure you'd of seen it. Now I feel awkward.'

'So do I. Do you want to tell me what this is about?'

'My daughter's got a subscription to this magazine, *Self*. And they printed an article that Kitty wrote about fathers and daughters talking to each other, and she well, she wrote about you. Laurel showed it to me.'

'My God.'

'It's ridiculous that I'm the one to tell you. I just thought . . .'

'It was bad?'

'No. No, she didn't say anything bad. I just didn't understand the whole idea of it. And I wondered what you thought.'

He got off the phone and walked back into the living room, shocked. His daughter Kitty was living in South Carolina working in a record store and making pots, vases and statuettes which she sold on commission. She had never written anything that he knew of, yet she'd apparently published an article in a national magazine about him without telling him. He lifted his arms and put them on the window sill; the air from the open window cooled his underarms. Outside, the Starlings' tiny dog marched officiously up and down the pavement, looking for someone to bark at. Maybe she had written an article about how wonderful he was, and she was too shy to show him right away. This was doubtful. Kitty was quiet but she wasn't shy. She was untactful and she could be aggressive. Uncertainty only made her doubly aggressive.

He turned the edge of one nostril over with his thumb and nervously stroked his nose hairs with one finger. He knew it was a nasty habit but it soothed him. When Kitty was a little girl he would do it to make her laugh. 'Well,' he'd say, 'do you think it's time we played with the hairs in our nose?' And she would giggle, holding her hands against her face, eyes sparkling over her knuckles.

Then she was 14, and as scornful and rejecting as any girl he had ever thrown a spitball at when he was that age. They didn't get along so well any more. Once, they were sitting in the rec room watching TV, he on the couch, she on the footstool. There was a Charlie Chan movie on TV, but he was mostly watching her back and her long, thick brown hair, which she had just washed and was brushing. She dropped her head forward from the neck to let the hair fall between her spread legs, and began slowly stroking it with a pink nylon brush.

'Say, don't you think it's time we played with the hairs in our nose?'

No reaction from bent back and hair.

'Who wants to play with the hairs in their nose?'

Nothing.

'Hairs in the nose, hairs in the nose,' he sang.

She bolted violently up from the stool. 'You are so gross you disgust me!' She stormed from the room, shoulders in a tailored jacket of indignation.

Sometimes he said it just to see her exasperation, to feel the adorable, futile outrage of her violated girl delicacy.

He wished that his wife would come home with the car so that he could drive to the store and buy a copy of *Self*. His car was being repaired and he could not walk to the little cluster of stores and parking lots that constituted 'town' in this heat. It would take a good 20 minutes and he would be completely worn out when he got there. He would find the magazine and stand there in the drugstore and read it and if it was something bad, he might not have the strength to walk back.

He went into the kitchen, opened a beer and brought it into the living room. His wife had been gone for over an hour, and God knows how much longer she would be. She could spend literally all day driving around the county doing nothing but buying a jar of honey or a bag of apples. Of course, he could call Kitty, but he'd probably just get her answering machine, and besides, he didn't want to talk to her before he understood the situation. He felt helplessness move through his body like a swimmer feels a large sea creature pass beneath him. How could she have done this to him? She knew how he dreaded exposure of any kind, she knew the way he guarded himself against strangers, the way he carefully drew all the curtains when twilight approached so that no one could see them walking through the house. She knew how ashamed he had been when, at 16, she had announced that she was lesbian.

The Starling dog was now across the street, yapping at the heels of a bow-legged old lady in a blue dress who was trying to walk down the street. 'Dammit,' he said. He left the window and got the afternoon opera station on the radio. They were in the final act of *La Bohème*.

He did not remember precisely when it had happened, but Kitty, his beautiful, happy little girl, turned into a glum, weird teenager that others kids picked on. She got skinny and ugly. Her blue eyes, which had been so sensitive and bright, turned filmy, as if the real Kitty had retreated so far from the surface that her eyes existed to shield rather than reflect her. It was as if she deliberately held her beauty away from them, only showing glimpses of it during unavoidable lapses, like the time she sat before the TV, daydreaming and lazily brushing her hair. At moments like this, her dormant charm broke his heart. It also annoyed him. What did she have to retreat from? They had both loved her. When she was little, and she couldn't sleep at night, Marsha would sit with her in bed for hours. She praised her stories and her drawings as if she were a genius. When Kitty was seven, she and her mother had special times, during which they went off together and talked about whatever Kitty wanted to talk about.

He tried to compare the sullen, morbid Kitty of 16 with the slender, self-possessed 28-year-old lesbian who wrote articles for *Self*. He pictured himself in court, waving a copy of *Self* before a shocked jury. The case would be taken up by the press. He saw the headlines: Dad

Sues Mag – Dyke Daughter Reveals . . . reveals what? What had Kitty found to say about him that was of interest to the entire country that she didn't want him to know about?

Anger overrode his helplessness. Kitty could be vicious. He hadn't seen her vicious side in years, but he knew it was there. He remembered the time he'd stood behind the half-open front door when 15-year-old Kitty sat hunched on the front steps with one of her few friends, a homely blonde who wore white lipstick and a white leather jacket. He had come to the door to view the weather and say something to the girls, but they were muttering so intently that curiosity got the better of him, and he hung back a moment to listen. 'At least your mom's smart,' said Kitty. 'My mom's not only a bitch, she's stupid.'

This after the lullabies and special times! It wasn't just an isolated incident either; every time he'd come home from work, his wife had something bad to say about Kitty. She hadn't set the table until she had been asked four times. She'd gone to Lois's house instead of coming straight home like she'd been told to do. She'd worn a dress that was short enough to show the tops of her pantyhose to school.

By the time Kitty came to dinner, looking as if she'd been doing slave labour all day, he would be mad at her. He couldn't help it. Here was his wife doing her damnedest to raise a family and cook dinner and here was this awful kid looking ugly, acting mean and not setting the table. It seemed unreasonable that she should turn out so badly after taking up so much time. Her afflicted expression made him angry too. What had anybody ever done to her?

He sat forward and gently gnawed the insides of his mouth as he listened to the dying girl in *La Bohème*. He saw his wife's car pull into the driveway. He walked to the back door, almost wringing his hands, and waited for her to come through the door. When she did, he snatched the grocery bag from her arm and said, 'Give me the keys.' She stood open-mouthed in the stairwell, looking at him with idiotic consternation. 'Give me the keys!'

'What is it Stew? What's happened?'

'I'll tell you when I get back.'

He got in the car and became part of it, this panting, mobile case propelling him through the incredibly complex and fast-moving world of other people, their houses, their childen, their dogs, their lives. He wasn't usually so aware of this unpleasant sense of disconnection between him and everyone else, but he had the feeling that it'd been there all along, underneath what he thought of most of the time. It was ironic that it should rear up so visibly at a time when there was in fact a mundane yet invasive and horribly real connection between him and everyone else in Wayne County: the hundreds of copies of *Self* magazine in countless drugstores, bookstores, groceries and libraries. It was as if there was a tentacle plugged into the side of the car, linking him with the random humans who picked up the magazine, possibly his very neighbours. He stopped at a crowded intersection, feeling like an ant in an enemy swarm.

Kitty had projected herself out of the house and into this swarm very early, ostensibly because life with him and Marsha had been so awful. Well it had been awful, but because of Kitty, not them. As if it wasn't enough to be sullen and dull, she turned into a lesbian. Kids followed her down the street jeering at her. Somebody dropped her books in a toilet. She got into a fist fight. Their neighbours gave them looks. This reaction seemed only to steel Kitty's grip on her new identity; it made her romanticise herself like the kid she was. She wrote poems about heroic women warriors, she brought home strange books and magazines which, among other things, seemed to glorify prostitutes. Marsha looked for them and threw them away. Kitty screamed at her, the tendons leaping out on her slender neck. He hit Kitty, Marsha tried to stop him and he yelled at her. Kitty leapt between them, as if to defend her mother. He grabbed her and shook her but he could not shake the conviction off her face.

Most of the time, though, they continued as always, eating dinner together, watching TV, making jokes. That was the worst thing; he would look at Kitty and see his daughter, now familiar in her withdrawn sullenness and feel comfort and affection. Then he would remember that she was a lesbian and a morass of complication and wrongness would come down between them, making it impossible for him to see her. Then she would be just Kitty again. He hated it.

She ran away at 16 and the police found her in the apartment of an 18-year-old body builder named Dolores who had a naked woman tatooed on her sinister bicep. Marsha made them put her in a mental hospital so psychiatrists could observe her, but he hated the psychiatrists – mean, supercilious sons of bitches who delighted in the trick question – so he took her back out. She finished school and they told her if she wanted to leave it was all right with them. She didn't waste any time getting out of the house.

She moved into an apartment near Detroit with a girl named George and took a job at a home for retarded kids. She would appear for visits with a huge bag of laundry every few weeks. She was thin and neurotically muscular, her body having the look of a fighting dog on a leash. She wore her hair like a boy's and wore black sunglasses, black leather half-gloves and leather belts. The only remnant of her beauty was her erect martial carriage and her efficient movements; she walked through a room like the commander of a guerilla force. She would sit at the dining room table with Marsha, drinking tea and having a laconic verbal conversation, her body speaking its precise martial language while the washing machine droned from the utility room and he wandered in and out trying to make sense of what she said. Sometimes she would stay into the evening to eat dinner and watch *All in the Family*. Then Marsha would send her home with a jar of homemade tapioca pudding or a bag of apples and oranges.

One day, instead of a visit they got a letter postmarked San Francisco. She had left George, she said. She listed strange details about her current environment and was vague about how she was supporting herself. He had nightmares about Kitty, with her brave, proudly muscular little body, lost among big fleshy women who danced naked in go-go bars and took drugs with needles. Terrible women whom his confused romantic daughter invested with oppressed heroism and intensely female glamour. He got up at night and stumbled into the bathroom for stomach medicine, the familiar darkness of the house heavy with menacing images that pressed about him, images that he saw reflected in his own expression when he turned on the bathroom light over the mirror.

Then one year she came home for Christmas. She came into the house with her luggage and a shopping bag of gifts for them and he saw that she was beautiful again. It was a beauty that both offended and titillated his senses. Her short spiky hair was streaked with purple, her dainty mouth was lipsticked, her nose and ears were pierced with amethyst and dangling silver. Her face had opened in thousands of petals. Her eyes shone with quick perception as she put down her bag and he knew that she had seen him see her beauty. She moved towards him with fluid hips, she embraced him for the first time in years. He felt her live, lithe body against him and his heart pulsed a message of blood and love into his deepest organs. 'Merry Christmas, Daddy,' she said. Her voice was husky and coarse, it reeked of knowledge and confidence. Her T-shirt said 'Chicks With Balls'. She was 22 years old.

She stayed for a week, discharging her strange jangling beauty into the house and changing the molecules of its air. She talked about the girls she shared an apartment with, her job at a coffee shop, how Californians were different from Michiganders. She talked about her friends: Lorraine who was so pretty men fell off their bicycles as they twisted their bodies for a better look at her; Judy, a martial arts expert and Meredith who was raising a child with her husband, Angela. She talked of poetry readings, ceramics classes, celebrations of spring.

He realised, as he watched her, that she was now doing things that were as bad or worse than the things that had made him angry at her five years before, yet they didn't quarrel. It seemed that a large white space existed between him and her, and that it was impossible to enter this space or to argue across it. Besides, she might never come back if he yelled at her.

Instead, he watched her, puzzling at the metamorphosis she had undergone. First she had been a beautiful, happy child turned homely, snotty, miserable adolescent. From there she had become a martinet girl with the eyes of a stifled pervert. Now she was a vibrant imp living, it seemed, in a world constructed of topsy-turvy junk pasted with rhinestones. Where had these three different people come from? Not even Marsha, who had spent so much time with her as a child, could trace the genesis of the new Kitty from the old one. Sometimes he bitterly reflected that he and Marsha weren't even real parents any more, but bereft old people rattling around in a house, connected not to a real child who was going to college, or who at least had some kind of understandable life, but a changeling who was the product of only their most obscure quirks, a being who came from recesses that neither of them suspected they'd had.

There were only a few cars in the parking lot. He wheeled through it with pointless deliberation before parking near the drugstore. He spent irritating seconds searching for *Self* until he realised that its airbrushed cover girl was grinning right at him. He stormed the table of contents, then headed for the back of the magazine. 'Speak Easy' was written sideways across the top of the appointed page in round turquoise letters. At the bottom was his daughter's name in a little box. 'Kitty Thorne is a ceramic artist living in South Carolina.' His hands were trembling.

It was hard for him to rationally ingest the beginning paragraphs which seemed, incredibly, to be about a phone conversation they'd had some time ago about the emptiness and selfishness of people who have sex but don't get married and have children. A few phrases that stood out clearly: '. . . My father may love me but he doesn't love the way I live.' '. . . even more complicated because I'm gay.' 'Because it still hurts me.'

For reasons he didn't understand, he felt a nervous smile tremble under his skin. He suppressed it.

'This hurt has its roots deep in our relationship, starting, I think, when I was a teenager.'

He had a horrible sensation of being in public so he paid for the thing and took it out to the car with him. He slowly drove to another spot in the lot, as far away from the drugstore as possible, picked up the magazine, and began again. She described 'the terrible difficulties' between him and her. She recounted, briefly and with hieroglyphic politeness, the fighting, the running away, the return, the tacit reconciliation.

'There is an emotional distance that we have both accepted and chosen to work around, hoping the occasional contact – love, anger, *something* – will get through.'

He put the magazine down and looked out the window. It was near dusk; most of the stores in the little mall lot were closed. There were only two other cars in the parking lot, and a big, slow, frowning woman with two grocery bags was getting ready to drive one away.

He was parked before a weedy piece of land at the edge of the parking lot. In it were rough, prickly weeds spread out like green tarantulas, young yellow dandelions, frail old dandelions and bunches of tough blue chickweed. Even in his distress he vaguely appreciated the beauty of the blue weeds against the cool white and grey sky. For a moment the sound of insects comforted him. Images of Kitty passed through his memory with terrible speed; her nine-year-old forehead bent over her dish of ice cream, her tiny nightgowned form ran up the stairs, her ringed hand brushed her face, the keys on her belt jiggled as she walked her slow blue-jeaned walk away from the house. Gone, all gone. The article went on to describe how Kitty hung up the phone feeling frustrated and then listed all the things she could've said to him to let him know how hurt she was, paving the way for 'real communication', all in ghastly talk show language. He was unable to put these words together with the Kitty he had last seen lounging around the house. She was 28 now and she no longer dyed her hair or wore jewels in her nose. Her demeanour was serious, bookish, almost old-maidish. Once he'd overheard her talking to Marsha and heard her say, 'So then this Italian girl gives me the once-over and says to Joanne, "You 'ang around with too many Wasps." And I said, "I'm not a Wasp, I'm white trash."'

'Speak for your goddamned self,' he'd said.

'If the worst occurred and my father was unable to respond to me in kind, I still would have done a good thing. I would have acknowledged my own needs and created the possibility to connect with what therapists call "the good parent" in myself.'

Well, if that was the kind of thing she was going to say to him, he was relieved she hadn't said it. But if she hadn't said it to him, why was she saying it to the rest of the country? He turned on the radio. It sang, 'Try to remember, and if you remember, then follow, follow.' He turned it off. He closed his eyes. When he was nine or 10 an uncle of his had told him, 'Everybody makes his own world. You see what you want to see and hear what you want to hear. You can do it right now. If you blink 10 times and then close your eyes real tight, you can see anything you want to see in front of you.' He'd tried it rather half-heartedly and hadn't seen anything but the vague suggestion of a yellowish-white ball moving creepily through the dark. At the time, he'd thought it was perhaps because he hadn't tried hard enough.

He had told Kitty to do the same thing, or something like it, when she was eight or nine. They were on the back porch sitting in striped lawn chairs, holding hands and watching the fireflies turn off and on. She closed her eyes for a long time. Then very seriously, she said, 'I see big balls of colour, like shaggy flowers. They're pink and red and . . . turquoise. I see an island with palm trees and pink rocks. There's dolphins and mermaids swimming in the water around it.' He'd been almost awed by her belief in this impossible vision. Then he was sad because she would never see what she wanted to see.

His memory floated back to his boyhood; he was walking down the middle of the street at dusk, sweating lightly after a basketball game. There were crickets and the muted barks of dogs and the low, affirming mumble of people on their front porches. He felt securely held by the warm light and its sounds, he felt an exquisite blend of happiness and sorrow that life could contain this perfect moment, and sadness that he would soon arrive home, walk into bright light and be on his way into the next day, with its loud noise and alarming possibility. He resolved to hold this evening walk in his mind for ever, to imprint all the sensations that occurred to him as he walked by the Oatlanders' house in a permanent place, so that he could always take it out and look at it. He dimly recalled feeling that if he could successfully do that, he could stop time and hold it.

He knew he had to go home soon. He didn't want to talk about the article with Marsha, but the idea of sitting in the house with her and not talking about it was hard to bear. He imagined the conversation grinding into being, a future conversation with Kitty gestating within it. The conversation was a vast, complex machine like those that occasionally appeared in his dreams; if only he could pull the switch everything would be all right, but he felt too stupefied by the weight and complexity of the thing to do so. Besides, in this case, everything might not be all right. He put the magazine under his seat and started the car.

Marsha was in her armchair reading. She looked up and the expression on her face seemed like the result of internal conflict as complicated and strong as his own, but cross-pulled in different directions, uncomprehending of him and what he knew. In his mind he withdrew from her so quickly that for a moment the familiar room was fraught with the inexplicable horror of a banal nightmare. Then the ordinariness of the scene threw the extraordinary event of the day into relief and he felt so angry and bewildered he could've howled.

'Everything all right, Stew?' asked Marsha.

'No, nothing is all right. I'm a tired old man in a shitty world I don't want to be in. I go out there, it's like walking on knives. Everything is an attack, the ugliness, the cheapness, the rudeness, everything.' He sensed her withdrawing from him into her own world of disgruntlement, her lips drawn together in that look of exasperated perseverance she'd gotten from her mother. Like Kitty, like everyone, she was leaving him. 'I don't have a real daughter and I don't have a real wife who's here with me because she's too busy running around on some –'

'We've been through this before. We agreed I could –'

'That was different! That was when we had two cars!' His voice tore through his throat in a jagged whiplash and came out a cracked half-scream. 'I don't have a car, remember? That means I'm stranded, all alone for hours and Norm Pisarro can just call me up and casually tell me that my lesbian daughter has just betrayed me in a national magazine and what do I think about that?' He wanted to punch the wall until his hand was bloody. He wanted Kitty to see the blood. Marsha's expression broke into soft open-mouthed consternation. The helplessness of it made his anger seem huge and terrible, then impotent and helpless itself. He sat down on the couch and instead of anger felt pain.

'What did Kitty do? What happened? What does Norm have –'

'She wrote an article in *Self* magazine about being a lesbian and her problems and something to do with me. I don't know, I could barely read the crap.'

Marsha looked down at her nails.

He looked at her and saw the aged beauty of her ivory skin, sagging under the weight of her years and her cockeyed bifocals, the emotional receptivity of her face, the dark down on her upper lip, the childish pearl buttons of her sweater, only the top button done.

'I'm surprised at Norm, that he would call you like that.'

'Oh, who the hell knows what he thought?' His heart was soothed and slowed by her words, even if they didn't address its real unhappiness.

'Here,' she said, 'let me rub your shoulders.'

He allowed her to approach him and they sat sideways on the couch. His weight balanced on the edge by his awkwardly planted legs, she sitting primly on one hip with her legs tightly crossed. The discomfort of the position negated the practical value of the massage, but he welcomed her touch. Marsha had strong, intelligent hands that spoke to his muscles of deep safety and love and the delight of physical life. In her effort, she leaned close and her sweatered breast touched him, releasing his tension almost against his will. Through half-closed eyes he observed her sneakers on the floor – he could not quite get over this phenomenon of adult women wearing what had been boy's shoes – in the dim light, one toe atop the other as though cuddling, their laces in pretty disorganisation.

Poor Kitty. It hadn't really been so bad that she hadn't set the table on time. He couldn't remember why he and Marsha had been so angry over the table. Unless it was Kitty's coldness, her always turning away, her sarcastic voice. But she was a teenager and that's what teenagers did. Well, it was too bad, but it couldn't be helped now.

He thought of his father. That was too bad too, and nobody was writing articles about that. There had been a distance between them too, so great and so absolute that the word 'distance' seemed inadequate to describe it. But that was probably because he had only known his father when he was a very young child; if his father had lived longer, perhaps they would've become closer. He could recall his father's face clearly only at the breakfast table, where it appeared silent and still except for lip and jaw motions, comforting in its constancy. His father ate his oatmeal with one hand working the spoon, one elbow on the table, eyes down, sometimes his other hand holding a cold rag to his head, which always hurt with what seemed to be a noble pain, willingly taken on with his duties as a husband and father. He had loved to stare at the big face with its deep lines and long earlobes, its thin lips, and loose, loopily chewing jaws. Its almost godlike stillness and expressionlessness filled him with admiration and reassurance until, one day, his father slowly looked up from his cereal, met his eyes and said, 'Stop staring at me, you little shit.'

In the other memories, his father was a large, heavy body with a vague oblong face. He saw him sleeping in the armchair in the living room, his large, hair-knuckled hands grazing the floor. He saw him walking up the front walk with the quick, clipped steps that he always used coming home from work, the straight-backed choppy gait that gave the big body an awesome mechanicalness. His shirt was wet under the arms, his head down, the eyes abstracted but alert, as though keeping careful watch on the outside world in case something nasty came at him, while he attended to the more important business inside.

'The good parent in yourself.' What did the well-meaning idiots who thought of these phrases mean by them? When a father dies, he is gone, there is no tiny, smiling daddy who appears, waving happily, in a secret pocket in your chest. Some kinds of loss are absolute. And no amount of self-realisation or self-expression will change that. As if she heard him, Marsha urgently pressed her weight into her hands and applied all her strength to relaxing his muscles. Her sweat and scented deodorant filtered through her sweater, which added its muted wooliness to her smell. 'All righty!' She rubbed his shoulders and patted him. He reached back and touched her hand in thanks.

Across from where they sat had once been a red chair, and in it had once sat Kitty, gripping her face in her hand, her expression mottled by tears. 'And if you ever try to come back here I'm going to spit in your face. I don't care if I'm on my deathbed, I'll still have the energy to spit in your face.'

Marsha's hands lingered on him for a moment. Then she moved and sat away from him on the couch.

NOTES ON THE AUTHORS

MARGARET ATWOOD was born in Ottawa in 1939 and now lives in Toronto. She has written more than 20 books, including poetry, fiction and non-fiction. She is best known for her novels *The Handmaid's Tale*, which was made into a film, *The Edible Woman*, *Life Before Man* and *Bodily Harm*. Her latest novel, *The Robber Bride*, was published in 1994 to outstanding reviews. She has also published three collections of short stories.

AMY BLOOM lives in Conneticut. Although a practising psychotherapist, she has not used her clients as material for her work but has kept their confidence: 'I think that being a sister, a mother and wife have more to do with what I write than being a therapist.' The result, in her first collection of short stories about family life, *Come to Me*, is both spellbinding storytelling and profoundly moving writing about love, longing and loss. 'Love is Not a Pie' was chosen by Alice Adams for the volume of *Best American Short Stories*, 1991.

ANGELA CARTER was born in 1940 and died in 1992. She read Engish at Bristol University, spent two years living in Japan, and from 1976 to 1978 was Fellow of Creative Writing at Sheffield University. Her first novel, *Shadow Dance*, was published in 1965, followed by *The Magic Toyshop*, *Several Perceptions*, *Heroes and Villains*, *Love*, *The Passion of the New Eve*, *Nights at the Circus* and *Wise Children*. She also published two collections of short stories and two works of non-fiction.

RACHEL CUSK was born to English parents in Canada in 1967, grew up in Los Angeles and East Anglia, and was educated at New College, Oxford. Her first novel, *Saving Agnes*, won the Whitbread First Novel Award in 1993. She reviews fiction regularly for *The Times* and her second novel, *The Temporary*, will be published in July 1995.

MARY GAITSKILL was born in Kentucky in 1954. Her mother had her committed to a psychiatric hospital after she was kicked out of boarding school at 15. She stayed there for two months before her parents decided they'd made a mistake. She then supported herself by working as a stripper and a go-go dancer until she had saved up enough to go to university to study journalism. She has published a collection of short stories called *Bad Behaviour* and a highly acclaimed novel, *Two Girls, Fat and Thin*.

BARBARA GOWDY, a Canadian, is the author of two novels. Her second, *Falling Angels* (described by the *Independent on Sunday* as reminiscent of early Margaret Atwood but with top spin), tells a tragicomic tale of three teenage girls living in the shadow of a drunken mother with an adulterous oaf of a father. The characters from her first collection of short stories, *We So Seldom Look on Love*, are all trying to come to terms with their bodies – a two-headed man, a woman with four legs and two vaginas, and a female-to-male transsexual. 'Presbyterian Crossing' is the most moving and perhaps the tamest story of the collection. Beneath her macabre imagination lies a deep awareness of how futile it is to deny one's individuality.

PAM HOUSTON After Pam Houston graduated from college in Ohio she rode up the east coast of America on a bike with a friend. When the friend dropped out for some 'real life', Houston kept on riding. 'I got in shape and kept going almost all the way to the west coast.' *Cowboys are My Weakness* is her first collection of short stories and it went straight into the American bestseller list. She's a part-time river guide and hunting guide, but not a hunter herself, and her short story 'How to Talk to a Hunter' was selected by Richard Ford for his volume of *Best American Short Stories*, 1990. Pam Houston also teaches creative writing at Denison University, Ohio.

ALISON LURIE was born in Chicago in 1926 and grew up in New York. She is currently Professor of English at Cornell University. She has written several novels, including *The Truth about Lorin Jones* and *Foreign Affairs*, which is set in London and won the Pulitzer Prize for Fiction in 1985. She is also the author of two works of non-fiction:

The Language of Clothes and a collection of essays called *Don't Tell the Grown-Ups*.

DAVID MAMET was born in Chicago in 1947. A Pulitzer Prize-winning playwright, screenplay writer and film director, his work is innovative, imaginative and frequently provocative. His recent plays include *Speed the Plow*, which starred Madonna when it was staged in New York and received rapturous applause at London's National Film Theatre in 1989, and the highly acclaimed and controversial *Oleanna*, his most recent play, which explores male–female conflicts. His films include *House of Games* and *The Untouchables*. Two collections of his essays have been published in Britain.

ELIZABETH MCCRACKEN, born in 1966, is a graduate of the Iowa Writers' Workshop and has had her short stories published in several American literary magazines. She lives in Provincetown, Massachusetts, and published her first collection in Britain in 1993. The stories in *Here's Your Hat What's Your Hurry* shock and amuse as a range of quirky outsiders search for identity and a sense of place.

LORRIE MOORE was born in 1957, brought up in New York State, and is now a Professor of English at the University of Wisconsin in Madison. She is the author of two collections of short stories, *Like Life* and *Self-Help*, and two novels, *Anagrams* and the highly acclaimed *Who Will Run the Frog Hospital?*. Much of her fiction relishes the differences between the sexes and the tender bonds that exist between people. Her work is frequently funny, sometimes profoundly sad, but it is always poignant.

JOSEPH O'CONNOR was born in Dublin in 1963 and now lives in London. In 1989 he won two top fiction awards in Ireland. *Cowboys and Indians*, his first novel, was published in 1991 and hailed as a comic masterpiece.

FRANK RONAN was born in 1963 in Ireland. His first novel, *The Men Who Loved Evelyn Cotton*, won the Irish *Times*/Aer Lingus Literature Prize and was followed by *A Picnic in Eden* and *The Better Angel*. He has had short stories published in a variety of magazines, in the collection *Telling Stories 2*, and broadcast on BBC Radio 4.

CAROL SHIELDS was born in Chicago but has lived for over 30 years in Canada with her husband and five children. Her work was first made available to a British audience in 1990 when *Mary Swann* was published to critical acclaim. That was quickly followed by *Happenstance*, *The Republic of Love* and *The Stone Diaries*, which was shortlisted for the 1993 Booker Prize.

HELEN SIMPSON was born in Bristol and read English at Oxford. After winning a talent competition sponsored by *Vogue* magazine she worked there for five years before going freelance. Her short stories have been published in numerous magazines, journals and anthologies, and her first collection, *Four Bare Legs in a Bed*, was published in 1990. With great sensitivity and deadpan wit, her stories look at the daily jostle between men and women, both in bed and out. In 1993 Helen Simpson was selected as one of the top 20 young British novelists in a promotion in UK bookshops.

TATYANA TOLSTAYA was born in 1951 and is a relative of Leo Tolstoy and granddaughter of Alexei Tolstoy. The entire edition of her first collection of short stories, *On the Golden Porch*, sold out within an hour of going on sale in the Soviet Union in 1991. It received high praise when published in Europe and America, and she has since published another collection, *Sleepwalker in a Fog*.

FAY WELDON was born in 1933 near Birmingham and spent much of her youth in New Zealand before she returned to Britain to attend St Andrews University. She worked as a waitress, secretary and market researcher before joining a leading advertising agency where she was responsible for the well-known slogan 'Go to work on an egg.' Her first novel, *The Fat Woman's Joke*, was published in 1968 and it was followed by an impressive and prolific output of 19 novels, including *Female Friends* and *The Life and Loves of a She Devil*, 20 television screenplays, including most notably *The Heart of the Country*, and a dazzling array of short stories. She also has four sons.

READ MORE IN PENGUIN

A CHOICE OF FICTION

Body of Glass Marge Piercy

'Outstanding . . . I have not read a more disturbing or moving novel about artificial intelligence since Mary Shelley's *Frankenstein* . . . It elevates its author to the pantheon of *haute* SF alongside Doris Lessing and Ursula Le Guin' – *Financial Times*

The Madness of a Seduced Woman Susan Fromberg Schaeffer

In her search for all-consuming, perfect love, Agnes Dempster, a beautiful young woman in turn-of-the-century Vermont, becomes infatuated with a man who, frightened by her intensity, betrays her. 'I can't remember a single other character in fiction with whom I have ever identified more . . . A great many women have tried to write *the* feminist novel. *This* is the novel they've been trying to write' – Margaret Forster

Now You Know Michael Frayn

'A constantly witty writer . . . Frayn's book can best be compared to a pin: it is small, shiny, sharp. Its impact will, one hopes, prick people into examining or re-examining one of the most teasing moral problems of our times' – *Spectator*

Brazzaville Beach William Boyd

'Hope Clearwater lives on an African beach reassessing the complicated, violent and tragic events which have occurred in her life. How much has she been responsible? How could she have forseen the dangers? . . . Boyd is a brilliant storyteller . . . a most serious book which stretches, tantalizes and delights' – *Financial Times*

Emily's Shoes Dermot Bolger

'A novel of enormous ambition, an attempt to create a folk history for those whose dark sexuality has banished them into the underworld of their own country . . . a serious and provocative work of fiction' – *Sunday Times*

READ MORE IN PENGUIN

A CHOICE OF FICTION

Crazy in Alabama Mark Childress

Way down South – in Industry, Alabama – 1965 was the year the orphan Peejoe discovered it wasn't sage to treat black people the same way you treated whites. Perhaps it was around the same time his Aunt Lucille arrived with her husband's head in a Tupperware box – he never could be sure . . . 'A truly wild, uplifting book' – *Time Out*

Memories of the Ford Administration John Updike

'Vintage Updike and a cracking good novel . . . Updike is always a polished performer. No other writer has explored the muddle of modern America with such honesty, clarity and plain good humour' – *Sunday Express*

The Children of Men P. D. James

'As taut, terrifying and ultimately convincing as anything in the dystopian genre. It is at once a piercing satire on our cosseted, faithless and trivially self-indulgent society and a most tender love story' – *Daily Mail*

The Only Problem Muriel Spark

Harvey Gotham had abandoned his beautiful wife Effie on the *autostrada* in Italy. Now, nearly a year later, ensconced in France where he is writing a monograph on the Book of Job, his solitude is interrupted by Effie's sister. Suddenly Harvey finds himself longing for the unpredictable pleasure's of Effie's company. But she has other ideas. 'One of this century's finest creators of the comic-metaphysical entertainment' – *The New York Times*

Collected Stories Beryl Bainbridge

Women in fox furs, not-quite-travelling salesmen, the twilight zone of genteel hotels and lodging houses – this is quintessential Bainbridge territory. This volume also contains the novella *Filthy Lucre*, written when the author was thirteen.